Borvo

An Anglo Saxon Tale

DNI Bradbury

authorHOUSE®

AuthorHouse™
1663 Liberty Drive
Bloomington, IN 47403
www.authorhouse.com
Phone: 1-800-839-8640

First published by AuthorHouse   07/05/2011

ISBN: 978-1-4567-8457-7 (sc)
ISBN: 978-1-4567-8458-4 (ebk)

Printed in the United States of America

Contents

Part Two

Part Three

Dedication

For Roy, Pippa and Russ

Acknowledgements

I wish to thank family and friends who have given me
encouragement and constructive advice.
Frankie, Lesley, Kathy, Chris, Sally, Viv and Denise.

Background to the action

The setting for the following fiction is the 9th century. The Romans had abandoned the islands of the Britons four centuries earlier. Different factions had fought, won and lost resulting in the emergence of several kingdoms occupying the mainland. The Angles and Saxons had been asked to help the indigenous peoples with their ongoing fight against the northern Picts and the Scots from the west. They settled and became the ruling race in most parts, with the exception of the islands' extremities.

The West Saxons held land to the south and west bordering Mercia and the Kentish lands. Their kings were law givers, strong and fair. From the north and east came the Vikings and Danes who also wanted these lands. Against this background there raged another quieter battle, the reforming Christians versus the pagans. Roman Christianity had already relegated those of the Celtic persuasion to a secondary status after the synod of Whitby in 664.

The following fiction is based around the reign of King Alfred the Great. It is not what might have happened, merely what could have happened. The main characters are fictional but the events of Alfred's reign are broadly what are deemed to have occurred. I have given the characters thoughts that are my invention. Alfred the Great's rule lasted from 871 to 899, the year of his death. The

Anglo Saxon Chronicles give his date of death as 901 but this is now thought to be erroneous. As with many historical facts there will always be people to debate on the veracity of each detail. Long may it be so.

DNIB/2011

Prologue

Bodies lay everywhere. The smell of blood filled the nostrils and made the youngest of the men retch. The king of the West Saxon had stood his ground but the cost had been high. Even he had lost his life and now his brother would be king. This war was not of their making. They were defending their lands against the invaders from across the seas. The raiders came, fought and moved on deeper into the countryside. Further and further they drove, relentless, into the kingdoms of the isles. Formidable opponents they were rarely defeated and many indigenous leaders had bought peace for their people rather than carrying on fighting at great human cost.

The new king sadly took on the mantle of saviour and was determined to protect his land. There was little time to mourn the passing of another kinsman, even though this time it was the king, his brother, who had died.

The burden on the young man was a heavy one and its outcome bought dear. His idea that God was on his side leant him the strength to go on. He had been sent to Rome as a child and had become a favourite of the pope. This had given him the inspiration to spread the wisdom of teaching to all his subjects. He would achieve this through education and example. The road was a long one. He understood the old ways and the people's need for the comfort it gave them. Their lives were part of the hills and valleys and they lived in harmony with Mother Nature. He knew with certainty that it would take many years before some could give up their worship of the earth's deities. He would need great forbearance. However, before any of his plans could be put into motion he needs must win the war.

He was given the news of his brother's death by a rider. Muddy and exhausted the man almost fell from his mount and gave the new king his obeisance. Immediately the young king fell to his knees to pray for his brother's soul. On rising he looked around at his men. He stood tall, his long fair hair blew across his face, he acknowledged their bowed heads as they recognised their new lord. They expected a lot from him. He knew that and he knew also that the odds were overwhelmingly against victory. He raised his sword and shield. They were both well cast by the strong arms of Saxon metal workers in the hottest fires. The beautifully honed metal glinted in the weak sun, as the rays caught the patterned sword it seemed to shine with a new intensity; the garnets in the golden hilt too took on the sun's fire as though heralding the shedding of more blood. With that flashing inspiration (and warning) in their eyes the men turned once more to prepare for battle.

Psalm 110
'He shall drink of the brook in the way: therefore shall he lift up the head.'

Part One

Dramatis Personae

The Family:

Borvo	named after one of the pagan river gods of healing
Elvina	Borvo's mother
Esmund	Borvo's father
Ayken	Borvo's elder brother whose name means oak
Sunniva	Borvo's sister named after the sun god
Gramma	Elvina's mother

Village characters:

Leofric	elder
Cynwise	his wife
Eldric	his son
Ealdyg	wild woman of the woods
Alric	one time lover of Ealdyg
Hild	Ayken's love
Godgyfu	Ayken and Hild's daughter
Aesc	Ayken's friend
Elfleda	Gramma's friend
Goaty	a simple soul

Others:

Brother Augustine	monk from Malmesburgh
Father Abbot	Malmesburgh
Seofon	wandering storyteller
The King	
Brand	king's minister
Oeric	thegn
Wilheard	soldier
Eorforheard	soldier
Eadwig	soldier
Aesfric	soldier
Konal	Danish soldier

Chapter One

Borvo is tested

The brook was lively and narrow. It tumbled over the stones that lined the floor of the valley. The water was clear and fresh. Small fish swam along in the sunlit waters. They were brightly coloured with streaks of silver and gold along their backs that caught and held the summer light. It was to this brook that one boy from the nearby village went every day to play in the cool water. He was tall for his age and stood out from the other boys because he had pale gold hair. All his friends and his family had dark hair and pale skin. He had been named for the ancient god of healing because the very hour that he was born his sister, who had been born with a weak leg, was so filled with joy at the birth of her brother that she got up from her stool by the open hearth and danced round the room. From that moment she had gradually increased her strength until she was almost completely cured. Thereafter she walked with only a slight limp which reminded people that she had once been lame. In those far off days only the strong or the lucky survived.

Their elder brother, too, was happy because it had been his job to help carry his sister whenever they had to journey far from home. Borvo's arrival in the family was therefore felt to be auspicious. At this time many of the old gods had been forgotten or supplanted by new ones. Raiders came and brought new ideas with them. Borvo's mother and father were not unusual in that they had their own gifts and knowledge passed down through the ages. They kept faith with the familiar gods of their upbringing.

It was high summer. Days were long and the brook was at its slowest. It had not rained for a while and the grass that fed the cattle, sheep and goats was getting very dry. Borvo's elder brother was a man, he was twenty four. He went with his father every day to tend the stock and help in the woods and fields. They grew corn, they kept goats for both milk and meat and they had sheep for wool and mutton. Their wool, and the wool of the local people, was among the finest in the whole of the south so every summer they took their fleeces to the big fair in the far off city. There they exchanged their wool for things they could not make themselves. In truth there was little that they could not fashion out of local materials but the excitement and the social gathering was enough to draw huge crowds from every direction. These fairs were full of story tellers and travellers from afar that brought important news from both their countries of origin or news about wars and fashion and politics. These were of vital importance to people who would remain isolated and uninformed without them. Borvo's village was only occasionally visited by travellers who too, told their story, and were made welcome for the news they brought and the fresh topics for gossip.

The next year Borvo would be fifteen then he would also accompany his father and brother to the fair. For now he was content to wander in the surrounding woods and fields and look out for all the plants that were special and used for healing and good health. His mother's mother had been a 'healing woman' in the distant village that had been their home, until the raids. After the burning they had been forced to move and travel until they found this place of acceptance and tolerance. Two generations later they were still settled. Even the indigenous peoples rarely moved on. Normally if the area remained safe and undiscovered then the villagers would be content. Borvo's grandmother had passed on her knowledge to her daughter and she in turn was hoping that her daughter would also be interested in the healing arts. This hope however was unfulfilled because Borvo's sister had spent a long time as an infant unable to move far or quickly and so she had sat for many hours learning how to sew. She was now, at the age of twenty two considered to be the best needlewoman in the area and many brought their fine cloth for her to sew into garments. Although she sewed the rough hewn tunics for everyday wear; she loved to take fine cloth and turn it into a work of art, for her stitching was so admired it was thought to rival any that might be found in the best established houses or even at court.

One summer morning when the day promised to be hot and sultry Borvo walked towards the brook that, although was not at its full winter height when it foamed and jumped fit to burst its banks, it had enough water to bring relief to the heat of the day. As he waded into the shallow waters he noticed that there was some unusual disturbance in the earth on the bank. The footprints were not any animal with which he was familiar. They were elongated and deep as though made by men who were heavily shod. He became alarmed as he realised that all the villagers wore rough footwear and did not possess such stout items. His sense of danger grew as he rounded a bend in the brook and came upon a figure in torn fighting dress lying face down in the mud. The man groaned and shivered despite the warmth of the day. Blood had seeped into the earth and his leather jerkin was also torn and red where his wound had bled. Lying some way off Borvo noticed was a torn garment of chainmail. This also made the boy uneasy as this clearly was someone of substance, even though at second glance he appeared to be a young man probably about the same age as Borvo's brother. Borvo looked around to see if he was alone. As there seemed to be no one else in sight he went to the man and touched him to wake him and tell him he would look after him. This was more serious than anything that Borvo had come across before. Normally he would consult with his family if he was unsure of a treatment. After all he was still learning. His mother and grandmother continually reminded him that even they were still learning. There was always something new that had to be faced.

The man's clothes were well made Borvo noticed as he tore at the shirt to push a handful of moss onto the wound to stem the flow of blood. He knew moss was all right but this was his first test of helping with a serious gash like this. He had seen his mother apply moss to cuts and watched as it helped with the healing process. Borvo prayed to the god, for whom he had been named, and as he prayed he worked to make the man comfortable so that he could think about what to do next. As the man started to regain consciousness Borvo sat away from him a little in case he lashed out in his misunderstanding. He might just think that Borvo was the aggressor. Very pale blue eyes opened and instantly Borvo saw the pain shine out. He was meant to help, he had been named for healing and so he did. With words of comfort and soothing the boy made the man comfortable with grasses and herbs from the old ways. Some he carried in his tunic, some grew by the brook and some were very near in the woodland that Borvo had known since he was able to walk. A sphagnum moss poultice was tied to the wound by strips of the man's shirt. Cold water mixed with feverfew helped to calm the man's fever and his thirst. Dry leaves were applied over the moss to mop up any blood that still seeped through. Agrimony and majorane from Gramma's store could be used later to help heal the wound and stave off infection. Words of comfort helped ease the man's anxiety. As the pain subsided the man was able to talk and asked Borvo who he was, where he came from and how he had grown to know so much about the healing arts. Rather overawed by the presence of such a man Borvo answered very few of the questions whilst remaining as polite as he could. He had been brought up on stories about family persecution and how his ancestors had learnt to evade hostility by clever use of language, deflection and, when all else failed they had moved on to friendlier villages.

Both Borvo and the man spoke the same language but with different accents. Borvo spoke slowly so the man would understand him more clearly. He told him he would go and fetch his parents so that they could be more help to him. There was no way that Borvo could physically move the tall, well set man. He smiled a reassuring smile as he left him as comfortable as he could. His last act was to pull a tree branch down lower so that the injured man would be sheltered from the hot summer sun. Borvo ran as fast as he could to his modest cottage and told his parents what had happened. His mother's face immediately showed fear and great anxiety whilst his father stood up, left his midday meal of barley bread and cheese from their goats. He strode around the small room in a state of preparedness. Borvo asked them why they had reacted in such a way and their only reply was, "You're too young to understand. We'll deal with this." Borvo insisted that he had some answer, he was after all fourteen and nearly grown to manhood. "I was born to heal. Don't tell me that my first real test is to be abandoned at a small sign of trouble. The man needs me, he needs you too, but if you won't come I'll go back alone. Gramma would have come with me if she was not so gampy, wouldn't you Gramma?" The elderly woman sitting bright eyed at the table nodded smiling with pride in her young grandson.

Borvo's parents looked at him with fresh eyes and then smiled to each other in silent assent. His father spoke, "Borvo, you are right.

We think the man must be healed. It will be dangerous though. There is news abroad that the king has lost his last battle and he is injured. There was talk in the village last night from a traveller. He brought the news." His father paused to take a deep breath, "Your man might well be a thegn or even the king himself. We'll come with you." So saying his parents gathered up the necessary herbs and ointments and rough blanket and went with him to the brook.

The three set out with wary tread and went swiftly to where Borvo had left the man. There were signs of where he had lain but the man was no longer there. It was as though he had been pulled or pulled himself along into the woods. They split up to look for the man and arranged to meet back at the cottage at dusk to speak further. They agreed on the call of the cuckoo as their signal that one of them had found their quarry. It was well past the time for the cuckoo so there would be no mistaking it for the real thing. As they went deeper into the wood they all felt quite alone and apprehensive. Borvo had keener eyes and ears than his parents and after an hour of searching he saw a dash of white deeper yet into the wood. This was a part he had not known before as it was almost in the middle of the trees. He went cautiously but knowing that he went to meet his destiny whatever that may be. He was more than a little surprised when he saw that the white he had seen was from his sister's dress. She was sitting with her back to a large oak and on her lap lay the head of a man. This was not Borvo's man but another and he too was injured. Borvo called his cuckoo call and went to help his sister tend the fallen man. This man was younger than the other, although in truth the other was barely past his mid twenties. Borvo's sister, named for the sun, Sunniva, had cleansed the man's wounds and had tied his arm to his chest with a strip of her skirt. She had then sat to cradle his head in her lap and wait for help. Sunniva, who had been out in the woods gathering plants and so was a fair distance from the village, had learnt at an early age to be patient as her lameness had held her back from doing what other youngsters took for granted. She was a gentle and loving young woman and had great faith in her family to find her wherever she was and however long it took. She waited patiently and she was not disappointed.

Sunniva and the young man had spoken a few words and she realised the importance of his master and leader. The king's army had been routed and they were in retreat. Well, this young man would be safe as long as she could hide him. She was rather taken with his gentle speech and kind face. Even in pain he had a quality that shone through and touched her heart. Sunniva felt excited and anxious and overwhelmed with a need to care for him and to be cared for by him. Borvo came upon this unexpected scene and immediately did what he could to make them more comfortable. He then set about finding enough fallen timber to fashion a litter to carry the patient to safety. It was some time before Borvo's parents found them. They were surprised to find Sunny as well as Borvo, whilst rather proud of the way their offspring had risen to this test there remained a deep seated dread of what may yet occur. As they carried the young man back to their cottage they tried to ask him where he thought his king might have gone. The only words they could get out of him were, "He must be saved!" When they had made the invalid as comfortable as they could Borvo decided that he had to retrace his steps and try to find the king, if such it was that he had helped by the brook. He would start his search there and try to gather some inspiration from the cool water. He had always gone there to think and it always gave him good messages. The babble of the brook spoke to him in ways that were little understood.

Chapter Two

Villagers rise to the challenge

As Borvo left the safety of the cottage, he looked back and smiled as he saw Sunniva sitting attentively by the thegn, Oeric, waiting to do any little thing to aid his comfort. He knew his sister well enough to know that she would not let any harm come to this young man if it were in her power to stop it. He carried that thought with him in his head as he approached the brook and so was not as careful as he might have been. He was grabbed roughly by the throat as someone put a strong arm round his neck and wrestled him to the ground. "'Tis just a lad, let him be." This came from an older man of the group. They were four in number and were dressed for battle. They were muddy, tired and bloody. The one who had spoken seemed to be in charge and peered at the boy's face. Borvo was now sitting up with his hands tied behind him and a soldier beside him holding a knife to his chest. "Yes, nought but a lad." He then spoke slowly with a strong and strange accent as though Borvo might be slow witted, "You seen a man hereabouts? Wounded? You understand me boy?" Borvo's quick mind took up the idea of dimmed wits and answered haltingly and with much concentration, "Mm, well sir, mm, um, I don't much know really. A man sir? No sir, no man sir. I come to look at the water sir. That's what I'm doing sir. Water sir. See. The brook sir." He hoped that the group might find it more bother than worth to deal with a cloddish boy that they let him go. This turned out to be the case. The soldier who had first caught Borvo seemed reluctant to release him but the older man said, "We need no more fools round here than I've got already. Fool, let him go. If it wasn't for you we wouldn't have lost the k . . . , the man, in the first place. Let him go I say. Unfast him." As the soldier cut the binding cords he added, "Run home boy and tell your village we are looking for a man, not trouble. We've enough trouble without some stupid villagers to deal with as well." As an afterthought he added, "We'll show no mercy if we're tricked."

Borvo did not need telling twice he ran off as fast as his legs could go. But he kept his wits and ran in the opposite direction from his village. He would not lead them there. He skirted round the outer edge of the wood and then, when he was sure they were following him he darted into the wood and led them through the deepest and darkest part so that before long he had lost them. He was young and agile, and they were battle worn and tired. When he was sure that he was not hunted any more he sat and thought about what to do next. He had to find the king but he also had to warn the village. He sat and prayed to the god of healing and the god answered him. At least that is how Borvo saw it as immediately after he had opened his eyes from praying he saw something that should not have been there. As he looked he saw a trail of blood, mostly hidden to the human eye but as he had fallen to his knees to pray he was lower down than usual. He followed the trail and found a hidden thicket where the wood was even more dense, he forced his way in and found the man, the king, semi conscious in the middle of the thick bushes. Borvo woke him up and put his hand over his mouth to stop him calling out. "Sire, ssh, quiet, I know, or at least I think I know who you are. There are men looking for you and they are not friends. They mean you harm. Stay here. Don't move any further, you will bleed too much. I must warn my village and then come back for you." He took his hand away and the king smiled weakly, "I am in your debt. Your name?" "Borvo, Sire. Named for the healing. I'll be back. I'll keep my word." As he stood up to go he added, "We have your thegn, Oeric, my sister is tending him. He will be well."

Borvo arrived back in the village as the sun was setting. He rushed to tell his parents what the situation was and in turn his father went to the other men of the village to warn them. He knew they were all loyal to the king and so there would be no trouble in keeping the secret. In fact several families had already offered help with extra food and coverings for the injured man. The help was accepted and the bond with the incomers deepened. They would always be incomers but also they were part of the village. Not there by right of birth but by right of humanity. It was their way and Borvo's family were grateful. They had known hardship and had fled from unfriendly society. Now they sighed and carried on the healing ways they had brought with them.

Borvo's mother packed up a bag of food and ointments for Borvo to take with him back to the king. Borvo's father wondered if the boy was old enough for such a task but his mother nodded her head and said he must be allowed this honour for he had found the king and started the treatment, it was time for him to grow up and prove himself. Borvo set out carrying his provisions in a leather pack that slung over his back enabling him to move quickly and unencumbered back to where he had left the injured king. He didn't go straight but took a circuitous path in case anyone had the idea of following him. He stopped often and looked around him, straining to hear as well as see if he was alone in his quest. It was late when he finally found the hidden copse where the king lay.

The king was still conscious and showed great relief when the boy returned. Borvo dressed the wounds with great care. His mother had given him extra instructions about what to do if he found certain signs of deterioration around any wound. Within an hour the king was much more comfortable and the two of them were sitting back drinking and eating the light meal prepared for them by Borvo's family.

"Tell me about your family boy." The command was clear, the king wished to know to whom he was indebted. So for the next hour Borvo told the king about his family's flight from oppression, his mother's gift of healing and his sister's excellent needlework. He spoke of his older brother, Ayken, and his prowess at all things physical as he was built tall and strong whilst Borvo was tall yet slender. Gradually the king relaxed and slept. Sleep would allow his body to heal; a fact drummed into Borvo by his grandmother, so he let the king start to heal himself in this way and kept watch throughout the night. As dawn broke the pale light crept through the dense woodland and the king awoke. Borvo had not slept at all and was exceedingly tired. They breakfasted off the remains of the food from the previous night. There was precious little so Borvo told the king he would run to the brook and fetch some clear water. He checked that the king was comfortable and left.

As Borvo approached the brook, his brook, the brook of inspiration, he became aware of voices echoing through the little valley where the brook squeezed past two small headlands of grassy earth. It was the native flint that gave the soil enough resistance to make the brook change its course and make a small detour. Borvo thanked his gods that morning for the bend in the brook as it gave him time to avoid detection from those who might wish him or the king harm. He sank deep onto his knees in the tall grass and waited. He listened and tried to understand the words that were not clear because of the noise of the running water. Borvo now lay, damp with dew, on his stomach and heard one strong voice tell the others that if they couldn't find the injured king their cause was lost. These five men were in fact loyal to the king but Borvo couldn't be sure. He edged away and left the men without having been noticed at all. He began to make his way back to the village to seek advice from his family when he came across the other small group of fighting men, four in all, who had captured him then let him go thinking him a 'lack-wit'. He once more fell to the ground and listened in to their conversation. Some of the words he did not understand but their meaning was clear in that they were looking for the group of men he had just left by the brook. He reasoned that if they were against the king then the first group of the morning were for the king. He desperately needed help but there was no one so he had to decide for himself. He went back to the brook and sat, out of sight to think clearly.

The brook was bright with the early morning sun, the sky was clear and the warmth of the sun began to make him want to sleep. He knew he could not give in to sleep just yet so he crawled to the edge of the bank and pushed his face into the reviving water. As he shook the droplets from his face he knew, clear as day, what he must do. He had to take a risk on the men round the corner; he had to avoid more bloodshed if he could. He approached the small ragged group and spoke calmly and softly so that they would understand his was a peaceful mission. Thankfully the man in charge did understand, although the other four men drew their knives in readiness for an attack. He bade them put away their weapons and raised his hand in greeting to Borvo. Quickly the man had summed up the boy and the fact that if he was up to no good then they could easily take him down. Borvo spoke with great emphasis and told the men of the other group of hostile soldiers who were minutes away from them. He offered to lead them into the woods where they would be safe. This may well have been a trap so they thanked him for his warning and decided to make their way down the brook and out of harms way. This would take them to the village and safety.

As they turned to go Borvo spoke with great agitation, "What would you do if you found the king?" One of the men sank to his knees and thanked his god. The leader looked curiously at Borvo and asked where he was from and who he was. Borvo very simply replied, "I am a healer." He paused as he saw the look of disbelief on their faces. He knew he was yet too young to claim such a gift, "Well, I'm learning to be a healer." He grinned and blushed. He then remembered his mission, "Do you have any sign that I can trust you?" The youngest of the group stepped forward and took from his belt a silver metal cross with a crown on top. Borvo had seen a similar piece on the belt of the king. "We must hurry," he urged the men, "Trust me and follow me, I'll take you to . . ." he could not finish as there was a sudden scuffle in the woods and a villager came into view hurrying after a wild boar. The boar was injured and justifiably angry at being hunted and hurt. He charged into the brook side clearing and sped across the water and off into the undergrowth on the other side. The villager stopped in his tracks and saw the unlikely gathering and grew anxious. He recognised Borvo and greeted him civilly. Borvo gathered up the men with a gesture and spoke to the man over his shoulder as they went into the woods, "Please get my parents and the village elders and tell them to listen to my father. These men are true, believe me, they are true." With that he dived into the shadows of the woods, quickly followed by the bemused but cautious soldiers.

As they went deeper into the wood the men began to doubt that they would ever find their way out again. Just as they were about to give up the boy turned and asked the leader to follow him. The man in charge told the others to wait and guard the place. As he followed Borvo into the hidden clearing he fell on his knees in an act of fealty. Borvo saw with great relief that the king knew and welcomed this man. Now his task was almost over he felt the need of his missed slumber. He asked the king if it would be acceptable for him to go back to the village and return with more help. He then made his weary and wary way back to his home.

As he drew close to the village he noticed a lot of activity and there seemed to be a gathering in the main thoroughfare, actually just a muddy lane that ran through the middle of the cluster of dwellings, and in the centre of this mass of villagers stood his parents and Ayken. Sunniva had not been persuaded to leave her charge who was still in some discomfort but healing nicely. Borvo knew he had to speak up but was a little nervous as he had not yet had cause to enter the world of adult discussion. He made his way to the middle of the people and spoke quietly in his father's ear. His father then held up his hand for silence and turned to offer his son to the crowd. Hesitantly Borvo spoke with a shaking voice and told the villagers that their king needed help and he could take them to him. They may not have believed him had not the carpenter, the failed huntsman of the morning, already set the scene and described in great detail how the boy had saved several of the king's men from the enemy. With great haste the villagers set about preparing a litter to carry the king and they made ready their homes in which to welcome the king and his men. This done they set off with Borvo and his father to bring the king back to the village.

Chapter Three

Borvo's vision

It was later that day that Borvo had time to rest and catch up on his lost sleep. He sauntered to the brook and lay down on the bank. Dangling his toes in the cool water he dozed and dreamt. About an hour into his well earned sleep he opened his eyes and felt that something had awakened him. The sun was still high in the sky so he thought that it must be mid afternoon. He rubbed his eyes to clear the sleepiness from them and then realised that he was not alone. He searched along the banks; both ways up and down stream, then felt a zephyr play about his face and neck. It was a still day and there was no breeze, yet he continued to feel the air around him, moving and seeming to play with him. The wind was cool and calming. He felt no fear.

The spirit came to him as though from a mist. He shook his head and his eyes cleared as the spirit sat by him on the bank of the brook. Borvo seemed encased in a cloud of calm. Any observer that might have seen such a look on his face may have considered that he was under a potent force; perhaps the young lad had discovered the dubious delights of fermented grain. This was not the case. His influence was a greater force than that, it came from another world, or maybe, just maybe it came from within him.

The boy was mystified as to why he had been chosen to receive such a powerful presence. His face wore a puzzled frown as he put out his hands in a questioning gesture of welcome. The spirit shimmered and settled again on the grass by the boy. Borvo waited. The spirit started to sing. The song had such a melody that Borvo became even more entranced. The tune was light and uplifting. Borvo was transported.

The First Song of Borvo

Listen carefully to my song
Find the place where you belong
I am hither, thither gone
You and yours must carry on

For me you were named and blessed
So you always will be best
Healing is the art you share
Generations have the care

Handed down from one another
Is the skill that seeks no other
We disarm and mend each rift
Healing harmony is the gift

I am with you here, benign
Ask the water for my sign
Your time is come, chosen now
Go and mend the royal bough

Borvo, Borvo take my water
When strife calls, spare no quarter
Stay your ground and proudly stand
Help will always be at hand

Listen carefully to my song
Find the place where you belong
I am hither, thither gone
You and yours must carry on!

The song played in and around the brook and in Borvo's head it seemed to dance with the ripples on the water. The words and the tune appeared to separate with the tune running away from the words then turning and chasing the song until they were one again. As they came back together the song played over and over in his mind until he knew he would never forget it. At last the boy slept a deep and untroubled sleep. The grassy bank both his pillow and his bed, the song from the water his destiny.

While their son slept Borvo's parents, Esmund and Elvina had been as busy as they ever could remember. In fact the whole village was in a state of preparedness. All was bustle as the poor huts were made ready to receive the injured king and his small band of soldiers. The villagers had little but they prepared to share their meagre existence with the strangers who needed them. It had been agreed that the largest of the huts should house the king as befitted his status. This was not Borvo's house but because of his and his family's involvement it was also agreed that Borvo and his parents should treat the king and his wounds.

It took the soldiers and the villagers several hours to bring the king to the settlement as they had to move very slowly so as not to open up his wound. Elvina had checked that her son's ministrations had been well done and that the dressings were still in place and effective. The long journey began. The king swooned in and out of consciousness. His guard who were ever present strode by the litter with alert eyes but increasingly weary tread. They had been at battle for weeks and needed this coming respite. Their current ordeal was not yet over though, as the party neared the edge of the woods the vanguard noticed an unusual disturbance in the floor of the pathway. He quickly assessed that there had been at least four booted men that had crossed the track within the last few hours. He knew they could not be the villagers and so concluded that the small band of the foe were close by. He signalled to the rest of the group to put the litter down and make ready to protect the king. Borvo's elder brother was in the party of villagers who accompanied the king. He was well built and athletic. Unlike the soldiers he was fresh and not at all battle weary. He volunteered to scout round to find out where the enemy were. He also knew these woods as well as any. Quickly and quietly he doubled back on the path, went into the thick trees to the east and made his way to where it was most likely that strangers might make camp.

His first thought was to go a clearing that was just a few hundred yards off the main track. Ayken, his name meaning 'made of oak', was mistaken in his first thought but when he realised he was wrong he moved swiftly onto the second place where they may be. Sure enough he smelt them before he saw them, the raggedy band had made a temporary encampment in a small rough area that was surrounded on all sides by strong, thick trees. Here the undergrowth had been cleared and the soldiers had made themselves as comfortable as they could. The smell that drew Ayken to their hideout was that of stale sweaty leather from their bodies and from the fish cooking over a small fire. The smoke from the fire wound its way up through the thick branches of the forest canopy and would never have given them away. Ayken stealthily found his way all around the camp and then went back to his own group. He spoke to the man in charge of the king's guard, "I'll need just one other fresh man to help me catch them and a stout length of twine. Quick we need to hurry; they are tired and so not as watchful as they should be. The one supposed to be on look out is very dozy. He can hardly keep his eyes open. The battle must have been a hard fought one!"

"Aye it was that lad." The older man pointed to the youngest of the soldiers, "Go with him Wilheard, do as he says, he knows these parts. Bring back our quarry and you'll be in the king's prayers tonight."

"Oh and they are behind you so it is probably safe to go on to the village." The two young men went off into the gathering evening with hope, wits and a length of twine.

Chapter Four

Of capture and a fresh enemy for Ayken

The village was astir with anticipation. The women had cooked as best they could in the time and waiting for the king's party were enough victuals to sustain an army, which in effect it was, however small. All was ready, the sheep broth, coarse bread, meat and mead were waiting for the returning group. None of them wanted to think of the king being hurt but there was excitement as they realised, without saying too much to each other, that this was an honour and a privilege. Of course if the other side won they would be killed, maimed and their huts burned. The survivors would move on until they found a kind village to take them in or they found a place where their particular skills would be welcome. All the adults knew this but they did not dwell on it for they would do their part and then see what the consequences might be.

The weary rescue party made its way along the village road to the hut that would receive the king. By the time he was safe the evening sun had dipped low behind the surrounding hills and the village and its people and livestock were bathed in the soft summer evening where shadows melt into the night and become one. The king was very pale by the time he was settled onto his wooden bed. Elvina took her place at the king's side to tend to his needs. Food was brought to all the soldiers and villagers who had affected the retreat. The soldiers had been billeted with the smith and his family. They had need of his skills and it was considered a sensible solution. Oeric was not yet able to meet with his comrades and so the village settled down to wait for news of young Wilheard and Ayken. The evening came and went and night fell dark and warm. The summer was well and truly at its hottest and the usual night breeze was absent. The exhausted younger soldiers slept, as did many of the settlement's inhabitants.

Ayken and Wilheard were of a similar age and strength. They did not know each other and Wilheard was inclined to believe that he was superior to Ayken. After all he was the king's thegn and Ayken was just a poor villager. It was therefore with some sense of mistreatment by his superior officer that Wilheard followed Ayken deep into the wood to find and capture the king's small band of enemies. Ayken had no such concept of inferiority as he set off through the trees; he was a straightforward young man and simply considered he was doing his duty to his king. As the two men neared the camp where the four rebels had settled Ayken motioned to Wilheard that they should be wary and as quiet as possible. This fuelled Wilheard's tired sense of propriety but he kept his counsel and did as he was instructed. They both dropped down to a crouching position and listened. The men were unaware of any intruder as they spoke with unguarded tongues. One hapless young man had been set as lookout but he was so tired that his head was forward on his chest and he was asleep. It took Ayken and Wilheard no time to knock him out and tie him up. Wilheard wanted to kill him. He pulled out a fine bladed knife and was seconds away from the deed when Ayken stopped him. He grabbed Wilheard's raised arm and there followed a silent tussle of wills which was won by Ayken, but only just. His slightly superior strength overcame the other and the thegn dropped his knife. Ayken picked it up and put it in his own belt. He began to feel uncomfortable with the other man and decided to stay beside or behind him as they moved quietly forward towards the rest of the group.

Luck was on the side of the king's men that night as another of the rebels decided to move away from the camp with the purpose of pissing, for this he went straight into the arms of the waiting captors. He was quickly bound but unfortunately he let out a cry to alert the remaining two companions. They were up and armed quickly for two very tired fighting men. Their stance was back to back as they protected each other's rear while waiting for an attack. Ayken and Wilheard moved to the centre of the camp and the four engaged in hand to hand fighting. Ayken had thrown Wilheard's knife back to him and got out his own inferior weapon. The struggle was over in a few minutes. The element of surprise and the comparative freshness of the king's men were enough to secure a victory. Soon all four invaders had their arms bound and then they were roped together. All were injured to some degree. The lookout had regained consciousness and sported a bloody wound to his head while the second man to be caught was the least injured being bruised but with no open wound. This one did stink however as the contents of his bladder had found its way down his legs as he'd had no time to piss before the fight. The two who had remained in the camp had several knife wounds, most of which were flesh deep only. One had sustained a deeper wound to his thigh and was bleeding profusely. Wilheard was bleeding from a gash in his upper arm and Ayken was aware of a pain in his side and a stickiness oozing through his jerkin. However such was the effect of the adrenaline flowing through their bodies that they kept going until all the work was done.

Ayken and Wilheard looked at their quarry, bound together in such a way that they could walk but not escape. They then looked at each other and for the first time smiled and nodded. Wilheard was exhausted from the short fight as he had been on the run with the king for many days, fighting or retreating. He had never questioned the king's decisions for he had utter faith in his lord and at this moment was proud of the work the two had done, even if he still thought on some level that he should have been in charge. Ayken was unaware of these thoughts in his companion and took his hand in a silent affirmation of a job well done. Wilheard gladly clasped his hand and then the two captors and their prize set off back through the woods to the village. It took them a couple of hours to make the journey back as their progress was slow. The man with the thigh wound bled heavily and had to be strapped up with a length of twine to try to hinder the bleeding. By the time they appeared in the village he was so weak that he collapsed as they unbound the group from each other.

As they limped into the village people came out of their cottages to greet them and help them. A small barn had been made secure for the men should Ayken and Wilheard be successful in their mission. It had not been only Elvina and Esmund who were concerned that they might not see their elder son alive again. The whole village realised that they had been holding their breath. Not only was the outcome the best for Borvo's family but also for the whole village. Had they failed then the enemy would have had no difficulty finding the village and realising that they had harboured the king. Their fate would have been dire in the extreme. So it was with relief and joy that they went out to welcome the victorious party.

The captives were safely in the barn with a proper guard. The wounds had been tended, such as they were. The man with the thigh wound had lost a lot of blood and slipped into unconsciousness during the night. Wilheard's arm was treated by Elvina and he was soon made comfortable in his billet with a bowl of food in front of him. Almost too tired to eat he thought about his actions and his companion and as he too slipped into the arms of Morpheus he thought he would speak to his commander and tell him of his considered disgrace in being made to obey a common man. Ayken meanwhile was being tended by his Gramma and she took off his jerkin and cleaned his wound. She applied all her skills to his injury and then had to leave it for time and the gods to decide on his fate. It was not a deep wound and she had done her best. As she sat back in her chair she took her nightly comphrey mixture then slept fitfully as she knew that should he take a turn for the worse during the night she had to be there to administer more medicine. Although she could no longer go out to the woods to gather herbs she had a generous supply brought to her by Borvo and Sunny. Each time they brought her a new supply she would tell them how to make potions and pastes with which to heal many hurts, both physical and those of the mind. Sunny listened but her skills lay elsewhere. Borvo thirsted for the knowledge and drank in every morsel that dropped from Gramma's lips.

So it was that the villagers, the king and his men and the invaders spent a sleep filled or anxious night. The dawn crept in with such light and hope that as the sky filled gradually with a warm pink and yellow glow its fingers crept into the dark interiors of the huts while people awoke and stretched and started the day. Cooking fires were lit, bed coverings were shaken and everyone went about their chores in the hope that they may learn more of the wounded. Children tried to steal glimpses of the prisoners, they strained their necks to catch sight of the king and some hovered around the doorway of Esmund and Elvina's cottage in the hope of seeing and speaking with Ayken. He was a popular young man with the children and rarely chastised them or shooed them away. Elvina left Borvo to tend the king while she went back to her home to check on her eldest son. She was concerned about his pallor and spoke softly with her mother about what she had done for him and what more could they do. Ayken stirred but his waking was feverish and

24

he quickly slumped once more into a troubled sleep. Between them mother and grandmother changed his dressings and made him as comfortable as they could. Elvina then made sure her mother was able to lie down to get her share of sleep as she had been semi vigilant all night. Elvina sent word to the king's hut to say she would stay with Ayken for the moment. Borvo was more than able to keep an eye on the king who was now sitting up and healing nicely. He was still weak but his command was returning and his very presence was rather too intimidating for some of the villagers. Mostly though they saw their king as a youngish man who needed their help and they were willing to lay down their lives for him.

Minister Brand was in charge of everything to do with the king's welfare. He was also in sole charge of his men. He was born to command and was the senior ealdorman of the king's witan council. These duties he carried out with great charm and strength. The villagers soon came to respect him for his own sake as well as for his position with the king. He had asked for help with guarding the Danes, for such were the invading soldiers. The morning brought sorry news for the prisoners as the man who has suffered the deep thigh wound had never regained consciousness and had died during the night. His body was taken out of the village and he was buried where his spirit could not interfere with the dead of the village. Of the remaining three prisoners there was one in command, one of low birth and a conscript. One of these was such a man for whom the invading army would give much; he was kinsman to one of their highest commanders.

On a practical level three prisoners were easier to manage than four. Brand considered that he had enough to do for the moment to keep the king safe and his whereabouts hidden. Whilst his scattered army needed to know he was alive the enemy did not need to know where he was. Brand decided to send a runner to where their comrades had last been seen to spread the word of the king's safety. Wilheard and Oeric were both wounded which left just him, Eadwig, Aesfric and Eoforheard. He needed Eorforheard and Aesfric to guard the prisoners. Eadwig was rather older than the others and not at all swift of foot. He was also too useful to have by him in case of crisis and so Wilheard, his least wounded young man, he sent on the dangerous, vital mission. His build was strong and, although not the swiftest of men, he was brave and built for sustained effort. He set off towards the east with the blessings of the villagers along with sustenance, such as they could spare.

Chapter Five

Borvo and the king

Borvo had spent the night in the king's room watching over him with his mother. Elvina had left at dawn to go to Ayken and so Borvo was alone with the king. He was not at all in awe of the man but he did have a healthy respect for him. The king seemed to him to have an aura about him that commanded respect, even in his weakened state. As Borvo greeted the day he began to hum the song he had received on the banks of the brook. He thought of the words and what they might mean. Singing the song, over and over again, made it all seem so real that he was caught up in his own world and neglected to notice the king raising himself up on one elbow and looking with fresh eyes at the youth who had saved him and his men. He was captivated by Borvo's singing and interrupted the third rendition of the song to ask him; "What manner of song is it you sing, Borvo?" Borvo thought that he might have stepped out of line so rather hesitatingly said, "Oh it's just something that came to me by the brook, yesterday when I slept."

"Ah, well, it sounds a song that reveres the old ways rather than the new." The king's voice was quiet and intense. Borvo's instinct was that he was treading on difficult adult ground and he became very wary of answering. He smiled and said, "Well, my Lord, dreams come unbidden, don't they?" The king looked at the youth and suddenly realised that he was speaking with a guardedness that had not been there before.

"Are you scared to be honest with me, Borvo?"

"Sir, I am being honest," the boy looked at the king and then disarmingly added, "Well, almost. Our family have fled many times from persecution so my parents have taught me to be, well, honest as much as I have to be." As an afterthought and by way of explanation he said, "We're strangers and healers you see. Not everyone welcomes us."

"Borvo, I am grateful that you are a healer and we will talk more of your 'ancient ways' when I have more strength. Now do you think I could eat before I pass out with hunger?" Borvo went out of the room to bring his lord bread and meat. He was thinking fast and decided that he must talk to his father before any more discussions with the king could take place. He was clever enough to realise that he would be no match for the king in a prolonged argument. He changed the subject, "Sir, I noticed in the night that some of your suffering is not from your wounds. Would you let my Gramma see you and offer you some relief? She is very good. I guess it is an old condition?" The king looked so surprised and at first said nothing in reply. He stared with renewed interest in this boy and then answered slowly with great deliberation, "You are right. I have long born the pain and discomfort for which no physician has been able to offer relief. I doubt your Gramma will be able to do so either." Borvo spoke no more.

Later that morning when the king had his minister with him Borvo took the opportunity to go and find his father to ask his advice. He found several of the village men talking and discussing the predicament in which they found themselves. There were four other men as well as Esmund, sitting in a group on the edge of the village where the cottages straggled into the meadow that led down to the beginnings of the wood. The woods rose up from the valley and covered the hillsides to the north and east of the village. To the west there were rock strewn hills and to the south were smaller hills with good grazing where they took their goats and sheep. The huts were mainly built of the rocks gathered from the hillside and wood from the forest. Clay mud turned into a sticky covering for the walls that helped to keep out the wind and rain. The roofs were covered with rough hewn thatch, brought from the salt marshes a days trek away and which lay between the village and the sea. It was an ideal spot for a settlement as they were protected on three sides from both bad weather and intruders. Only a few travellers got through the thick woods or over the hills therefore up to now the villagers had felt relatively safe. Now the dilemma was thrust upon them as to what to do with the king and his men and to maintain the villagers' safety. It did not occur to any of them not to help the king but they were facing a problem to which they had, as yet, no answer.

After a while the men decided that the only way was to ask the king's man, minister Brand, what they should do and how they might consult the king. It was at this moment that Borvo came upon the men and spoke with his father about his 'dream'.

"Father, I need help. I am not up to arguing with the King. Tell me what I ought to be saying."

"Why, Borvo, what has the King done to alarm you so?"

Borvo's father was concerned as he looked at his son's face. There was a pale, anxious quality which had not been there before.

"Not here father, let's go home and talk there."

"Well son, I'll have to explain to the others why I'm leaving in a hurry. Run home and wait for me there."

Borvo ran home and waited rather uncertainly for his father to return. He knew there was much for the village to discuss. A passing traveller, who was dressed as a brother from the abbey in the town of Malmesburgh had, only last month, told the small community of a bid to outlaw all worship other than that favoured by the court. The monk had been a lay brother only but sent on a mission for the abbot. He knew little of the ways of either the church or the king but loved to gossip and be thought of as more important than he was. From this unlikely source the villagers tended not to believe his story that spoke of such stringent measures. Always their way was to accept and incorporate any one with views of the old ways as well as tolerate or embrace the ideas that were new.

The villagers had built a separate place out of wood where they could gather and pray. It happened to be on the site of an old cairn where people had gathered for time without number to worship as their will took them. As the village carpenter was a convert the rough table held a beautifully carved cross. They needed no other symbol. Recently, in the last few years there had been an increasing number of people passing through with tales that the old path and the gods that abounded in days gone by were less evident than they had been. The village elders had met many times and discussed the problems that were brought to them by travellers. They always decided that their way was to carry on, accepting those who came with whatever was in their hearts. It was this acceptance and friendliness that had attracted Borvo's family and encouraged them to stay. Moreover the village needed healers as the last 'wise' person to live among them had fallen prey to a wild boar and been gored. The attack had severed an artery and the 'wise man' had bled to death. Since that time the villagers had relied on vague ideas gleaned from observing the man at his work. They had come to realise that the presence of someone with the old ways was preferable if not vital to the wellbeing of the whole community.

Chapter Six

Escape and bloodshed

Sunniva had dressed Oeric's wounds earlier that morning, the second day after the king and his men had been brought to the village. On the advice of her Gramma she had mixed leaves from the majorane and comphrey plants with hot water and made a paste with which to soothe his wounds. He now slept with greater comfort and his face had begun to lose the grey colour which had so alarmed this young woman. She sat by his pallet and smoothed the rough woollen cover over his chest; he stirred but did not wake. She smiled a smile so tender that she herself was surprised at how he made her feel. They had exchanged but few words and most of the time they had spent in each other's company had been full of pain and fear. Now as the morning sun rose in the sky and filtered through the warm air in the cottage there seemed to be time for peaceful reflection and healing quiet. It was onto this tranquil scene that Borvo brought his own disruptive anxiety.

"Sunny, I've got to . . ." He stopped abruptly as his lovely gentle sister turned on him with a ferocious look of rebuke;

"Hush, Borvo," then turning back to her charge she added, "he sleeps."

She took up her sewing and carried on as though she and Oeric were the only two people in the world.

"Oh, well, that's good then." Borvo responded rather sulkily and as he felt that he was intruding he went outside and sat under a tree and waited for his father. As he sat and contemplated all the strange things that were going on he thought momentarily of his sister's face when she looked at the king's man. He had never seen her look so at anyone although many young men had tried to make her like them, she had treated them all with grace and distance. This small village of twenty huts that had welcomed them in and made them safe was no longer a sanctuary. Borvo felt that it closed in on him and he had to fight down a strong instinct to flee. In that moment he knew that his future was not in the village. He saw a town with many more people and roads that crossed and led out to more dwellings than he had ever seen in one place. There were bridges and rivers that seemed to surround the town. This was in his mind as Esmund came upon his son and was struck by the consternation in his young face. He sat down next to him on the ground; "Why Borvo, you are troubled. Tell me and we will work it out. How has the king upset you? What has he said?"

Borvo repeated the conversation with the king then lapsed again into silence. He looked at his father then away and stared into the distance.

"I feel that I will leave here very soon. There is a need in me to go. It has just come over me." He continued to gaze into the north and into his future.

From his birth Esmund had known that Borvo would be the one to break his heart or make him proud, he still didn't know which it was to be. Deep down Esmund understood that his son's destiny had caught up with him and he had to find his own path. Ayken, his older son, was born to use his strong physical frame in either work or fighting. This too he accepted. He considered his daughter.

Sunniva was talented with the needle but because of her lameness he had always expected her to remain within the family. He had seen the look of a woman on her face when she tended the young soldier. Suddenly he felt that he may lose all his children in a very short space of time. It saddened him but he sighed and asked the gods to help them all as they made their way. He mentally shook his thoughts from him and concentrated on Borvo who was talking again.

"When you and Ayken next go north can I come with you? I have a picture in my head that won't leave me. I think it is the place that calls me."

Esmund took a long time to reply. Eventually he said, "We don't know what is going to happen, Borvo. There is great trouble at the moment and we have to make sure the king and his men get to safety. But, yes, I think we can take you with us. It is time." He smiled a rather wistful smile and patted his son's head. "About the king and his god. It is best to be careful. Many don't want our ways to continue. Ask questions if you wish but keep in mind what is in your soul. Perhaps one day you will tell me about the brook?"

Borvo looked startled and then laughed. "I suppose I must get my . . . my gifts from you. I thought it was just Gramma."

"Borvo, you are a mixture of us all with an extra piece that is just your own. You are all special. Remember that, won't you?" Esmund stood up and stretched.

"We have agreed a plan with the king's minister. We need to prepare. Go to your mother and help her then go back to the king and see what needs to be done with his wounds. We may need to gather more plants for the healing."

The rest of the day was busy for the whole village. Men talked and made preparations for the king and his men on their journey to find and hopefully meet with the rest of their supporters. The young and fit were made ready to fight to protect the king. Being such a small village there were only eight men fit enough for fighting but they were keen to help and were caught up in the excitement of the moment. None thought of the danger or that some may not return. On that day when their king needed them more than the goats and the crops in the fields, that day they felt invincible.

Women talked and prepared food and mended clothing to enable the village men and the king's men to go forth with as much protection as they could. There was little to spare but what they had they gave. The king was wounded but he was mending and knew the sacrifices that the villagers were making on his behalf. When the battles were over he would not forget them. He spoke with minister Brand and made him promise to compensate the village should he, the king, not make it through. Brand was an honourable man and agreed that whatever was in his power so to do would be done. It was the third day since the king had been brought to the village. It was decided that after one more day for healing the group would set out. They hoped against hope that Wilheard would return by then to report on the rest of the king's men. If he didn't they would take a chance and go anyway. It was more dangerous to stay than to go.

Another late summer morning dawned misty and chill. The hills that looked over the village were lost in the early light. Where the forest lay the trees were almost completely hidden except for some very tall beech trees that had grown over the rest in an effort to reach the light. There were sounds of life coming from the cottages as the villagers went about their usual early morning chores as well as making preparations for the departure of the king, his men and the village volunteers the next day. It had been decided that the prisoners would be kept back in the village until more of the king's men could be sent to escort them safely. Prisoners were valuable and useful for barter and exchange when dealing with this particular enemy.

One of the young men not going on the journey with the others was Goaty. He had been named purely for his kind and gentle way with the goats. His parents had long since gone and he was part of the village by adoption. He was accepted for who he was, slow and gentle. When he was born his mother believed that the gods had kept something back for themselves and so named him as special but few could remember what that name had been. His mother had wandered off one day and her shawl was found drifting in the river on the far side of the southern downland. Goaty lived in poor circumstances at the very western end of the settlement. His wooden cottage was but one room where he had his straw mattress on the floor by the meagre central hearth. The edges of his mattress had been singed by flying chips of burning wood over the years but he loved the warmth and so took no heed of any advice and stayed close by the fire. His work took him to the surrounding hills for most of the day and he was rewarded with food and clothing by the owners of the goats. They had little enough for themselves but it was an isolated village and they took care of their own. At the time of the king's stay Goaty was about twenty summers old. No one knew for certain and it was of no real significance. He was who he was and that was that.

Goaty was always one of the first in the village to rise and tend his one goat before he helped others with theirs. She was a young nanny who gave him milk and slept in the one room cottage with him. He'd had a stray dog once but that had died and so now it was just the two of them. The morning of the expedition Goaty was woken by an unusual stirring outside his cottage. There was no fabric at the window, all that kept the weather out was a rough wooden shutter fixed there by one of the older men who had taken pity on the orphaned boy years before. The boy had steadfastly refused to leave the hovel that he had shared with his mother so until he was considered old enough to be on his own the village took care of him and shared with him what they had.

The Danes had been kept in a secure barn guarded by the very strong village smith and two of the king's men, Eoforheard and Aesfric. Seasoned fighters the Danes were very resourceful. Injured but determined not to remain prisoners for long they whispered together and sought every opportunity to find a weakness in the guards. Just before dawn on the fateful day they waited until the smith went to piss in the nearby thicket. Eoforheard was always tense at these times as he knew that in a fight he and Aesfric could not take on the three men and win. His comfort was in the knowledge that they were bound by strong leather straps both hands and feet. Aesfric decided that he too needed to go outside and relieve himself. Eoforheard was left alone and nervous.

Just a few moments into his solitary vigil one of the men groaned and his eyes rolled and he started to shake as though in a fever. His actions became increasingly agitated which put Eoforheard into a quandary. Neither the smith nor Aesfric had returned. The noise from the prisoner became louder and louder. To lose a prisoner through neglect was frowned upon as they could be used to barter with and so he decided to investigate. As he approached the writhing man the others silently freed their already loosed bonds and hit Eoforheard savagely over the head. His last thoughts were clouded in a red mist as he lost consciousness. Within seconds the smith came running back in to the barn to see the three men disappear out through the window space. The smith was built for strength not speed and so it was no contest for the three leaner, battle hardened, men to outrun him. As the smith lumbered to the nearest hut he gave a shout of alarm. Aesfric had come round the side of the small barn and run straight into them. They swiftly knocked him out and ran on. The earliest risers came out to see what the commotion was about. Within minutes there was a general buzz as people ran to and fro trying to take in what was happening. Brand ran out of his lodgings and went to the barn to find a young village man sitting on the earthen floor cradling Eorforheard in his lap. The injured man's blood had already seeped out to cover the smock and leggings of the villager. Brand turned to a passing child and told him to run as fast as he could to the hut of 'The Healers' who were to come with their medicines to tend the wounded king's man in the small barn. Aesfric was nowhere to be seen.

Chapter Seven

Flight after carnage

The three fleeing soldiers initially made good progress out of the village. Their flight was inspired by the need to get back to their leader and the adrenaline that pushes on all who are in great fear for their lives. It was this 'kill or be killed' thought running through them like fire that gave them no second thought about knocking down and cudgelling the village simpleton who had mysteriously appeared before them out of the mist. Goaty, once disturbed by the unusual sounds of the morning with which he was always in tune, had gone outside to make sure that his nanny goat was not in any difficulty. She always had free run of the hovel and surrounding land and rarely came inside once the may had blossomed. After Goaty's brief encounter with the runaways he lay in a pool of blood with his she goat standing beside him bleating a forlorn sound of doom.

As the three crashed into the woods they slowed down both because of the undergrowth and their minor sores that they had sustained from their fight with Ayken and Wilheard. The leader of the troop decided that the two of them who were least injured would go ahead more quickly and so he ordered his wounded man to stay and draw off the inevitable chasing party. Brand

and some of the village men gave chase. They passed by Goaty's cottage and saw that people were attending to yet another victim of the desperate men and so they ran on. The resources of this little village were being stretched to the limit but the king must be saved and he must get back to lead his remaining loyal people to regain his kingdom. Brand would do what he could after the war was won. The village men knew the woods much better than the soldiers and it took but half an hour before they found the badly wounded soldier. Brand had no sympathy for his wounds. He ordered Esmund to bind him where he lay and then follow the party to find the others. Esmund made him as comfortable as he could; his human compassion would not allow him to hurt the young man any further even though he had caused such torment to others. He prayed for help as he ran on after the disappearing group. The other two prisoners had decided to split up to confuse their pursuers. The leader, who was the nephew of one of their commanders, had most of the cunning and so managed to avoid being captured on that morning. The other fellow made for the brook so that he could drink and make his way up the water course so that he wouldn't leave any boot prints.

Borvo had been sent out early that morning to pick the leaves of the herbs and flowers whilst they still had the dew on them. He had finished his task and was sitting on the wet bank of the brook singing his special song in his head. The mist swirled around him. He turned his head at the sudden noise and thought for an instant that Borvo the God had come to speak with him again. As the figure lumbered out of the mist he realised that it was the rough soldier who had taken him prisoner before. Borvo got up, threw his bundle of herbs into the water as an offering, and ran for all his worth. He made his way deep into the forest and didn't stop until he was well clear of the danger. As he ran blindly deeper than ever before into the forest he noticed that the trees were of a different kind from those near his village. He ran and walked and stumbled along with the fear of being caught greater than the fear of being lost.

Brand and the others came upon the rough soldier as he lay panting under a thicket quite near to where he had startled Borvo. He had been too complacent thinking he knew the enemy and had no sense to keep going. It was now well past sunrise and the morning was almost half over before they struggled back to the village with the two hostages. Brand had made the decision to abandon the chase for the third prisoner. He looked at the men with him and decided that they should use strategy rather than force to outwit the man. Brand had little man power at his disposal and he must use it to best advantage.

Esmund, Ayken and the other villagers were exhausted when they returned to the village. Brand immediately went to the king and had counsel with him. The plans for leaving were postponed for another day to allow the villagers to rest and get back their strength. It would be a long trek when they finally set out. There were other advantages in delay as it would give the king one more day to regain his strength which was already well on the way to being fully restored thanks to his treatment. The king was intrigued by the incomers. He was also impressed by the way the village had accepted them and defended them.

Elvina had organised a low pallet in the barn for Eorforheard. She decided his injuries were too severe for him to be moved. His pallet was placed by the window where he could get fresh air and sunlight to improve his recovery. Whether he would make a full recovery was beyond her knowledge but she had done her best with the medicine available to her. She had bound his head wound with the healing moss and tied clean linen around it to stop any movement of the broken skull. He may not regain all his wits but she would go and look for some rare herbs when she was released from the initial tasks. She needed more knit-bone for an infusion.

She also needed more rosemary and chamomile for the inevitable headache and for mending the blood ways. She had also told Borvo to make sure that he brought back yarrow which was excellent for stopping bleeding. Never before had she found the need for so many of her skills. She had helped with battle wounds before but this time she realised that this was a different test as she had become very attached to the young soldiers and they had acted with great courage and respect for the humble villagers. This impressed her more than any battle bravado.

With Esmund and Ayken in pursuit of the prisoners and Borvo out collecting herbs it was left to Gramma to deal with Goaty's injuries. His wounds were similar to those of Eorforheard but rather more severe. Gramma tended the young man with her own blend of mosses and herbs very like her daughter had done for Eorforheard. Once she had done all she could, she and another matron of the village took it in turns to sit with him and make sure that he was never alone. Any sign of change in his condition needed prompt attention. Any delay could result in disastrous consequences. Already they may be too late but they had to try. This gentle soul did not deserve such treatment. His life had been hard enough. As Gramma sat by him she began to chant. Tunes and words from her childhood gathered in her thoughts and she carefully let them hang in the air and surround her sleeping charge. He was deep in a place where few could get to him. His only chance was Gramma's will with the help of her gods. She chanted and hummed the ancient tunes until she was too weary to continue. She then let herself fall into a renewing slumber. These times lasted but half an hour but they were enough to sustain her through her vigil. Borvo had told her of his encounter with Borvo the God by the brook. She considered her grandson as she sat by this lost young man. How he had grown to be such a good healer in so short of time made her think that he must be the one. In every generation there was one with special powers that stood out from the rest. All the line had the gift of healing. All the line had intuition and skills. Borvo was different. He looked different and he acted differently from the rest of the family. As the day wore on she wondered why he was so long in coming back with the plants they all needed. Elfleda came back to take her turn at sitting with Goaty and Gramma shuffled off to find out what was happening with the rest of the family and indeed the whole village. She was stiff from sitting so long in one place and she needed her tincture of comphrey to help her own aches. As she returned to the family cottage she found only Sunniva and Oeric. Sunniva was helping Oeric take tentative steps outside in the pale spring sunshine. He had made great strides in his recovery thanks to Sunniva's devotion and now was making rapid progress to full health with the help of stripped saplings fashioned for him by Ayken. Gramma noticed his colour was improving and she nodded. He would be all right. Sunniva's colour was high and she knew full well why that was so. She had seen many young women blush so when in the presence of their love. Oeric didn't know it yet but Sunny considered they were destined to be together. As he could now be left Gramma sent Sunniva to find out what was going on. She would take her medicine and then be well enough to start again in a while. She sat down and dozed. Oeric sat in the sunshine and closed his eyes.

Sunniva found her mother in the barn bending over the stricken Eorforheard. His head was swathed in cloth and his face was ashen. There was a blood soaked smock abandoned nearby where the young man who first found him had taken it off as soon as he could. Still in shock from finding such a sight he had walked out in a daze and left it where it lay. Elvina was listening to Eorforheard's breathing. Suddenly she stood up and sighed. She turned and saw her daughter, "He will have his chance now. His breathing is shallow but regular again." She didn't smile but put her hand out to Sunniva and grasped it for giving and receiving comfort. "How is Oeric today?" It was then that Elvina smiled as she watched her daughter's colour heighten as she replied, "He has taken steps outside and I have left him sitting in the sun. Gramma says he will be well."

"Good. You've done well. You like him daughter?" Elvina knew the answer but wanted to force Sunniva into confessing. It was a gentle teasing but threw Sunniva into confusion.

"Oh, yes, no, I hardly know how I . . . I like him well enough he's . . . well he Oh Mam, Mam, Mam, he's . . . he's . . . isn't he?"

Laughing Elvina agreed that he was.

Chapter Eight

Borvo is lost but Ealdyg finds her man

Konal, the leader of the prisoners, was lost. He had stumbled further and further into the woods until he was exhausted. Weeks of fighting followed by incarceration had taken its toll. He was not a young man any more. He had seen more than thirty summers and wanted nothing more than to return home to his plump wife and five children. There had been more but his eldest son had joined the fighting and had been killed at the battle in the east just as they landed their ships on the coast. The foolhardy locals had tried to either fight or run away. Most of those that fought were killed and those that ran away when inevitably captured, also met the same fate. Konal was tired of it all. As he had set fire to his son's body he longed to go home. He knew his leader would countenance no such sentiment and so he buried his feelings deep in his heart along with memories of his son, swung his sword with the best of the men and trudged on, burning, killing or enslaving until the countryside was won. This last western lord seemed trickier than most. They had not found it easy and the terrain helped the natives not the invading army. He thought that there may be few of the West Saxon's left but still they would not give in. He admired their lord as a great strategist, or may be he was just lucky. As he sat with his back against a large tree his thoughts ranged back and forth. There was little light coming through the canopy of the forest. He guessed it must be late in the day but without the sky as a reference he felt unsure.

Konal slept and fell into a fever. Delirious he thought that he was being soothed by a soft white hand. Cool water brushed his face and a rough earthenware vessel put to his dry lips. The drink was cool. It was not water or ale. Deep in his fevered brain an alarm rang and he tried to push the hand away but he had no strength left. He groaned, drank and slept once more. Ealdyg had lived in the forest nearly all her life. She was old now and loved nothing more than sitting in her humble hut, living off the land and spinning. Once she had loved a man but he had gone to fight and never returned. She remembered something else as well, a shadow, a face but then it was gone. She had gone from her father's home when both her mother and father had died. She'd sought help to bury them and then stayed in the forest weaving the stories in her head of what might have been. There had been a time when she'd left but that was so long ago. All in all now she was content. The animals and birds loved her or at least they didn't run away and were not afraid of her. She would settle for that. As the light went out of her eyes she stayed closer to her hut and mixed her broth with herbs to keep out the cold and help her dreams. Sometimes the dreams became reality and she was young again, hope stirred in her breast at these times and she walked with a lighter tread. It was during one of her dreamy times that she had found Konal. Of course it was her Alric come back to her. She made him comfortable where he lay and ran back and forth to her hut to fetch a rough cover for him until he could be moved. The cool herb tea she had given him was an infusion of feverfew and majorane. This would bring down his fever and then he would recognise her. As she soothed his brow she repeated his name over and over like a lullaby. Konal slept and as he slept his fever abated and his sleep became calm and restoring.

Ealdyg sat on the ground next to Konal, wrapped herself in a blanket and she too slept. Day turned into night and night into day. Brand and his men had long since given up looking for the one prisoner. They were back in the village deciding what to do next with an even more depleted stock of sound men with which to carry on the fight. They must get back to the place where they had agreed to meet and reform. Brand knew that the young healer, Borvo, was lost in the forest. He prayed that he would not meet up with Konal. No quarter would be given. In this war it was kill or be killed. In the case of the youth it might be that he was a prize worth keeping which would be perhaps even worse than death. Brand shivered at the thought and carried on with his duties pushing the evil out of his mind. Esmund had taken his older son Ayken back into the forest to search for Borvo but secretly he had little hope. The forest was vast and stretched over the hills in seemingly manageable pockets of gentle woodland that ran on and on one into the other.

Borvo rested. As he ran on through the trees he thought that at one time he heard people calling his name. He went cautiously to where he imagined the sound to come from. Then he heard it no more. For Borvo, as for Konal and Ealdyg, day turned into night. The resourceful youth decided to make himself comfortable with whatever he could find and rest. When he felt restored he would try to find his way home. He prayed to his god for himself and for his family. These were strange and exhausting times and he was confused by the last few days. After his exhortation to the gods he felt more hopeful and he too slept.

That night there was little sleep for Esmund and the rest of his family. Elvina and Gramma worked tirelessly to heal the men wounded by Konal and his men. Esmund and Ayken were still searching for Borvo until well past darkness when they too decided to come back and make another early start the following day. Sunniva sat and sewed to take her mind off both her feelings for Oeric and her concern for her younger brother.

Chapter Nine

Plans and hopes but a light goes out

Brand had been closeted with the king for most of the afternoon.

"My Lord, there has been much commotion today as I am sure you have heard." The king was sitting up on his pallet and seemed much improved, almost ready to take complete charge again. His wound, tended by Borvo and his family, had healed well. There was some ache but there had been no more bleeding and the bruises were a riot of colour as they healed.

"I know that the prisoners escaped and that they left two badly injured. I have also heard that young Borvo is missing. What is being done for all these poor people? I have been praying but as yet have found no solace in prayer."

"Borvo's mother tends Eorforheard. He was too ill to move so he is well cared for in the barn. The villagers seem ever resourceful. I admire them. Their straightforward approach to matters is refreshing. There is also a simple man who tends the goats. His condition seems desperate. We picked up two of the prisoners who are now securely bound and tied to a cart in a smaller hut. One prisoner died from his wounds and their leader is missing." Brand stopped to reflect. The king said nothing.

"This enemy seem in poor condition. They were strong when they started but their campaign has been long and they seem battle weary." Brand's eyes shone with renewed light, "If only we could regroup we could have them on the run. We ought to get going as soon as we may. Konal may well get back to his people and tell them what he knows."

The king smiled a weary smile, "You are right of course but I need to know how the villagers are and what has happened to Borvo." He paused. It was his way not to make hurried or ill considered decisions.

"Tomorrow we will set out as planned with whoever we can. Tell the village that we appreciate their loyalty and when we are successful we will make sure they are recompensed. Will you seek now to find out about the boy? I have an idea that may suit him if I can get him to think away from his pagan gods. It will be a long road I think as they have been driven away by many in their lives."

Brand looked surprised. Again the king smiled and said, "I have not been idle even though I've been limited in my movement. People do gossip and none too softly if they think you're ears are stopped by sleep."

Brand left the king to finish his meal and set out to find Elvina. She was as he suspected tending the young soldier, Eorforheard. She turned round at his approach and she put a finger to her lips, "He is restless but I have given him a draught and he should settle. I have good thoughts about him and hope that the wound is not too deep. Not like Goaty. He is very bad. My mother tends him." As she spoke her smile charmed the older man and he felt a warmth towards this woman for which he felt guilty. They walked out of the barn and towards Elvina's hut at the other end of the village. The evening was drawing in and as the summer day gave way to evening the light began to change the colour of the surrounding hills to a soft lilac streaked with dark green and broom yellow. Brand asked

49

after Borvo. Elvina's face became taut and the worry that she had suppressed surfaced to take over her whole being. "Esmund and Ayken search for him. They will do their best." She sighed, "He is at home in the forest but even he may go too far and in the mists of this morning he could get lost."

"The king asks after him. We will go in the early morning tomorrow. Pray God we will have news of him by then. I believe the king will want to hear word even after we have gone."

Elvina looked ever more anxious, "He is too young to leave home yet. We do not want to lose him. He has much to learn."

"Be easy Elvina, the king would not harm him, he is a good man. Let it go for now but my words are by way of a warning. But hold him as long as you can. He is gifted."

Brand walked back to the hut where the king was now up and about testing his strength and planning his next move in the fight to save his people and beloved Wessex.

As Elvina entered their cottage she saw that her mother was not in her usual seat. She addressed her daughter, "Sunny, where is Gramma? Have father and Ayken returned yet? Is there any news at all?"

Sunniva put down her sewing and got up to embrace her mother, "Sit down Mother and I'll get you some broth, it's been ready for a while. No news of Borvo, father and Ayken have yet to return but Gramma is with Goaty. It's not good. He's very bad."

"Perhaps I should . . ."

"Mother, go nowhere until you've eaten. You'll be no good to any if you collapse."

Elvina sank back into the seat by the fire. She seemed to notice something else, "Where's Oeric?"

Sunniva blushed, "Oh, he's gone to find Minister Brand and tell him he is fit for duty. He thanks us for our care and . . ." at the next statement Sunniva blushed even deeper, "and he says he will come back to thank us properly one day soon." She stared into the fire then added, "He took my hand and then he kissed me. I didn't know what to do so I . . . well I kissed him too."

Elvina stopped eating and held out her hand to her daughter. No words were necessary. She squeezed her hand, the hand that was so talented and gentle and smiled her approval. She finished her broth, cleared away the bowl and then went to find her mother to see if she could help her with Goaty.

Gramma was in Goaty's hut. She had made it as comfortable as she could. The fire was alight with burning logs and there were fresh rushes on the floor. Her bones ached with tiredness but she had her charge and she would stick with him until there was an end to it. Either he would recover or he would not. She had done all that was in her considerable power but there were limits. Goaty had a deep wound to his head, a high fever and his skin was cold and wet. None of these were good signs but if he was to go into the next world then Gramma would sing to him and placate the spirits with her old songs. These she hummed as she worked on him. She had done all she could, now it was up to Goaty and his gods. His she-goat had been milked and Gramma offered a small cup to Goaty in the hope that the familiar smell might get through to him and if not bring him back then give him comfort wherever he was going.

As Elvina approached the poor hut at the very end of the village she recognised her mother's singing and chanting. The old songs always reappeared at times of great crisis so she entered knowing that Goaty was in a very bad way.

Chapter Ten

Borvo is found while Ayken leaves

Ealdyg was asleep with her head resting against the great bole of the oak tree. Its many tangled roots formed a comfortable place for her to lie in and not roll away as she slipped into unconsciousness. Konal passed a restless night but his fever broke at some point and he awoke rested and oddly at peace with himself. He looked over to his side and saw the old woman against the tree. He moved his body slightly to get a more comfortable position and unwittingly touched her. Her head lolled to one side coming to rest at an unnatural angle. He had seen enough death to know that she slept the deep sleep of the dead. Her face was as pale as the moon but she smiled and had obviously died happy. Konal was unaware of her story and so did not realise that she felt that she had found her love who, after all the years and against all odds, had returned to find her. She had died content. She was but forty five years old.

Konal on the other hand was left in a quandary. He found that he was tied to the tree by leather straps that had been knotted on the opposite side of the trunk from where he lay. What was more uncomfortable was that the old woman had similarly tied herself to him, presumably so that he would not run away. All this puzzled him greatly but he was a practical man and so made himself as easy as he could while he thought of a way out of his predicament.

As he settled back on the forest floor, he realised that the old woman had taken his sword and knife. She must have put them somewhere safe, probably in her hut. He could see the wooden shack if he twisted his head and looked over his shoulder. The leather straps were damp with dew and had tightened so that they were tight against his skin. He had endured worse tortures but he was very vulnerable and so shook his head to clear his thoughts in an effort to hurry his thinking. Ealdyg flopped beside him. This too caused him concern as her body was giving up its smell and this was not pleasant. He had a healthy respect for the passing of life but his foremost thoughts were of getting back to his group and passing on the important news of their enemy's condition. As he twisted round once more to try to loose his bonds he saw a shadow flit across in front of the hut. It was a slight form that ran and then hid behind the next tree. It was some moment before the figure reappeared, this time closer to where he lay but still outside his reach. He sighed a great sigh of relief when he recognised the young healer from the Saxon village. Borvo stood just far enough away to gauge the circumstances of the man. He did not yet know that he and his men had all but killed the young soldier and Goaty. He did not yet know of the recapture of the other two. All Borvo saw as he looked down was the dead form of Ealdyg and the odd tryst of the two figures. What he should have done was leave the man to his fate. He should have run back to the village as fast as he could and get help. Borvo was a young boy, maybe wise beyond his years in many things, but still with much to learn.

Borvo knew Ealdyg as did all the villagers. She lived a good way into the forest and occasionally would be helped by the villagers. They knew she was mad but they considered her harmless and looked out for her when they could. On her very rare visits to the village she would walk along the outskirts of the settlement and work her way back to her hut having picked up the bundles of clothes and food left for her by the first oak tree that marked the start of the wood. Borvo summoned up the courage to speak to the tethered man, "Did you kill her?" he asked. He accompanied his words with gestures to make sure he was understood. Konal shook his head. The older man tapped his head to indicate his fever of the night and held out his bonded hands and legs. Borvo was tired. He went back to the hut and collected up the man's sword and knife. He threw the knife down just out of reach of the man and then he ran with all his remaining strength towards the village. He knew the direction from Ealdyg's place. It was a long run but he could do it. The king may depend on him. As Borvo ran he took less care than usual and fell over a root which trapped his foot and left him with a broken ankle. He could run no further. He cried in agony and with frustration. He crawled to the nearest tree and put his back to it and waited.

Meanwhile Konal had seen his trusty blade and was determined to get it therefore he strained with all his considerable muscle ignoring the deep cuts in his arm made by the stretched leather until he finally reached it. He picked it up and managed to saw through his bonds. He stood and stretched. His legs and back ached. Konal waited until the sensation came back to his limbs then ran off after the boy. He had an idea that he would capture the youth and take him hostage. His men could always do with a healer. Ealdyg he left where she lay. Hers was an ignominious end to a sad life.

Ayken and Esmund set off as soon as it was light to restart their search for Borvo. They followed a new path that morning and swept through to the little used south eastern track that led eventually to Ealdyg's hut. They stayed within shouting distance of each other and called periodically both to each other and to Borvo. They would not give up until they found him, whatever his fate. Anxiety lent strength to their legs and backs. It was mid morning when they stopped to drink the water they carried and talked to reassure each other about the successful outcome of their quest. Borvo must not be lost, he had to be found. As Ayken sat and Esmund stood by the poorly distinguished path they both began to despair. They had been searching all last evening and now it was well into the morning and still there was no trace of him. Their voices were low but carried on the wind and it was then that Borvo's hopes rose. Surely it was his father's voice he could hear. Perhaps he was dreaming. No he was wide awake and in pain. He decided it was safe to call out. Esmund heard it first, the plaintive cry of his younger son. "Come Ayken, that's him. This way." Esmund ran off hotly pursued by Ayken. As they came upon the small clearing which in truth was no more that a widening of the path they rushed to Borvo and knelt down and hugged him. As they did so Borvo cried out in both physical pain and a warning shout as he had just seen Konal leap into the path brandishing his knife. Ayken whirled round, Borvo held out Konal's sword to him which the younger boy had kept by him. The older brother took the sword and there followed a fierce but very short fight. Ayken was stronger than Konal but he lacked the killer instinct. He did not give way but could not kill the older man. Konal was on the ground and Ayken turned to find something with which to bind the man when Konal leapt to his feet and sped off through the under growth. He had enough sense to know that captured he would be no good to his leader and if he stayed the younger man would eventually realise he must be killed. Esmund stood back to let Ayken fight as he had no weapon, save his knife, and thought that anyway he would get in his son's way.

As Konal took off through the trees Esmund moved swiftly to unpack his own supply of food and drink and give it to Ayken. "Borvo and I will be all right. Follow and come back to tell Minister Brand where he leads you. May the gods bless you and be with you."

As an afterthought he added, "And the king's god as well. You may need all the help they can give." The two men hugged and Ayken ran off to follow the Dane. As he watched his elder son disappear into the forest Esmund's heart was heavy as he wondered if he would see him alive again. Esmund turned to where Borvo sat and smiled at him. "You need the attention of your Gramma." So saying he lifted Borvo gently onto his back and set off for the difficult journey homeward. Borvo told his father about finding Konal and Ealdyg tied together by her hut; one alive and the other smiling in death. Esmund didn't answer at first then decided to tell Borvo the truth about Ealdyg. All the elders knew but had decided not to tell the young hut dwellers in case any news got to the wrong ears and caused more distress than there had already been.

Their journey was necessarily slow as Borvo was no longer the small child that had ridden his father's back for fun. He was tall and slender certainly but his muscles were well developed and he weighed heavily on Esmund's shoulders. By the time they regained the village Borvo's face was deathly pale and he was sweating profusely from a high temperature. Esmund also was sweating but only from exertion. He was happy to be relieved of his burden and left his younger son in the care of his mother, Gramma and sister and went to find the elders of the village. So much had happened and in such a short time that of necessity they must keep up with the day's events. The king would be interested too in Ayken's quest. He would be less interested in Ealdyg's death and funeral arrangements.

The king had sunk to his knees after speaking with Esmund and Brand. He prayed that the young Ayken would be well and return with news that would help finish this constant battle with the invaders. He had learned so much from being in this simple village. He knew now what one of his main tasks was when he had time to think about other things; things other than fighting and war. He wanted peace above all but then stability and education for as many as could understand. He knew he would need help but put any such thoughts to the back of his mind, first he must win the battle, find a way to stop the Danes ever coming back.

Once Esmund had finished with the king and his minister he went to the hut of one of the elders, Leofric. Outwardly Leofric was a rough man who had spent all his time working hard on the land to make a good life for his family. He was also an honest and wise man to whom the rest of the village looked for leadership. Leofric accepted his role with crude understanding of human nature. His opinion was usually fair. Esmund spoke with him and told him of Ealdyg's death tied to the invader.

"Oh, so it is over then. She must have thought that he had come back. A life wasted in hoping that sent her mad. It was the baby that did it. Once she had him she went off into a world of her own. There was no turning her back to this cruel world. What about her son? How is he do you know?"

Esmund spoke of Borvo's injury and how he had rushed straight to the king when he came back, "I hadn't the time to inquire after him. I'll go now and come back with news but we have to bring her back its only right."

Leofric took a long time to answer and said, "Yes, we have to. We will use the litter that bore the king here. She would have liked that in her days of understanding."

Borvo was asleep in his bed when Esmund went back to his cottage. Gramma was gone and so was his wife, only Sunny remained sitting by Borvo and watching him. Esmund placed a kiss on her forehead and then went out to Goaty's hut to speak with Gramma. As he approached the poor hut he saw dim candle light moving rhythmically to and fro across the open doorway. Low chanting hovered in the air then disappeared leaving a profound silence. From all this he knew that Goaty had gone on to the next life. His injuries must have been too great for the skills of Gramma. Everyone had to die sooner or later and this was Goaty's time. Esmund felt a sense of the fates weaving their threads and pulling mortal spirits this way and that. It was meant to be so. Goaty and Ealdyg would be reconciled with each other on their journey to the next world. She could no more help her madness then he could his distressed birth and simple understanding. It had been a traumatic birth for Ealdyg and when Goaty finally came forth into the light he was damaged. Ealdyg's lover had walked away from them and never looked back. The elder villagers remembered the strong back walking into the hills without a glance at the woman who loved him to insanity and the poor child that would bear his frame but not his wits. Ealdyg had tried to care for the baby but she was too often in her own world of dreams and so the village took him on and Leofric, his uncle, made sure that he was well cared for and that no harm came to him until he could fend for himself. Leofric organised the litter and the men that would bring his sister back to her home. It would be her final journey with the son who had been no compensation for her abandonment. As Ealdyg's body came nearer to the village more and more people came to light their way with tapers throwing small flickers of welcome. By now the whole village, young and old, knew of Goaty's story. Gramma and Elfleda bathed and made ready Goaty's body for the ceremony the following day. He had never regained consciousness although Gramma felt a small response when she held his hand at one stage but even so she kept up an almost endless singing and chanting and talking with him just in case he heard the love in her voice. She hoped that this would send him on his way knowing that he was cared for. The plaintive cry of Goaty's she-goat was distressing to hear. She had been milked and tethered in case she wandered off but nothing would still her cries until the morning when she was calmer and thankfully quiet.

Chapter Eleven

Two kinds of departure

Minister Brand woke to a beautiful clear summer day. It was already warm and he had a feeling of well being and good portents for the coming journey. He rose, dressed and then prayed briefly before he sought his lord to finalise their departure. The king had expressed a desire to leave as soon as possible after the first meal so that they could make the meeting place before darkness fell. Luckily it was summer so the nights were short and they would make good headway. Brand had told the king about Ealdyg and her estranged son, Goaty. They were to be buried that day. The king had been relieved to hear that cremation practice had died out in the village some years before. The dead were given burials in a cleared part of the small southern woodlands that were in no way any size at all compared to those of the north and east.

Some of the villagers had accepted the concept of one god worship and took part in services when any visiting monk found his way to their remote settlement. There had been a regular cleric that visited them every quarter. He unfortunately had died some months earlier and there had been no one to replace him. He had given Leofric the task of recording every death and noting where they lay in the clearing for the dead. He always blessed the plot and the mutual trust between him and the villagers was profound. They occasionally visited the abbey in the town to the north when they took their stock and corn to market. Others though kept to their old ways and some planted their feet firmly in both camps because they couldn't decide which was in the right. A very few had had such a hard life making enough to eat and struggling to clothe their children or put a roof over their heads that they tended not to believe in any kind of deity as they felt abandoned by any and all of them. Ealdyg had become too withdrawn from society to make any rational judgement and Goaty had liked the concept of a caring father figure so Leofric, himself the first village convert, decided to give them as Christian a burial as he could. It was high summer and so the bodies could not be left unburied. The graves had been dug the night before and all was prepared for a joint departure the same morning that the king and the village men designated to accompany him were also to start their onward journey.

The king and all who went with him left the village while the dew was still on the grass. They were well provided for with food and drink for the day. Any lingering sore or healing wound had been tended by Elvira and the man given any salve that might help relieve any future irritation. All the villagers came out of their huts to see the small band of brave men go to their destiny. They knew that of the men who left with the king it was possible that not all would return and those that did may well be hurt or changed in some way.

As the tramp of feet faded into the woodland Leofric gathered everyone left to form a procession to the burial ground. The cart containing the two wooden boxes was drawn in front by a donkey. Leofric and his wife walked close by the back of the cart with everyone else following behind. It was a slow walk because Leofric understood how much Gramma had done for Goaty and it was important that she was able to keep up with the procession with dignity. Both Ealdyg and Goaty had wooden crosses placed on their chests with pots of ointment and food to help them with their journey on into the next world. Leofric led the service, such as it was. He had been told by the now late cleric that a cross was all the dead needed for their next journey but it would take a long time for the rest of the superstitions to die out and so he tolerated the grave goods that harkened back and were testament to a different view.

"Ealdyg, my sister. Goaty, her son. You lived your lives as best you could. It was a poor life for you both but we did what we could. God and Jesus bless you and forgive you. Your souls may be joined in the next life. Amen"

Then both boxes were laid in the ground and covered with earth. Some crossed themselves as they had seen the monks do, others silently prayed to Mother Earth to take the departed ones in and help them on their way. Gramma stepped up and spoke some old words over the graves. None would reproach her. It was over. There would be no more pain for either of them. Leofric on the other hand would always feel the guilt of wondering if he could have made any difference to the outcome of his sister's life. His was a rough understanding but as he laboured in the fields he would occasionally reflect on his actions and whether he could have done more.

On this day however he had other things to demand his attention. His son was one of those that had gone with the king. When he and his wife and younger children sat down to their evening meal he wondered if he would see him again. One look at his wife's closed face told him that she, too, thought of their firstborn.

In Elvina's hut there was tense calm. Esmund had described the fight between Ayken and Konal and told of how he feared for Ayken in that, although he was built to fight, he lacked the killer drive that would finish off his opponent before his opponent finished him. They had, he told them, to trust to the gods to spare him until he learnt to survive, even at the expense of killing another. Elvina was deeply troubled. Whichever way she looked at the problem either her strong athletic son would be killed before he learnt to kill or he would return a changed man with the blood of others upon him. Gramma saw her daughter's dilemma and without the need for speech she painfully hauled her bent frame from her chair and went to put her hand on her daughter's arm, caressing and soothing but without ever saying; "It will not be so," because they all knew that it would. One way or another Ayken, the Ayken they knew, would be lost to them. Borvo slept a deep healing sleep. Esmund was fashioning a crutch even as they sat and spoke of their other son his hands were busy. So it was that in the morning Borvo would look out from his pallet and see his means of getting around. He was young and would mend quickly. They would give him knit bone in the morning and its properties of advancing the healing were well known. He would be well. It was not yet time to tell him that before the king's party had left he had sent word by way of Minister Brand that when he was ready he would send for the young healer. They were all deeply troubled by the king's interest in Borvo but had no way of resisting the attention without moving on as their forefathers had done. They were settled now and didn't want to leave. There would be a way. They must try hard to find it.

Sunniva had been kept busy all day with sewing for the departing soldiers and also finishing the cloth to dress the bodies of the hapless Ealdyg and Goaty. She also had made sure she was busy with as many chores as she could because she didn't want to think that she might not see Oeric again. He had held her hand and smiled but said no more to her. He had not taken the opportunity to kiss her again. She knew that he may not survive and this was his reason but she would have welcomed a sign or a token of his intentions. Oeric's intentions were clear to all but his duty was to the king and to fight he would go with a conscience that was free from burden. He buried his feelings for Sunny and went willingly to fight for the king and his home.

Chapter Twelve

End of summer

It had been two months since the king and his men had lain and mended in the village. The summer was now coming to an end. It had been a good summer, warm sun was nightly refreshed by rain and the harvest was going to be a good one. The village was preparing for more hard work as they laboured well into the evening to make ready for the gathering in. A weary traveller had brought news of the battles that kept the king and his men busy defending their small kingdom. There was no particular news of the village men and boys who had walked so willingly away behind the king. However the stories told were mainly of success for the king and so with that the villagers had to be content.

Borvo had recovered quickly from his broken ankle and had spent the summer working hard in the fields as he had to try to replace his absent older brother. The only sign of any injury came when he was tired and his foot turned on itself giving him a less than graceful hesitation in his stride. Elvina watched as her younger son took up the mantle of his older brother. Her heart ached when she thought of what may befall Ayken. She swallowed her anger that her lithe younger son should have been damaged so that he no longer ran with the grace of one of the forest deer.

As Borvo worked he realised how lucky they had been to have his brother's strength. He himself had grown but would never be as tall or as strong as Ayken. When he had time he listened to his Gramma while she told him about the herbs and plants and tried to learn much that would see him through the coming years. He knew he was not long for the country life. Sometimes he ached to be away and at other times he knew and wanted only this bucolic simplicity. He went daily to the brook to think and commune with the spirit of the place. Increasingly he felt that the spirit was guiding him to fulfil his destiny. There had been other songs, snatches in the wind, but nothing compared to that definite waking dream at the time of the king. After the harvest celebrations he would talk to his parents about his future. They would not want to lose him so quickly but he would try very hard to make them see that he just had to go. He would miss the brook but the ideas and the words of the spirit he would keep close to his heart always.

After the king's visit the villagers had taken the new religion to their hearts more than before. The little wooden building that some had used to gather together to pray in with the visiting cleric was more widely used. A new cleric had begun to visit the village more regularly. It was a long way from any centre of religion but he usually managed to get to them every few months. At these times he would bless the departed and the new born children and bless any union between men and women. Brother Augustine, as he was known, was round and jolly and came to the village on a small pony. His figure suggested that walking was not his first option for travel. He was not a simple man in any way but he was relaxed about his flock. He noticed signs still of the 'old ways' but thought that, in time, they would be forgotten or merge with the new and so he turned away from any conflict and just let the people 'be' as they wished to be.

This was not the case in settlements closer to religious centres but this village was fortunate in its cleric. Borvo listened to Brother Augustine and took in the message of kindness mixed with anger and retribution of the new god. Augustine, being the lazy fellow that he was, spoke mainly of the good and the tolerant in the religion. He was not mentally prepared to fight with any belligerence for his beliefs. It was a good life and he was well content. So it was that Borvo took on the simple message of peace and love and learned nothing of fiery intolerance.

Brother Augustine had promised to come back to bless the harvest and preparations were made for the occasion. It had been a good summer and the grain was stored in every conceivable barn and loft. Cattle fodder was prepared and stored to keep until it was needed in the winter. Most of the beasts would be used for feed to keep the villagers alive during the long winter months. The best were kept back for breeding and starting again the next year. Late winter was always lean in terms of food but generally they managed to survive. Some of the old would die as would the less robust children, but it was the way and it was accepted with resignation.

Along with Brother Augustine there would be another welcome addition to the harvest celebrations. Every year a travelling wanderer would turn up just as the harvest was all safely stored away. He never offered to help but he sang and told tales for his supper and bed. The villagers would welcome him with their usual glee and after the revels he would be the most popular man in the area. His stories not only kept alive the traditions of the countryside but somehow the villagers felt that he was a link to the ancient ones. He made everything right as though by speaking the old tongue and through telling the well loved tales he brought stability with him. His stories were a mixture of kings long gone, gods and demons, dragons and riddles. Above all the youngsters loved the riddles. They would follow him about and try to guess what the answers were before he had even told his tales. Apart from the laughter and good food the celebrations were a time for the village to get to hear the news from the rest of the kingdom. They themselves could and did go journeying to find out what was happening to the rest of their precious land. But late summer had been so busy that any news was welcome. This year the expectations were heightened as they longed to hear of the battles but most of all of their loved ones who still had not reappeared since leaving with the king. Ayken had not returned so it was assumed he was with the king's party or had met a poor end at Konal's hands. There was no news.

The day of feasting dawned and with the dawn came another day of late summer sun. The brook was nearly run dry since there had been so little rain that year. Much of the water had been used for the crops and the animals and now that the crops were in they needed rain. Borvo and some of the other boys went to the brook and decided to offer something to the river god and ask for rain to swell his winding course back to the sea. They each gathered a token from their homes. The blacksmith's son took a nail, the baker a pot and so on. Borvo gathered a handful of comphrey as it was his Gramma's special plant and he thought that would carry more weight with the river god than any other. The boys stood by the deepest part of the slow moving brook and wished for rain and the safe return of their brothers and fathers. Since the fighting men had left the village these boys of middle years, not quite men but no longer children had worked hard for their families and the village and it was due to their efforts that the harvest would be almost as good as before when their stronger older kin had been in charge. The villagers were proud of them although there were occasions when all of them, almost without exception, had sneaked off to wander the woods or seek relief from the endless hot days of toil.

Whilst the boys were seeking help from the spirit of the brook the women were preparing the food for the evening's supper.

Brother Augustine had arrived the night before and had found accommodation with Leofric. It was a poor bed but better than sleeping in the barn. There was to be a service in the small wooden church before the feasting and so the monk spent much of the day speaking with those that sought his guidance and preparing for the simple service of thanksgiving. He had his usual conversation with Leofric about those that still sought the old ways.

"Well Leofric, do they still look both ways, back and forth?" Leofric always had the same answer to give although he had accepted Christianity he took his tolerance from Augustine, "Yes Brother, but they still like to come to the church. Their spirit is good whatever they call it." As an afterthought he added, "There is little dissent now just the usual arguments when too much of the fermented apple or ale is in their bellies."

Brother Augustine smiled his usual fat smile and nodded. He was content and what if his new Prior had asked too many questions about his flock, part of the truth was sometimes all that was needed to keep a quiet life. Brother Augustine loved calm waters, his faith was sincere but with insight born of great wisdom he knew that forcing people to abandon deeply held ideas was no way to introduce his loving god. There was a slight unease in the back of his mind when he thought of his new Prior. His god seemed to be a ferocious and unforgiving god so Augustine would do as much as he could to keep him from his many villages where the old and the new merged with less distinction than the purist would like or indeed countenance.

Chapter Thirteen

Friendships forged, enemies endured

The battles had been long and bloody. Skirmishes and full blown head on clashes had resulted in withdrawal by both sides as their fighting men were exhausted and needed to regain strength and purpose. If there was no result soon the autumn would be upon them with its warnings of winter and then no one would win except the cold and hunger. Having been laid up in his western retreat the king had taken the fight to the enemy and was holding his own and even gaining ground. The men of the northern town that bordered the Mercian kingdom had rallied and given the tired battle weary horde fresh hope, fresh men and faith in victory. The abbey there was a place where the king found renewed purpose. He prayed that God would help his kingdom and steady his resolve. He was busy fighting for survival. He knew the enemy were still pagan. He knew that if they won then great damage would be done, not only to his people but to their newly found and sometimes shaky belief in the new religion. No quarter would be spared. He had to find the way to win the war. He took time to reflect on the men from the village where he had recovered from his injuries. They had proven themselves full of valour and that despite being only roughly taught in fighting but they had soon learnt. The two who had stood out from the rest were Ayken, the brother of the young healer, Borvo and the son of Leofric, the elder, who was called Eldric.

Wilheard had got through to the king's headquarters in the northwest of the kingdom and had delivered the vital message that the king was alive, slightly injured and was on his way back to lead them to victory. During the subsequent fighting Wilheard also fought bravely although his chagrin with Ayken never left him and he was always ready to speak out against him as a country clod who knew nothing of battle. Bands of fighting men need to pull together and use their energy against the enemy not each other. The king and Brand knew of the animosity but could not take the time to keep the two apart. They had to trust that no harm would come of it and that the need to survive would be paramount.

Eorforheard was so grateful to Ayken's mother for healing him; he was almost back to new, that his friendship with Ayken caused further intense irritation to Wilheard. Eorforheard was still able to join the battle but his injuries had left him with a lazy left arm and poor sight in his left eye. His speech was also slower than previously but the king needed every loyal man he could get and so the young Eorforheard was included in each skirmish, albeit mainly as back up and to the rear so that he would not incapacitate the rest. He was however extremely good at observing any untoward movement by renegades and would move in to finish them off with his right hand wielding his heavy sword. Occasionally he would bring his left arm up to help hold the sword with its swirling pattern and brilliant edge as he swung it over the hapless victim. It was often the last thing they saw. He found that the more he used his left arm the stronger it became. At night he, Ayken, Eldric and the other men would sit round the fire and tell stories of their lives. The village men would tell of harvests, wild beasts of the forests and of survival. The king's men would tell of bloody hand to hand fighting, periods of pursuit, flight and at times interminable waiting. Theirs too were stories of survival each tale intertwined and giving all who gathered a purpose. Some were born to till and others to fight, it had always been so.

As Ayken fought he thought of his family, his village and his sweetheart. He had lain with her that summer and it was understood that she would be part of his family when they returned. She readily agreed to his plans for them and they had parted with great passion. The coupling had been fruitful but Ayken was as yet unaware that as she, Hild, now helped with the harvest supper her belly showed signs of swelling.

Chapter Fourteen

Welcome visitors

Seofon, the travelling story teller arrived in the village just as the afternoon sun was lowering to the horizon. He was named for the number seven. He was the seventh son of twelve children and his parents had run out of energy when trying to think of a different name for him and so he remained, Seofon. As a young boy he had discovered his gift for mimicry and had quickly used his talent to make a living away from his home village on the western shores. He travelled the length and breadth of the different kingdoms and always he found someone to feed him in return for news and a merry tale. A few comely widows had spun his garments in the hope of him staying but he took their generosity, was briefly as generous with his gratitude in nightly comfort then disappeared like snow in harvest as quickly gone as he came. His brain was razor sharp and he remembered every by way and secret path that would lead to where he wished to go. He knew each hostelry that would give him shelter for a story and he never forgot those who had done him good or indeed those who had harmed him. In short, he lived by his wits.

As he came up the main village road he was surrounded by youngsters who begged him immediately to tell them a riddle. He was weary and in dire need of refreshment but he was a patient man of forty summers and so sat down by the smith's hut and asked them to work out one of his riddles.

> "I am turned and coiled and smoothed and baked
> Red I start then with white I'm caked
> A handle sits where lips do dwell
> Gentle now, treat me well.
> What am I?"

Seofon sang this simple rhyme softly and by the time he was finished the noisy youngsters were spellbound. It was not that difficult for the brighter ones to work out the riddle but Seofon's personality was hypnotic. He held his audience enthralled.

The smith's wife came out and saw him with the children and offered him a glass of ale. This he readily accepted and so continued to sit where he was until he saw the people gathering for their harvest supper celebrations. Brother Augustine had come to join him and they sat and passed the time of day talking about their travels and what they had heard on the road.

"Well brother I've been north recently and have heard that the king has made such progress that he is willing to make a pact with the invaders. An end to this continuing uncertain and bloody state would be welcome." Seofon spoke with authority but also with respect. He liked Augustine and saw that his way was tolerance without loss of integrity.

Brother Augustine also liked Seofon. He enjoyed his stories and was a good ally if they met on the road. "You may be right Seofon. An end to this constant invasion threat will be a welcome relief. The king seems to have worked miracles though. It was only a few months ago that he was in this very village, wounded and with only a few loyal men to his name and to watch his back." He paused to scratch his chin where a drop of ale had dribbled down, "the men of Malmesburgh rallied and went off to fight with the king. They have been relentless. I doubt the king would have triumphed without them." He sat and neither spoke for a while then Augustine added as an afterthought, "The monks' prayers I'm sure would have helped as well. The new abbot is very keen."

"You don't speak with warmth when you mention him brother. Is he not worthy?" Seofon always wanted to know who fitted in with whom as it may be useful to his survival.

"Oh, yes, so worthy that I doubt any can keep up with him. Not me for certain sure." Augustine smiled, sighed and drank some more. Both men enjoyed the warm evening sun on their faces. As they supped their ale they were joined by the men of the village who had finished their work and were now waiting for the revels to start. More ale was dispensed and more news sought from the incomers. These times were vital for the village. It was important that they kept up with affairs especially now since their own brothers and sons were away fighting with the king. It had been a hot hard summer without them. Now they wanted to hear news that they were coming back. Neither of the news carriers could say with any certainty that this was the case. All the comfort that they could bring was that the king may make a treaty. With this they had to be content.

The mutton was as tender as lamb and was served with barley bread. Nettle and burdock had been added for flavour and digestion. Ale and cider were drunk with relish and the time had come for Seofon to tell of his travels and the news of the battles. He knew what was expected of him and he rose to walk among the assembled villagers so that his stories of gods, dragons, good and bad men, mythical kings and daring deeds would have more impact if he could surprise the audience with sudden turns and twists, swirling, shouting at them then letting his voice drop so that they had to strain to hear his words. Just as the children had been spellbound earlier he held the adults, too, in the palm of his hand. The dragon was slain, the hero was triumphant and good had beaten the bad back to their slimy pits.

Seofon sat down and took more ale. His face was red both from his exertions and the copious ale; as he wiped the sweat from his brow he saw movement in the doorway of the barn. Soon everyone had sensed there were newcomers and had turned to defend themselves against any intruders. They were so fired up by Seofon's tales that they imagined monsters where there were none. Half the revellers had leapt to their feet ready for action when through the open doorway came a group of very weary men. They were back, but how they had changed. Those who had been little more than boys when they left were now men and nothing could give them back their youthful innocence. They had done unimaginable things and seen such darkness in men's souls that it had bitten deep into their own.

Chapter Fifteen

Peace Treaty?

The deed was done. The leaders had met and agreed a peaceful co-existence. The West Saxons would live in harmony with the invaders. They would each keep to their own areas and would not raid into their neighbour's lands. The kingdoms would be safe once more, their people able to till the land, rear their sheep and produce the finest wool for export. Men would be at home with their growing broods and would talk of fighting but never hunger for it. They had done their duty and given their arms to help their king. Some would always thirst for more bloodshed and some hated the idea of making a pact with the enemy. They would have fought on until no one was left standing, the fields red with blood and there would be more widows and grieving children than ever before in living memory. The travelling storytellers would talk of despair not hope and there would be gloom over the countryside.

This was not the king's way. He had fought and lost members of his family. He had seen the effect of fighting on young men. They turned up to stand with their fellow Saxons, boys with down on their chins. They went home hardened men with strong beards and darkness in their hearts. He had watched the grief as a widow took the body of her husband and said goodbye to it in the ground. He did not want this for his people. He wanted security and education and time for religious devotion. A monk had been sent for to be at his side and to lead his country into better ways. It was a rare moment for the king as he sat and contemplated the future and all that he had to do. His minister came to him with speech of affairs that needed his attention.

"Brand, have you remembered our promise to the villagers? What have we done for them but bring them sorrow? We sent back their men with darkness in their eyes. Give them rights over the woodlands and the rivers. They are too small for a charter but we will give them one anyway and they will be recognised as citizens wherever they travel in this land."

"Yes my lord, it is in hand. They will not suffer again as they have done before. Such generosity when they themselves had so little. It was their devotion that helped us see what we were fighting for." His minister had suffered in the last battle and walked with a stiff back and rigid leg. No longer a young man he was in middle age and had a certain ease of conversation when talking with his lord. Their respect was mutual. Brand continued his thoughts out loud, "What of the young healer? You had plans for him I think."

The king looked away out of the window and contemplated for a while, "There is time enough. He will keep. Let him have his winter at home, then next spring will be his time. There is to be a child in the family so let them have their joy."

As Brand started to speak the king smiled and asked his own question, "How did I know about the child? I sent a messenger there and he came back with news of the entire village. I wanted to know about them but also whether any had heard of the runaway, Konal. His chief was keen to have him back and thought I had him. He is connected to their royal house and is wanted for many reasons."

Brand smiled, it was like his king to keep a check on details. His smile soon froze on his face as he heard the king say next, "He will be a monk at Malmesburgh. They could do with him there." Brand protested. He had seen the light in the boy's eyes when he went to the brook. He was a child of the earth and would hate the ways of the monks, especially the rigid abbot who took delight in terrorising the young and old alike under his charge. "My lord, is that wise? He is so . . ." As Brand sought the appropriate word the king turned a set face towards him, "He cannot be left to waste his talent and it will bring discipline and learning that he would not otherwise have. He will be under my protection; he will come to no harm. The abbot is harsh but fair. All will be well."

Brand knew that this was not the case but understood when he had said enough. There were other ways of protecting people and he would see to it that Borvo was well looked after. He liked the boy and thought it a shame that he had to give up his simple life to fit in with the king's passion. He knew that the king burned with fervour for the church and wanted to do all he could to set his people on the 'right path'. He said none of this and made his exit, slowly and with stiff dignity. There was much to do to prepare the right people in the right place for the appointed time.

As Brand left the king's chamber he hurried through his mind to place the people who would be useful to him. The bishop of Winchester, yes, he would do to start with, as Brand thought of his long time friend he smiled, clasped his hands together and said, "Yes, he'll do, he'll do. He won't let me down." He walked slowly away to his own quarters.

Chapter Sixteen

More welcome returns

Hild had longed for Ayken's return. She knew he would be happy with her news and that he would honour his commitment to her. She couldn't have been mistaken in his love and passion for her. She had told her parents of the forthcoming child. They in turn had been formally to visit Esmund and Elvina. There had been agreement for marriage and so plans were made that as soon as Ayken returned the coupling would be official and the baby well born.

The night had been a long one following on from a day that was full of hard work. All was merriment as the harvest supper and entertainment took its usual turn. Hild was tired, the baby had started to move that very day and she had been on her feet for hours. As the supper drew to its conclusion she sat down amidst the food debris although there was little wasted. She heard the finishing story from Seofon. It was a good one and she was thrilled to hear the ending. She would slip away and go to her bed. Her clothes felt heavy on her and she longed to lay in her shift and drift away to dream of the day that Ayken came home. She heard the hush fall over the barn and it took her a while to understand what was happening. She looked through the smoky room and saw strangers at the door. They walked in as though they expected a welcome, seven weary dirty men stood in complete silence before the assembled apprehensive village.

Their leader spoke to Leofric, "What no welcome for your son?" Leofric didn't hesitate; he ran to Eldric and embraced him as though he would never let him go. "God be thanked, you are home." Cynwise, Leofric's wife came forward and her joy was overwhelming. No one in the room remained untouched by the happiness that beamed from her. The relief from months of worry overcame her and she kissed her son then ran from the hall into the night air. This all happened in a moment, the atmosphere now seemed full of talking, laughing and greeting. One man stood apart. Ayken was a changed man. He had left the village as an eager follower of the king, ready to do what was necessary to defeat the enemy. He returned with darkness in his eyes and a burden on his spirit that was not to be easily moved. Elvina and Esmund went to him, put their arms around him and led him from the festivities. Borvo looked on; he did not understand what was happening so he searched for Sunny and Gramma. They were both on their feet and gathered him up with them as they all left to go home and be with Ayken. Hild made her way through the crowd and followed on behind. Sunny realised that she was following them and waited for her, she put her arm through Hild's and they walked together. She was to be part of the family and so she had the right to see both good and bad, for surely Sunny thought, there was bad to come.

Eldric looked over his father's shoulder at the retreating form of his friend. He broke away from his family and went after Ayken. He said nothing to him but put a hand on his shoulder. Ayken turned, looked deep into Eldric's eyes and said, "It was well done." As he turned once more to leave he added, "You're a good man."

Eldric went back to the throng of well wishers and asked for quiet. He had been a rumbustuous boy with dark auburn hair and a cheeky grin that delighted all even when he was in trouble. Now he exuded an air of leadership and gravity. He had returned fully grown in maturity. He spoke to the village, "We are happy to return although one less in number than when we left. There is no way to deny that we lost our friend, Aesc. He died in the final battle. Fighting to protect us, he fell." Eldric swallowed and continued, "His family must be proud of him. He did not let them down. Ayken held him until his breath came to him no more. This, of all the things we did and saw, has affected Ayken and driven a dark sword deep into his mind. He will take time to come back to us in his full strength. Honour him as the rest of us, he did so much; . . . and so much, he may never be able to . . . tell all." Eldric's voice tailed off and he turned to his comrades, saluted them all and then left. His mother waited outside for him and when Leofric joined them they went home to revel in each other's company. Each had feared that they might not see each other again. It was a profound joy.

People drifted away from the festivities. Hild's parents looked for her and then decided to go to Elvina's cottage to look for her. They knew she was smitten with Ayken and had accepted their daughter's choice. If they were part of the new family then it was their right to be there. They didn't fully understand the 'healers' but respected them and indeed were a little in awe of them and their powers. They were superstitious and easily afraid of what they could not experience themselves or fully understand.

Brother Augustine and Seofon sat together. They had both drunk a fair quantity of ale but quickly sobered up when the village men returned. Augustine was the first to speak, "I think it safe to say that this will be remembered for many years, not for your splendid story though, but for the real drama. I don't know whether to go to them or not. They are steadfastly not of the faith." He wiped his hot brow with his sleeve, a mixture of copious ale, food and sultry weather was making him feel uncomfortable and sleepy. "They are spiritual though. Honest people." He lay down on some straw, folded his arms around his fat belly and added through a yawn, "I'll go to them in the morning. They need the night to settle." With that he went to sleep.

Seofon looked at him in disbelief. He was instantly sober and needed to walk before he could find any slumber. He strolled around the village. Some candles were burning, mostly those of the families where the men had returned. Aesc's family sat in their cottage, numb with grief. The light from their fire lit their faces. They were in shock and all were silent. They looked at each other and knew not what to say or do. Aesc's father paced the small area until he was too confined and left to walk the fields and woods until dawn. Seofon followed him to make sure that he would be well.

Some slept, some talked, others wept and two men walked until the sun rose, for one of them at least the world would not seem the same again. His lively, only son had given his life for his friends. The honour that gave to his memory was bitter sweet.

Chapter Seventeen

Welcome and not so welcome arrivals

It was time for Hild to give birth. She and Ayken had gone through the ceremony and now they were husband and wife. Although Ayken had accepted his role in wooing Hild and giving her a child he nevertheless was unenthusiastic about life in general. He had come back from fighting alongside the king's men with darkness in his heart and soul that ran so deep his family despaired of ever seeing the happy young man they knew and loved so well. Hild loved him, she had always loved him. From the time she saw him tend the flock or walk through the woods or emerge from fishing grinning from ear to ear as he swung his catch over his shoulder. They had gradually come to an understanding. They had lain together with great passion that summer and when the emotion of going away to fight had overcome them.

Strongly built, Ayken's heart was not in killing, except to put food on the table, but even then he respected his prey and honoured it before butchery. Hild was round and taller than most although not even up to Ayken's shoulder, she walked with a grace that attracted most young men who saw her but she only had eyes for Ayken. They made their home in a hut built by their families towards the edge of the settlement. As the final thatch went on Hild felt a surge of belonging. She looked at Ayken and smiled; "Well my man, here we are and may it bring us joy." Not one to avoid the problems of life she added; "May it break through your darkness and bring you light back into your heart." As she spoke she touched his face and planted a kiss on his bearded cheek. "We will have patience although your son kicks as though he is ready." Ayken stared at her swollen belly and for the first time reached out and touched her. It was fleeting but it was a caress. That simple action gave her hope that the final part of his healing had begun.

Borvo walked up to his brother and laid a hand on his arm; "You never speak of the fighting but I know you did well. Everyone says so." As he paused and looked into his brother's sad eyes he added with wisdom beyond his years; "Try to forgive yourself. We won't make you a hero if you don't want us to but you won't stop people praising you for your courage. Welcome back." Ayken sighed and with an enormous effort smiled at his young sapling of a brother who had outgrown most of his clothes although not outwards, only up. It wasn't lack of food that kept him slender but a restless energy that overtook him so that he couldn't be still. He knew he was to leave but when was not in his own hands so he wandered the woods, took comfort from the brook, did his work for the family and the village and waited.

Hild gave birth in the middle of the night a month after they had moved into the cottage. She was surrounded by her female relatives who gave her the attention and help that she needed. Elvina prepared a remedy to advance the healing as after the birth was a fearful time for infection. The little girl was born healthy and strong and entered into life with enthusiastic gusto. When Ayken was allowed to see her he immediately took her in his arms and vowed to protect her as long as he had strength in his body. After the fields of bloody battle that sat heavy in his memory she was a breath of new life that swept the rest away and gave him such comfort. At that moment he really did begin to heal, and as Borvo had suggested, he began to forgive himself for the formidable fighting machine that he had become and that had been so surprising to him. Hild struggled for a few days after the birth during which time all worried for her but then she rallied and gradually came back to full health. Ayken had no special powers from his family and was keen on acceptance so they named their daughter to please Hild, she would be called Godgyfu, a gift from god.

As the late winter sun shone through the open door of the cottage Ayken looked in on Hild and Godgyfu, both serenely asleep. He quietly walked in and dropped something on Hild's lap. He reached out and almost touched her hair but thought better not disturb her, let her sleep. Later when Hild awoke she looked at the baby then contentedly sighing she stretched and then felt something pressing on her skirts. Lying there was a beautiful amethyst necklace. She had seen a similar one round Gramma's old craggy neck. It was supposed to have healing powers but she had given little credence to this thinking that it was the person who had the healing not the stones. However, she delightedly twisted the stones round her neck and fastened them with a knot. Her joy was not only in the gift but the fact of the gift. Ayken surely was mended now. She rose to start preparing the family meal.

Sunny had sewn beautiful stitches all round the edge of the blanket that Hild used for Godgyfu. She spent most of her time as she had before the king and his men had disrupted their lives with sewing and helping her Gramma with her concoctions. Gramma noticed a far away look in her eyes but did not press her granddaughter. She knew what was in her mind and felt great sorrow for her anguish. Oeric had not returned to see her and he had not sent any word back via Ayken when the fighting was over.

She settled for family helpmeet and aunt to Godgyfu in whom all found joy.

Sunny worried for Borvo too. He spent many hours away from the village, wandering and thinking. He became distracted and distant. The boy was growing up and away. It would not be long she thought before he was no longer physically with them. She sewed tunics for him so that when he left he would be well clothed. It was all she could do and the occupation helped her forget her own pain.

The spring was very nearly upon them. The stores that had been well stocked and the food laid down for the long harsh winter that the trees laden with berries had foretold were depleted. Elvina and Esmund had collected herbs and roots for the winter ills that may befall the village. It had been a busy time as they set about making tinctures and ointments in preparation. Gramma had become increasingly immobile and her pains increased. She missed nothing by way of family humours but became rather more irritable as her joints gave her little respite from pain.

Autumn had given way to winter and the villagers had settled to essential tasks and the winter occupations of weaving and storytelling. Survival was a mixture of good harvest, good neighbours and luck. This particular winter had been mild and wet. The stored grain became fusty but still edible. Designated animals were slaughtered for their meat and by luck and good management the village got through. The feasting in midwinter had been modest but even more enjoyable than usual because most of the men had returned to rejoin their families. Only the family of Aesc still mourned but even they were wont to join in and try to regain some composure. There would always be an ache in their hearts but they must carry on. Life was harsh but there was beauty in their lives from the hills and the woods and the sky. They were country folk who had learned to live with a natural order that gave the year a pattern that in itself was comforting and healing.

The frosty days of February gave way to the cold winds of March. The trees in the woods showed signs of new life and the villagers began to mend winter torn hedges and let the livestock out into the fields from the cramped conditions of their winter quarters. Borvo had spent the winter fretting and becoming increasingly withdrawn. Sunny sewed until her fingers were sore so determined was she not to have any waking moment that was not occupied. Gramma regained some better temper with the warmer weather and increasingly took to spending some time each day with Hild and Godgyfu. The child grew and flourished and took on the look of both her parents although favouring Hild with her thick brown hair. Ayken looked forward to a fresh year and one in which he could occupy his time with the things he loved rather than fighting.

One dull and dreary rainy March day two horsemen rode into the village and tied their horses to the iron rings outside the smith's cottage. Brand and Eorforheard dismounted and went to seek Leofric to offer greetings and explain the reason for their journey. Borvo saw them arrive and immediately took off to go to the brook so that he might have some time on his own. He knew what was going to happen and although waiting for them all winter, now the time had come he felt anxious and ill prepared.

Chapter Eighteen

Call for Augustine

Brother Augustine slept when he could through long services and even longer sermons it seemed. His Father Abbot was a stern man, newly come to the Abbey of Malmesburgh. He replaced an old man, generous to a fault and wise, who had died suddenly a year since from an attack of dysentery. Augustine missed him as a fellow brother and as a counsellor. Rarely did he ask the new Father for advice. In fact he tried very hard to stay out of his way for fear of a sermon on severity and how strict they must be with the novices so that they may learn through hardship. Augustine felt that the opposite was true but his pleas had fallen on deaf ears and so he kept his thoughts to himself and spent much of his time travelling the road to tend his far flung flock. He enjoyed the encounters on the road and found great comfort in the welcome he received in the villages of his ministry. Those were the people who mattered to him and his kindness in dealing with them was appreciated and drew more to the church than any heavy weight sermon filled with the idea of wretched or dire consequences.

He had prayed so hard for the fighting to be over and for the king to be victorious. God surely was on the side of the oppressed rather than the aggressor. He was a learned man but even so he was mystified by the many things that others saw from the teaching that he sometimes wondered if they had read the same words as he had. But lately he had spent less time studying and more and more time administering to others which was a welcome relief from the abbey tensions. Even so he sometimes missed the time for revelling in the written word as he had previously been wont to do. A call from within the chapter house brought him back to the present and he shook his heavy frame and went to see what his Father Abbot had need of him this time. As he made his way to the dark room within he reflected on why life had to be so complicated. His surprise was evident when Father Abbot explained his mission to him.

"Brother, I have a task. The king has sent word that a young boy will be joining us and you are required to bring him here to start his novitiate." Augustine stared at him as this was not one of his usual responsibilities. There were others much worthier than he to bring youngsters in. Augustine would try to put them off whilst the current incumbent reigned.

"Why is this task to fall to me, Father?" Augustine used few words when conversing with the Abbot as without warning he would find himself trapped by a slip of the tongue in a convulsion of scripture.

"Minister Brand has ordered it to be so. The king takes a special interest in the youth and you know him of old. He is Borvo of the woodland settlement two day's ride from here." Augustine's heart sank as he remembered the young boy, full of life and promise. He also knew he would hate it in the abbey as he was a spirit of the woods and the river steeped in the colourful ways of his ancestors. He had heard that the king favoured the boy and his gifts. So this was to be his prize for helping the king in his hour of need. Well as long as Augustine was around he would look out for Borvo. He began to welcome his charge as he considered that he might be able to ease the youth into the difficult life here and there were compensations. He would read, learn how to script and be taught philosophy. Perhaps it was not such a bad thing. By the time Augustine was packed and ready for the road he had convinced himself that all would be well.

He set off hopefully.

Chapter Nineteen

Brand's Two Speeches

Brand was seated on a smooth wooden chair that had a colourful woollen cloth over it. It was the best that the village had to offer. Leofric was seated on a settle alongside him, Esmund sat close by. The rest stood around the meeting house and listened with interest and apprehension as to what could bring so important an entourage to their village when peace had been declared. Some feared that the king might want more of their sons to fight or protect the borders, so newly agreed. Theirs was a small, close knit community and even one loss was felt by all. They all accepted that death was part of life's pattern but last year they had lost more than they bargained for. Goaty and Aesc were sorely missed and Ealdyg was spoken of with respect, principally because she had a cursed life and was Leofric's sister. They felt for him, most of course felt relief that she no longer suffered the torment of longing and waiting which had so turned her mind. These then were some of the thoughts that stumbled into their thinking as they waited for the minister to speak.

Brand had argued long and hard with the king about the village. Although the king had honourable intentions he occasionally put things to one side when affairs of state became too onerous. Finally Brand had his attention and they verbally fought until both were equally satisfied with the outcome. Brand knew that the village would welcome most of what he had to say. But there was one area that the king had insisted upon that he knew would cause concern. But eventually his people would accept that this was the fate of some and so would weave it into their stories and somehow make it a source of pride, for indeed in many ways it was an honour to be so noticed. However, first he must explain the king's offer to the village and its reward of loyalty in a time of great trouble.

Leofric called for silence and then formally introduced Brand to speak with the villagers. Brand rose with a studied dignity as befitted the occasion. He wished to convey by his actions the deep respect he felt they deserved. He lifted his hand in greeting and began his address, "Loyal men and women, the king greets you through me, his minister. He sends his gratitude with me and asks that I make known to you the high affection in which he holds you." Brand paused, looked round at the crowd and smiled at them. Some smiled back with relief and others gave a restrained cheer and welcome. They all remembered his careful handling of them last year and gave him the respect he had earned then. Brand continued, "Our king is mindful of your circumstances and he has graciously decided that, although you are small he will grant you a charter, you will have special rights over the surrounding woods for forage and hunting," here Brand paused for an inward smile, he knew that they regularly took advantage of all that the woods had to offer, he continued "you will have had your sport there before, we understand that but this will give you rights in your own name rather than that of your local overlord." An appreciative murmur grew to laughter amongst some as it was well known that their overlord was noticeable by his absence; except of course at quarter days when their tythes were due. He then sent his steward to collect all they owed. In truth they were not onerous but he gave nothing back to this out of the way corner of his domain therefore they were not well disposed towards him.

Brand became serious, "The king also wishes to ensure that your young have full advantage of his kindness and has therefore sent to the abbot of Malmesburgh to send out a regular brother to tend to your holy needs and the education of the children." He knew what he had to say next was going to be alarming to a few but he heartily approved himself so he ploughed on, "Both boys and girls will be taught by the brother to read and write the scriptures and sign their own names. Boys will be taught the simple rules of numbers to help them with future trade so that none may take advantage of his loyal people." Gasps were heard from some of the assembled company but many were in favour of the proposals. Why not, didn't their womenfolk fight alongside them when needed, no it was the proper reward for their children and for this they were grateful. Brand had one last thing to say about this before his final and expected blow. "The small church will be built on. There will be a room where the brother may teach the young. For this the king will pay. He desires only one more gift from you in that he take Borvo to be a monk at Malmesburgh under his protection. He thinks his special ways will be a greater gift for many if he has learning and the discipline of the abbey." At these words many shuffled uncomfortably and looked with great sadness on Elvina and Esmund. Borvo's parents had bright eyes full of tears but refused to shed them. Only Gramma allowed hers to fall unchecked.

Borvo himself had returned from the brook and was standing outside listening. He was overcome with both fear and excitement. This was the start of his destiny and he understood that this path was the one he must follow. As the meeting broke up and refreshment was laid on for Brand and his companion before their trek back to the king, Brand sought out Elvina and Esmund. As they stood a little apart from the rest he spoke quietly "Special greetings to you both," he bowed graciously although he did not need to do so, "I tried to persuade the king to leave him longer but he will have him." He drew them further away from the crowd so that only they could hear his words, "I have spoken with the Bishop of Winchester and he has promised to look out for the boy. Brother Augustine is even now on his way to bring your son to the Abbey. I have also ensured that he will be apprentice to the infirmary. There he will learn much and also give the rather ancient incumbent much to add to his already copious knowledge. I can do no more at the present time but I beg you, if you hear of anything alarming you must get word to me and I will protect him as much as I can." He saw the pain in their faces and added, "The abbot is a severe man and intolerant of the old ways, but he is fair in most things, tell Borvo to be wary and comply, if only outwardly, there will be much that he will gain in terms of scribing and reading. It will be of great consequence in the future, I can't explain more please trust me." Elvina took his hand and pressed it to her cheek in grateful thanks for his concern for her precious son. She was too full of emotion to speak. Esmund then clasped the same hand and thanked him. Brand felt even more than before that this family were truly blessed and he was fortunate in knowing them; he still felt great warmth for Elvina and her touch had sent thrills through his ageing body that reminded him of his youth. Casually he introduced the matter of their other children and caught up on the news of Ayken and Sunny. When asked outright about Oeric he said that he could not answer and made his excuses and went to speak with Leofric.

Sunny had been standing within earshot of the group and turned away quickly so that her tears would fall in private. She would go to see Hild and the child; this always gave her joy and would take her mind off the inner pain. Ayken walked up just as his sister was running blindly away from the meeting hall. When he was told what had taken place both in terms of Brand's protection and Oeric's silence he went straightway to his cottage to offer a shoulder to Sunny. He wanted to be with Borvo but there would be time enough for that painful parting. Ayken had recovered his equilibrium and his even temper had returned. Always deep within would be the horror of the battlefield but he was healed enough to live the life that he would always choose above any other; herdsman, family man and protector of the weak. Hild had proven herself to his equal in most things. He was physically stronger but she had strength in all other areas that was a match for him and in love she forgave him many oversights of attention. Life had to be lived and survival was the key. Together they were a force to be reckoned with and their families and their village (which after all was an extension of the family) meant the world to them. Elvina and Esmund were very happy in their daughter-in-law and had welcomed her as one of their own. Hild's parents were mostly relaxed with them all and the two families had become more understanding of, and tolerant about, their differences.

Easter had been set that year for early in the fourth month and this was to be when Brother Augustine came, took the Easter services and went away with Borvo. There was only one week to go and there was much to do. Borvo was relieved that he was not to go with the minister. He respected him but would be much more relaxed travelling with Brother Augustine. After much discussion it had been decided that despite the busy time of year Ayken would go with Borvo and Augustine and Esmund would double up his efforts on Ayken's behalf with his stock and his planting. The thought was that if the abbot saw Ayken, a heralded fighting man on behalf of the king, standing as brother to Borvo he would be reminded that he was not friendless and perhaps go more kindly with him. They were all troubled by the abbot's reputation but knew that they had no choice in the matter. So it was decided. Gramma taught Borvo as much as she could and packaged up some familiar and commonly held potions to take with him. He would need no personal possessions as they were not allowed so Sunny did not even have the joy of sewing for her younger brother. She had sewn all winter but these things she put away for when he might need them. Lovingly she lay them in a rough wooden chest and filled it with dried lavender to help preserve them. It was always in this way that she demonstrated her love and this she was denied. Her distress was overwhelming but she buried it deep within her and carried on. Well, she was ever practical so she must think of some other way to send Borvo off with good heart.

Borvo spent the last week in his village helping his father in the fields and listening to Gramma when she thought of one more thing that he ought to know. Her anxiety for her grandson was demonstrated by her demanding his attention whenever he came near her. Somehow the week passed and Elvina found time to walk with Borvo in the hills and speak with him without any one else listening in. She had a difficult task ahead of her and she needed to know that she had his undivided attention.

As they walked in the chilly early spring they took comfort in their isolation, albeit temporary, from the hustle and bustle of the wider family. The wind played about them making Elvina snuggle more closely into her shawl. Borvo didn't seem to notice the cold. He was bright and in his eyes was a distance that saddened his mother when she looked into them. She turned and found a bank on which to sit and patted the place beside her. Borvo reluctantly gave up the wonderful feeling of purpose that he felt from striding over the hills and sat down.

"My son, we must talk, you and I, and it will not be easy for me to tell you what you need to know." Elvina, breathed deeply and now she had started found it easier to go on. Borvo kept looking into the distant hills. He felt that if he looked at his mother she may falter.

"Borvo, you are about to go into the world where people are not always as . . . as safe as the villagers. Some of course will be good and kind but others may see you and wish to take advantage of you. They may see you as young and unworldly and try to take your money, your life or, or your . . ." she paused searching for the right words to convey the horror she had conjured in her mind, "or your innocence. Physically they may . . ." Borvo turned and held out his hand to his mother to stop her anguish.

"Mother, Ayken gave me a similar warning a few weeks ago when it was clear that the time may soon come for me to leave." He blushed, "In fact he described what I must not allow anyone to do to me." Then he laughed, "He said some monks were rotten with it. Don't worry I shall be careful."

Elvina held her son close and continued, rather relieved and also grateful to Ayken, "Minister Brand told your father that you are under his protection and that of the Bishop of Winchester so you must get word to any of us should anything untoward befall you. In any thing my dear son, in any thing."

"I will mother. You know that even if they had not called for me to go now I had to go soon anyway. I felt it last year. My future is not here, not yet anyway, I have to leave and this is as good a way as any."

Neither one of them said any more for the next few minutes as they sat together in loving silence. Finally Elvina spoke, "About Sunny. Borvo, your sister is deeply sad about Oeric. She thought they had an understanding but there has been no word and Ayken will say nothing so we don't know if he knows nothing or just will not say. Borvo, take the time to make a tender farewell with her and if you hear anything about Oeric try to let her know, good or bad, either will break her pain of not knowing and eventually will calm her."

"I will, she deserves to be happy." After another pause he added, "I'm rather scared but excited as well. Honour the gods for me, go to the brook with Sunny and Godgyfu and speak to me there through the water. I will try to make you glad you had me as your second son." With that they began the walk back through the spring countryside which was alive with young leaves, buds and nesting birds. The inevitable cycle of nature calmed them as they drank in its permanence.

Chapter Twenty

Borvo begins his journey

Malmesburgh was a thriving market town that had been well established for several centuries. It was not the nearest but it was the fairest market that was available for the villagers. The journey to market, driving their sheep and carts took two days and so when they went to Malmesburgh they always stayed away for several nights as they set up their pens and stalls and sold their wares. It served also as a place where the isolated villagers from all over the region could meet and exchange news of the invasions at the same time they would talk of more local issues. The cost of crossing the bridge into the town was always good for a topic of interest to all. The town burghers had just put the pavage tax up by one quarter of a penny. It had caused unrest but like so many such taxes people got used to them and they became the new norm.

Augustine and Borvo had set off from the village at dawn. There was a long way to go and although the monk had a substantial pony the boy was required to walk. They began the journey, one with excited fear coursing through his body and the other with resignation at the deed. In his heart he knew that Borvo would undoubtedly benefit from education. He was a very bright young man and had plenty of spirit. As they made their slow pace through the woods and then the rolling hills of the inner lands he reflected that the boy would need every ounce of his natural wit and cunning to survive. The twin guardians of secrets, fear and obedience, were not conducive to open protection of the vulnerable. However on this crisp spring morning there was a long way to go and much to enjoy, as was his wont he would worry about things as they happened. Augustine looked forward to resting by a small inn by the river where he was well known and was usually supplied with a good ale and substantial mutton pie. The host was always keen to serve a man of the cloth especially if he was generous with his blessings and blind to small transgressions of doctrine.

Borvo had other thoughts as they went on their way. He was sad to leave the woods behind. His parting from his family and the villagers had been almost unbearable. Ayken was supposed to be accompanying them to the town but a last minute hitch with Godgyfu had delayed his departure. He had promised Borvo that he would catch them up on the road. So far there was no sign of him and Borvo was anxious, both for himself but also for his niece. The more he thought of those he had left behind the more he wondered why he had been chosen by the king for special attention. However, the morning was nearly over and the sun was high in the sky. To Augustine this meant that his midday meal was beckoning. He had explained to Ayken where the inn was and so they settled down to take their food and wait for the elder brother to overtake them. Borvo was glad to stop. Walking all day did not tire him but the anxiety leant extra weight to each step. Augustine had drunk his ale and folded his chubby arms across his fat belly and was dozing noisily in the corner of the inn's ale room. Borvo had eaten his fill which was considerably less than his companion and was restless for the outside air. Inside was friendly but rather rank. He wandered out to the river and found a dry oak stump on which to sit and wait for Ayken. He looked back at the way they had come and watched and longed for the journey to be going the other way. He knew he had to leave at some point but reality was unsettling.

As he sat and watched he felt sleepy and his head nodded on his chest. He dreamt of the brook and its cool waters and how he always gained strength from its nearness. He heard the slow movement of this wider river and was drawn to open his eyes. There in the middle of the river was an eddy. It was a still day and the river lazy so there should be no dramatic movement. But there it was. Moving across the water to where he sat. Up from the middle of the disturbed water there rose a form. It came to him, engulfed him. Inside Borvo's head there came the familiar words of the song from his favourite protector.

The Second Song of Borvo

Listen carefully to my song
Find the place where you belong
I am hither thither gone
You and yours must carry on

For me you were named and blessed
So you always will be best
Healing is the art you share
Generations have the care

Beware of monk in garden green
Take care of boy at midnight seen
All the words that you will hear
Will be twisted not so clear

Keep wise counsel Borvo boy
You are meant to spread much joy
Make the best of what you can
Very soon will stand the man

Wisdom is deep in your soul
You will counsel that's your goal
King will give his precious jewel
Be thus kind and never cruel

Listen carefully to my song
For now stay where you belong
I am hither thither gone
You and yours must carry on

A shadow crossed Borvo's face and he was startled awake. Unsettled he looked up and saw a stranger staring down at him. He struggled to stand and move away from this threatening form. "Boy? You all right?" A man in his late twenties was stretching out a hand to take hold of him; Borvo cried out in alarm and moved back towards the river. At that moment another larger impressive figure loomed up behind the stranger and swung him round holding him in such a grip that the older man had no chance of moving. Borvo relaxed, "Ayken, oh Ayken" with that he stumbled back even more and fell headlong into the river. Ayken thrust the man away from him, onto the ground and went to help his young brother up from the muddy water. "Half a day young Borvo, half a day and there you are in trouble already." Smiling he pulled the youngster onto the bank and gently held his shoulder while he turned to see who had dared to touch a member of his family. The stranger was still lying where he had been thrown, winded and a little afraid of this powerful man. As he sat up he gabbled, "I was sent by the monk to find his charge. He seemed to be asleep and I worried he would fall in the water." All Ayken would say was, "He may be yet a boy but he is well protected, remember that and tell anyone who would cause him harm."

He turned to the sorry looking youth and hurried him inside to find a way of cleaning him up. When they spoke with Augustine he denied having spoken to any of his charge. There were many who trod the road looking for suitable vulnerable people to kidnap and sell into slavery. A good living was to be had and so they decided that this man was such a villain. It pained Ayken's heart to the core to think of what might have happened to Borvo. He gave Augustine a strong word in the matter of taking care with his brother to which the monk replied with abject sadness at his own mortal weakness for food and ale. His dejection would not last long but his present contrition was real enough.

When Borvo had been reassured about Godgyfu he concentrated on trying to dry his clothes so that he would continue his journey in a modicum of comfort. As soon as they were alone Ayken asked him if he had another vision. "I saw you from the other bank and was going to call out but you seemed to be in one of your reveries. Take care young one; there are those who will be afraid of such things."

Borvo considered his brother's words and nodded, "There is much that I must learn but I will keep my secret. Do you really think the man was out to sell me?"

"Well whoever he was he has gone now, even the innkeeper didn't know him." Ayken went to speak with Augustine and when he returned he said, "We will stay here an extra night, the mistress will wash your clothes and you will appear in the town a day late but refreshed and clean. It is best. Augustine will make an excuse to the abbot and all will be as it should be." Borvo visibly relaxed and later set about his supper with great relish. As did Augustine but then that was no surprise.

The morning of their departure broke clear and cool and the trio set off for the town with full bellies and more outward cheer than any of them felt. Malmesburgh was busy with its weekly market and people. The weary trio entered the town over the bridge to the south west of the town and made their way towards the abbey. Augustine understood the sights and sounds were new to Borvo so he took his time and let them wander the roads drinking in the excitement of it all. Borvo was intrigued with everything that he saw and was so engrossed with the market town that the smell of the people, animals and detritus hardly registered with him at all. Colourful stalls sat alongside penned animals, sweetmeats were laid out on another, fine cloth, jars and pots and beads swam before his eyes. So many strangers gathered in one place seemed to the callow youth to be the most unexpected sight of all. One stall held a collection of bones and amulets that the seller was trying to imbue with religious meaning. "Finger of St Peter, piece of Christ's robe, oil from Jerusalem!" he repeated these over and over hoping to encourage good fortune for the buyer but also for himself. People were clustered around his wares and he seemed to be doing a good trade.

Augustine pointed and quietly remarked, "Do not speak of this to the abbot as he is against such items that he himself does not offer. It takes money from the abbey purse." Borvo nodded and said nothing. He understood that silence was preferable and would often be taken for assent. He would keep his counsel although he was deeply moved by the fact that this town was the very one of his former vision when he knew he would have to leave the village. He was on his course and that was a small crumb of comfort to him in his present anxiety. In the night at the inn he had told Ayken of his new vision and discussed it with him. Ayken was concerned that his brother was learning far too young about the outside world. He naturally wanted to protect him and knew that he couldn't. He just said to him that if he walked in his own path and kept faith with his own idea of what was good and what was bad then he would be proud of him. He must now decide whenever he was confronted with problems as he would not be able to ask his family. They had taught him well and with that they must be content.

The abbey doors were heavy but well oiled. As the great oak slowly opened it revealed a life that was instantly quieter than the town over the wall. Sandals flapped on earth and flagstone as monks went about their daily tasks. They seemed not to notice the new arrivals but each one gave them a sidelong glance. It was not a silent Order but there was no excess chatter; however the discipline of the daily offices did not naturally stamp out common human curiosity. Ayken and Borvo were well aware of the interest they had caused and shuffled uneasily in the courtyard until they were invited by a gesture from Augustine to enter the abbey building. The darkness after the bright sunlight was disconcerting and at first they found it difficult to see the abbot with his prior waiting to greet them seated at the end of a long well scrubbed table.

Augustine had gone to seek an audience with the abbot as soon as they entered the abbey. The abbot was a spare man in mid life who looked at both Ayken and Borvo with interest but no smile. He greeted them but as they were of poor stock he wasted little time. "You are well recommended by no higher authority than the king's man himself so you will stay here and learn. The infirmerer will be your teacher and you will be called Brother Mark. I am your father now and you will obey all that I say." So saying he turned to Ayken and said, "He is in our charge. Go back to your village with our blessing." Ayken was slightly in awe of this powerful man but his feelings for Borvo overcame all others and he bowed and said, "He is well protected Father, make sure no harm comes to him. I leave him to you." He embraced Borvo and went unsteadily out of the abbey; quickly in case any should see the tear in his eye and also because the monks made him feel uncomfortable and confined.

The newly named Brother Mark watched him go with trepidation but he bowed his head to the abbot and stood waiting for further instruction. The surprised and rather affronted abbot spoke only to Augustine, "Brother take the boy and make sure he understands what is required of him." So saying he turned and walked slowly away dismissing all thoughts of the young man's comfort but still wondering why such as he had fallen in so good a favour with the king's man. He would have to be watched.

End of part one

Part Two

Five years have passed and Brother Mark has distinguished himself as a scholar and as an able helpmeet for Brother Andrew the Infirmerer. He has survived the rigours of the monastic life. This is mainly due to the watchful eye of Brother Augustine, Minister Brand and his brother Ayken.

His own reticence on things spiritual has also saved him from uncomfortable penance on more than one occasion.

The king has now sent for him and he is due to set out for court with very little idea as to why he has been summoned. He hopes that it will be to heal and travel, to learn more and to be set free from the cloistered life that has given him so much but at great personal cost.

Dramatis Personae Part Two:

Alric	novice at Malmesburgh befriended by Borvo
Aescwine	second child for Hild and Ayken
Beadmund	Minister Brand's third son
Godric	young son of Beadmund
Aedylpryd	youngest daughter of Minister Brand
Rimilda	wife to Minister Brand
Elfgifu	mother of Ayken's dead friend Aesc
Esric	father to Aesc and husband of Elfgifu
Ealhfrith	Bishop of Winchester
Brother Simeon	monk at Winchester Abbey
Princess Aethelgifu	daughter to the king

Chapter Twenty One

A friendship forged for ever

Brother Mark had been immured in his thirst for knowledge ever since he stepped through the abbey doors. He hated the confinement of monastic life but realised that without it he would be hindered in his quest. He took to Brother Andrew immediately. They had tirelessly worked together to bring on the healing herbs in the abbey gardens, they had shared their understanding of tending the sick. They had concocted tinctures, salves, ointments and so much more as they revelled in each other's company. Brother Andrew was old and needed the younger man's strength. Together they had been a force to be reckoned with inside the abbey. It had somehow got out among the other monks that Brother Mark was well protected from outside, not only was he favoured at court but his family were strong and willing to look after his interests. Many young novices were orphans and friendless. Although the first few months of Borvo's incarceration were hard he had survived the regime. He had kept his counsel as he had promised himself and he had flourished.

Now he had to leave the abbey and go to the king. Never for one moment had he forgotten the vision of the river by the inn. He kept his mind open and his eyes ever alert for danger. His initial puzzlement at the words settled into patient waiting. He knew that his time would come and as sure as night follows day it had. One night, about two years after his entry into the life, he had been awoken by an urgent pain in his belly. The beans he had had for supper the previous evening had not settled well. There was a new cook at the abbey and he turned out to be a poor substitute for his predecessor. As he sat up on his apology for a bed his eyes got used to the darkness, there was little moonlight that night, he felt rather than saw that the bed in the corner was empty. Normally it was occupied by the youngest of the novices who was a slightly built, pious child. Anxious for his wellbeing Brother Mark rose and went silently down the worn steps which led to the outside. He heard a small muffled cry and following his instincts he made his way to the garden beyond the chapter house where he witnessed something that made his blood run cold. Two men, one a monk and one a lay brother, had hold of the child and were trying to strip him and assault him. His young pale limbs were threshing about in panic but his head was covered with a sack. Brother Mark knew he had to stop them but also that he was no match for the men. He thought quickly and pretended that he was not alone. It was an old trick but one that might just work. He shouted at the two men and made his voice loud enough to wake any light sleeper in the abbey. As he rushed forward to help the boy the lay brother ran away but the monk stood his ground. It was not in Brother Mark's nature to be violent but he had to threaten the monk to go away so he picked up a piece of wood and raised it above his head in a threatening manner. There was no need to go further as at that moment two sleepy monks came round the corner to investigate the disturbance. Immediately they jumped to the wrong conclusion and held Brother Mark. The boy was in shock and could not speak; he lay on the ground, half naked and shivering. Gently they covered him and carried him to the infirmary. Brother Mark was thrown unceremoniously into a locked room to wait for justice. As he hit the stone wall of the tiny cell he lost consciousness and slipped into the rank reeds on the floor and there he stayed until early light, cold, damp and hurt. The assailants who had been cowled and therefore unrecognisable melted away into the night.

As morning broke Brother Mark was hauled roughly before the abbot. Although the abbot was a harsh man he was, in essence, fair. "Well Brother, what occurred to make you adopt such a threatening posture?"

Brother Mark was surprised by his conciliatory tone unaware that this was the abbot's device in all matters to put people off guard after which they would give themselves away.

"Father, I woke to find Alric gone from his bed. I heard a disturbance, followed the noise and came upon the attempt to assault him. I could only think of making a noise and using the wood to threaten them in the hope they would run. I am no match for two strong men."

"There were two?"

"Yes Father. The lay brother ran away but the other stood his ground. Is there no one missing this morning?"

The abbot turned to Augustine who confirmed that one of the lay brothers had not appeared for his early meal and that one of the brothers was also missing. He was a monk who normally worked in the kitchens. "And how fares the youth?" Again Augustine spoke, "He only will say that Brother Mark saved him, he repeats it over and over." With no word of apology the abbot turned away and said, "Brother Mark you are free to resume your duties." The audience was over. Borvo was resurrected at that moment. He had never sought this life and now he was determined it would end. He felt the injustice of his uncomfortable incarceration so he threw off his habit and stood in defiance. He almost shouted at the abbot,

"What about Alric? Is this justice? Who will find the monk and bring him to book?"

The abbot turned, stared at Borvo but could not risk annoying those that were above his own station. Although he himself was high born he had a healthy respect for the king. Again he ignored Borvo, turned to Augustine and said, "Explain our justice and make sure that Alric is given into the care of Brother Mark as he has his welfare at heart." He paused then added, "Explain also that one more outburst will find result in a discipline that will test his mettle."

It was later in the day that word came from the town that a body had been found floating in the river, a monk's habit lay on the bank by the bridge with his sandals neatly piled on top. The lay brother was never heard of again and no story ever came to the abbey as to his fate. Alric recovered and became Mark's shadow. He helped Mark and Andrew in the garden and although he had been destined to help elsewhere his timidity turned the hearts of all so they let him be where he was at peace. He lacked sharp wit and would never have made a scholar but his tenderness with plants was greatly appreciated by the others.

It took sometime for all the brothers to be comfortable in Mark's company. He had been mixed up in a terrible event and some chose to believe that he was not as innocent as he declared. He had also shouted at the abbot and tore his habit. Such disruptive behaviour was unsettling and resulted in much gossip and innuendo that were harmful to him for a while. Augustine did his best to quell any rumours if they reached his ears. After a few months much was forgotten as the monks all settled down and the work of the abbey went on as usual.

As Brother Mark reflected on the past five years he thought of the times when he was allowed to go home to the village. It had changed a little in size as its prosperity increased. The school had been a mixed blessing in that given an opportunity to learn and understand some of the young people preferred to try their fortune in the towns. He saw the changes but kept his emotions distant from them. This was no longer his world. Only when he threw off his vestment and sandals and waded into the cooling brook did he feel at peace. It was there that he had learnt to deal with the scripture that he was constantly taught. It was believable, a good story, as were so many of the stories about the gods. He made silent assent when it was needed but his love of the woods, rivers and space of the country was so much a part of his soul that he could never, ever deny its existence. He did what many before him had done, and what countless others to come would do, he made an accommodation in his heart and married the two ideas together. Sitting by his brook he delved deeply into his very being. He argued with himself, he argued with his new teaching; he brought his old ways learnt through his Gramma to the surface and examined each and every detail and so on until he ached to know the truth.

Agonising over the harsh discipline of the one and the freedom of the other he lost hours, days in contemplation. Elvina and Esmund let him be. They loved having their son home for a short while but they knew they could never keep him or contain him. He had much to learn but so much more to give. His life was destined to be a broad landscape, he could not, would not settle for such simplicity as theirs, at least not until he had found what was deep inside him. They fed him, loved him and discussed his life at the abbey. It sounded unduly restrictive to them but Borvo (he would always be Borvo to them) appeared to have accepted the discipline in order to embrace the education he received. He always walked back to them and so by the time he arrived in the village he was limping badly on his weak ankle. It constantly broke Elvina's heart to see him gamp from the woods but then she saw the smile on his face and his joy at their meeting. She would then put aside her own misgivings and make his stay as healing as she knew how.

Uncle Borvo revelled in his niece. Godgyfu who was a happy, chubby child and as she grew she favoured Hild in stature but Elvina in face, Elvina being the more slightly built and with much more grace than her daughter-in-law. When Godgyfu was three years old Ayken and Hild had another child. This was a son and they called him Aescwine. There was no discussion about it. Ayken just said the name as he was born and Hild accepted. She knew his darkness was buried deep so this was a good sign in her mind. Ayken had cradled his friend Aesc in his last futile attempts to live and so perhaps she thought this would give him an opportunity to make amends. He couldn't save his friend but he could honour him in his son. As he grew there was no doubt that he was Ayken's son, he seemed to be built like a mountain, huge and calm.

Brother Mark had plenty of time for reflection now. He had been relieved of his duties at the infirmary. He was no longer required to sit in the library for hours copying manuscript. It was unusual in the abbey for a brother to have two occupations. It had been a specific request, one that could not be refused, by the Bishop of Winchester who was a boyhood friend of Minister Brand and godfather to his children. Mark was expected to attend the daily offices which he did with a quiet heart. It gave him time for peaceful reflection. He had often wondered if the rest of the brothers had similar thoughts to his own. He understood the need in him to believe in a god or gods but they blurred into one. Jesus would become a god of the river as well as his own spiritual patron. Jesus was everywhere, the holy spirit was everywhere, his ancient gods and goddesses were everywhere. Were they one and the same? Borvo thought they were. Brother Mark tried to reason it out.

As he thought of all these past years he made a conscious effort to put it all behind him. He was thinking only of the good times.

There had been bad, bad times and he was loath to bring them to the front of his thinking. He shuddered as he put aside, once more, the horrific images that he carried in the dark recesses of his mind. He must concentrate on the matter in hand. His abbot had given him a task and he must fulfil it. The king had sent for him to come to court which was at Winchester for the summer. He was to walk there as a pilgrimage via the abbey of Sarum. Accompanied by Alric who would not leave his side they intended to make full use of their freedom and lack of order. He was to take his bed roll, his precious bag of herbs, a psalter and some few shillings for essential food. Lodging he was expected to beg for or sleep under the stars. Alric's only baggage was his bedroll. He must rely on god and Brother Mark to keep him and protect him. The call had been perfunctory when it came. He was aware that his time at the abbey was drawing to a close. The old abbot had died from fever in the previous winter. He was mourned by the brothers as, despite his severity of faith, he had been a fair if not a warm leader. It was the general feeling amongst the brothers that 'better the devil you know as a worse one may appear'.

So Brother Mark and Alric, one early summer morning, set off from Malmesburgh for their long journey to Winchester. Mark felt that he would never see the abbey again. He trod with a light and measured step. Alric was still undersized for his age and not over muscled. His devotion to Mark would take him a long way. As they left the abbey, having made their farewells, a soft summer rain began and by the time they stopped for a midday rest their habits were soaked through. The two companions sheltered under an enormous hedge and ate their bread and drank their ale. Despite the rain they were not downhearted as it was warm rain and for the first time in a long time they felt a sense of freedom. Alric was slow and believed everything that Mark told him although on occasions Mark caught a glimpse of light in his companions eyes that he seemed keen to mask. Mark wanted to throw off his abbey name and revert to Borvo but knew this was not the time to do so. He recognised that it was a way of obliterating the past and was deeply aware of his own identity. In all the five years he had never forgotten who he was. He just accepted that to learn and understand all that he was privileged to learn his was a passage to the light. For him the spiritual world was a mixture of all he had ever known, and with this he was comfortable, searching for more truth always but essentially comfortable with the journey.

Chapter Twenty Two

Gramma Disappears

The village had prospered in the last five years. They basked in the glory of their successful dealing with the king and his men. Leofric had grown old and was well respected as the head of the village. Eldric had grown also to become mature and wise. He took every opportunity to build Ayken up in the stories told during the long dark nights of winter. Ayken detested the idea of hero worship but he could not escape the local fame that Eldric's stories gave him. Hild was proud but wary as she understood that her husband had taken a long time to get back to the gentle quiet man she loved. All this talk of the fighting kept him from finally healing. No entreaty seemed to made headway with Eldric, he was perhaps aware that by talking of Ayken's exploits he also had to tell of his own and he had been no mean fighter.

As the village had settled into peace it had increased in size but not lost its essence and feeling of being one extended family group. There were now two roads, the main thoroughfare as before but now there was a second that cut away from the centre towards the south. Even Goaty's old hut had been taken over and enlarged by a needy family. Leofric had been reluctant at first but then realised that time moves on and his sister and her son would always be remembered as long as he lived and as long as Seofon included their story in his visits to entertain the cottage people. The smith had taken on a young boy as help, a potter had set up again now there was more trade and generally there was more bustle although nothing compared with the town. The village retained its feeling of peace and seclusion.

When Borvo visited from the abbey he always made sure to pay his respects to Leofric and pass on any news that might be of interest. Leofric was grateful for this honour as he realised how favoured Borvo was and might be even greater in the future. Many an hour did he talk with Esmund about his younger son. They speculated well into the night on the plans that the king might have for him. Any glory would shine a little on the village and in times of trouble, no one believed that they were over, and this was important for their continued good fortune.

One huge burden that hung over the village was the loss of Gramma. They knew not whether she was alive or dead. One day she had gone missing and no attempt to find her had any success. It had been four years after Borvo left that she had disappeared. Her pains had increased to an unbearable level. Even her skills had been unable to afford her any relief. Elvina was frantic with worry but as time went on she accepted that it was in the hands of the gods and she must wait. She regularly went to the brook and made an offering. The action gave her some little peace. In her heart she wondered if her mother had taken herself off to die alone with dignity. She longed to find her and honour her but, for now, it was not to be. They had searched as long and as far as they could but all to no avail.

Another source of pain and pride for the family was the departure of Sunny. Minister Brand had come to them one day in late autumn and asked if she would join his household as companion and sewing mistress to his wife and daughter. She had agreed and left the village only a year after Borvo. It was with a heavy heart that Sunny left her family. She had given up all hope of Oeric coming back to claim her. She no longer laughed as before. She no longer stood at the edge of the wood longing to see him come riding out of the trees and sweep her away with his passion. She died a little inside each time. She had embraced sadness. When Brand put his offer to her, through Esmund, she brightened as hope surged through her. If she was within reach of the court she may see him again and their love would be rekindled. Brand made no mention of Oeric and Esmund did not ask. It was agreed that it would be good for all concerned as Sunny was still the finest seamstress and no one could take that away from her. She would tutor Brand's daughter in the craft and help the other servants improve their sewing. Sunny left her home with both regret and renewed hope.

The first weeks were exciting for Sunny. She instantly liked the daughter of the household who was unprepossessing in appearance and ungainly to the point of awkward. Her mother, Rimilda, had given up on her and spent her time drifting from minor task to minor task. She wore silver jewellery, necklace, arm bangles and a ring made of a Roman coin, no longer legal tender but good for decoration. A seemingly shallow woman who had married Brand for his status she nonetheless had given him children, this last daughter though had been a mistake. The others were away and married. Five in all there were three sons and one other daughter who had left their home as soon as they might. Brand respected Rimilda as his wife and would not dishonour her in any way. One of the sons named, Beadmund, had married young and lost his wife in childbirth. He now lived with his wife's family who helped him care for his son. The infant was strong and survived whilst his mother gave her life for his. He was now five years old, and went by the name of Godric.

Aedylpryd knew she was a disappointment to her mother and tried to keep out of her way. As soon as Sunny appeared, who seemed against all the odds to like her, she blossomed. Sunny's quiet way of encouragement suited the young girl and they were instant friends. Occasionally Rimilda would stop their sewing to relieve her own boredom and insist that Sunny entertain her with stories of life in the village. The arrangement of the buildings that they inhabited was such that Brand and his wife had their separate quarters that were well insulated from the prevailing westerly winds with finely woven woollen cloth dyed in the colours of the earth, reds, oranges and green. The central fire kept damp and cold at bay and created a soft light by which they read or sewed, laughed, chatted and quarrelled.

So life settled into a new pattern and Sunny became more content than she had imagined. One day Brand had a visitor and when he was seated at the long table for the evening meal Sunny passed and recognised Oeric. She was so shaken that she gave a small shriek and fled outside to the grounds surrounding Brand's long main dwelling. Oeric caught up with her as she was about to disappear from sight into a copse of trees. He pulled at her sleeve and she stopped, turned and stared at him, burst into tears and pushed him away. "Sunniva, I didn't know how to tell you. I was promised to another. From childhood it was understood." Oeric dropped his hands in a helpless gesture, "For the good of the families." Sunny's tearful face tore at his heart. She stumbled out some incoherent words then turned and walked back with great composure to the house, went to her room and wept until she was spent.

In the morning Oeric waited for Sunny and insisted that they walk together. "I do not love her. She is my wife in name only. I lie with her to produce a son, not for love. I knew you were here and came to ask you to . . ." here he paused and held out his hand to her, "I want to ask you to be mine, as my love. I am not able to leave her but I would always love you." Sunny became still and as cold as stone. She backed away from the only man she could ever love, shook her head and turned and left him staring after her. The retreating figure broke his heart. He had been sure that she would accept his proposal. His confidence shattered he went to take his leave from Brand and Rimilda. He briefly told Brand what had occurred and was further surprised by Brand telling him in no uncertain terms that he was a fool and should have known that she would not take him in such circumstances.

After this desolate period from which it took Sunny a few weeks to recover, she once again revelled in the company of Aedylpryd. She would stay and help make this unfortunate girl into an independent woman. All was change but as people grew up and made homes and families all was in essence the same.

Chapter Twenty Three

One more tender parting

News spread as wildfire sweeps through a forest in drought. The Danes had broken the treaty. Battles had begun again and men were being called upon, once more to go and fight for their freedom. People of the village were stunned by the tales from a passing traveller. Not Seofon this time, he was busy elsewhere, it was an itinerant wanderer who just stumbled upon the spreading number of houses by accident. Leofric held council with Esmund, Eldric and the other men of the village. Words floated around the long barn and to Elvina they became a morass of agitation. How could it be that they must give up their young men to fight once more? Peace seemed so transient to her although five years of comparative calm was in itself unusual for those times of the raiders.

Ayken would go, Eldric and others also would muster under the banner of their hitherto absent thegn. They would make their way to a point east of Malmesburgh and gather there with the other groups massing together to form a fighting force to quell, once and for all the less than honourable foe. For it was the Danes who broke the treaty and the Danes must therefore be beaten back to their agreed boundary. All the king wanted was to see his family and his kingdom settle down and learn, read books in their own tongue and honour god and one another. It was rumoured that he spent so much time kneeling with his Welsh monk that he had let the border patrols become lax. What truth there was in this only the king and his ministers knew but the result was there for all to see, more conflict.

The village men set off three days after receiving the news. Ayken made a tender farewell to his growing family. Godgyfu hugged her father with her chubby arms and kissed him sweetly on his hairy face. She stroked his long hair and whispered lovingly in his ear. Hild lifted Aescwine to him and he hugged his son with tears in his eyes. Would he ever see them again he wondered as he kissed Hild and bade her protect them at all costs. Esmund stepped up and vowed to keep watch over his son's family while he was gone. He also embraced Ayken and offered him both solace and encouragement. Elvina stood by and gently kissed her son. She said nothing; Ayken felt her silence more than all the words. He turned away and went to join the departing party. As he left the village he cursed all Danes that took him away from such sweet life. Had he not fought enough last time? His bitterness increased with each step. By the time they had met up with other bands of men his heart was stone and woe betide any Dane who came near his sword.

Brother Mark and Alric had been on the road for five days and were having a wondrous time. They slept, ate and drank simply. They searched the highways and byways for herbs and berries. Borvo emerged from his confining habit to talk to Alric about his life before Malmesburgh. It seemed safe to do so now they were away from the abbey. Alric took in all that Borvo told him and as the days passed he longed to go there and see for himself what wonderful company there might be there for him. Gradually they made their way towards their goal, but they were in no hurry. On the sixth day they were aware of more bustle on the roads, more groups of men gathering, extra vigilant guardians of any settlement questioning all travellers, suspicious even of a monk and a boy. As the two friends stopped one evening at an inn Brother Mark determined from overheard conversation that there was fresh trouble with the Danes. He immediately thought of Konal, lying tied to a dead woman and a tree. His memory triggered both a smile and a shiver as he then remembered how Ayken and Konal had fought in the woods. There was new danger with each step they took towards Winchester. He must think of Alric's safety. He would be no good in any fighting force and he was too vulnerable to be left to his own devices. As he lay in the inn that night Mark thought long and hard about his young companion. Court would be a nightmare for him, he would be scorned for his lack of wits and his slight frame bent under the yoke of heavy domesticity. He realised that he must eventually get to the king but that a detour might just be in order. After all his orders were clear in their determination for him to get to court but there had been no timescale set down for him.

After they had taken bread, cheese and water for their early meal they set off once more upon the road. It took Alric some time to realise that the sun was coming from a different direction than usual. He asked Brother Mark why this was so and received the answer, "All will be clear. Have patience my young friend." He trusted this kind man and so he happily fell into step and they proceeded to head south then west. As they went they met more and more of the fighting groups going in the opposite direction. Brother Mark decided that it would be best to keep to the little known routes and so he struck away across country towards his beloved woods. Two days later, having slept out under the stars in the balmy summer night, they arrived at the eastern edge of the trees. Alric had developed a cough which troubled him a great deal. Mark stopped and breathed huge breaths as though he couldn't get enough of the precious air into his lungs then set about finding some meadowsweet. This would make a fragrant tea which would help Alric's condition. They slept one more night in the woods then emerged half a day later into the clearing by the village.

Elvina had been inconsolable after saying goodbye to the last of her children. She thought she was dreaming as she wandered through the main road with Godgyfu by her side. She shook her head to clear it then realised she was not dreaming, it really was Borvo come back, still dressed as a monk but his tonsure was growing out and his hair nearly back to fullness. He was accompanied by a young strip of a boy who held onto his habit as though he would fall if he let go. The youth was bent over coughing as though he would bring up his guts. As Elvina started to go forward to embrace her son Godgyfu beat her to it. She ran and flung her arms round her favourite uncle and screamed with delight. Elvina moved in, hugged Borvo and then took charge of Alric as Borvo explained who he was and why they had come.

"He's in my charge Mother and I thought it safest for him to stay with you while the battles are fought again. He is not strong. Alric." This was all he could manage as Godgyfu was smothering his face with her excited kisses.

Elivina took Alric's hand and smiling said, "Welcome young Alric, let us go and tend your cough." They all went happily to their hut and settled down to talk and rest and treat Alric's ailment.

Later as they sat in the hut, having caught up with the news of the renewed fighting Brother Mark spoke about his young charge. He reminded them about the attack on him and how he had been his shadow ever since. They remembered and welcomed the youth with kindness. "Well Borvo, what are we to do with him?"

"Mother, Father, I know that you have lost us all for now but we will be back with you one day. He is in need of love and care." As he smiled at Alric he added, "He is useful too. I have taught him much about how to make ointments and so forth." Alric lay on his side having been given another infusion of meadowsweet. He was calmer now and smiling around him. He spoke for the first time without hesitation, "Thank you for taking me in. I dare not go where Brother Mark is going." He breathed deeply, coughed, then added, "Simply, I would die." All the family were astonished but did not pursue the conversation. Hild came in at that moment with Aescwine and all was happy chaos once more.

It was some time later that Esmund, Elvina and Borvo went out into the evening sun to stroll and talk. "Mother, father, I have to go to court. It is my destiny. I will stay here a few days to recover from the journey and to make sure Alric is all right. Then I will go." Esmund held his son's shoulder in a bond of affection and reassured him that they would look after his companion. "That is good" replied his son "but I had another thought on the road here. You have Hild and the children to brighten your days even though we are all gone for the present. Aesc's parents will never have that joy again. If you asked Elfgifu to help look after Alric they may take to each other and he would then fill their days." Elvina laughed and said she would certainly seek the help of the other woman. "She may be willing but I am not sure about Esric. He descended into gloom from which he rarely escapes. It will be harder." All Borvo would say was, "We will see. We must try."

The next day Elfgifu appeared at the hut entrance early to take her turn at nursing the sick youth. His fever was up and he looked pale. The grief stricken woman went forward, sat by his side and held his slender hand in her own which was roughened by years of toil but still able to be tender. She immediately took to Alric as she tended his fever and waited for it to break. Esric came once to see his wife tend another then left without a word and came no more. The next few days saw an improvement in Alric's fever and cough while Borvo helped with the animals and in the fields and also found time to play with his nephew and niece. Late in the evenings he would find his way to the brook where he needed the solitude. Its presence never failed to calm him and lead him to profound thought. A passage he had recently copied out from the gospel of one called Mark; spoke of the kingdom to which they all aspired after death. It would belong to any one who was kind to children. After this reflection he decided to tackle Esric head on and plead with him about Alric. He was taciturn but Borvo was relentless when he thought he was right, it was in the scripture after all.

The following morning Borvo went to Esric's field and spoke with him. "I must leave soon and Alric needs a home. He needs love and care and in return he will help you and Elfgifu, he had some healing too. Will you help him and me?" Esric did not answer for a long time. Borvo just stood and held out his hand to him in supplication. He let him take time. Finally when Borvo had decided that even he was mistaken the older man looked deep into Borvo's face, what he saw there convinced him that he was worthy and he nodded. "It is hard to lose your only son. I nearly lost Elfgifu when we had Aesc. I see that she needs Alric as much as he needs her. I will protect them both. I was going to deny you when you came to me as I was sure you would. You are a good man Borvo. It is for you." Borvo was very moved by such a long speech from this man. "It is for you too Esric, you too deserve more. Alric will repay in kind that you do not yet know. I am grateful." He left the man with his sheep and his crops and returned to tell his family the good news. He was only slightly aware that Esric had seen something in his eyes that was immensely powerful. If it was a god given gift then he must use it wisely.

As Borvo came upon his home he saw Alric sitting outside in the fresh air with Elfgifu sitting beside him. Their bodies were in caring harmony which pleasant sight made his news even more welcome. When later that evening all the family were gathered in the cottage to say goodbye to Alric before he moved in with his new 'family' the youngster stood up everyone became quiet. As he looked hesitantly around him he straightened his lean frame and spoke, "Brother Mark, You have cared for me but I am tired of walking all over the land. I will stay here and wait for you. I will go with these good people and make you proud of me." His simplicity was touching. "I learnt a long time ago that to appear more clever than those around you meant a beating so I became a 'lackwit'. The beatings stopped. Only now am I able to begin again to be myself. I have learnt so much from you Brother Mark and you will always have my loyalty unto death. I would like to help your family also with their healing. My grandmother was a healer and paid for it with her life. They didn't understand."

He had said enough. Elvina put her arms around his shoulders and guided him to Elfgifu and Esric. "Come with us Alric, make your home with us, and wait for your friend to return. You will help us with the sheep and goats. We will be together." Elfgifu's face was alive for the first time since Aesc had died. The three walked out into the summer night to begin afresh.

"He is very trusting of you, Borvo." This from Esmund. "Yes father that is why I couldn't take him to court. He would be torn to pieces by everyone. I must go back. But I can stay for a short while." As he contemplated this turn of events he added softly, almost to himself, "Why could he not trust me with this?" Neither parent said anything as they knew that there were some things that must be worked out alone, then they would mean more. The next few days would be bitter sweet, full of joy at reunion and sorrow at the coming parting. Not a second was wasted.

Chapter Twenty Four

A companion for Seofon

Men and boys from all over Wessex, some mercenaries from further afield, and the regular fighting men loyal to the king were gathering. From every corner of the small kingdom they came. Anglo Saxons, some Britons all with either swords, staves, shields of many sorts and knives. Theirs was a tradition of magnificently worked metal that had strength and beauty in its forging. Quietly at first then with increasing noise they came, raggedy bands led by local men following on with their overlords, all loyal to the king, most wishing they could stay at home and not have the need to fight once more for freedom. Plaited, helmeted, some in chain mail, stout leather over jerkins with minds and hearts on the job in hand. It was fatal in battle to remember the soft times. The wives, children, aged parents, trusty hound, village life of tillage and husbandry were all too distracting. The men had to steel themselves to fight, they knew what they were fighting for but to remember details would be costly. On they walked towards the gathering point. As the smaller bands of men met then they formed into larger units. Cooks and camp followers brought up the rear of each growing unit. The call had gone out and they had responded.

One of the number for whom this had an interest beyond fighting was Seofon. He joined with a band of men from Malmesburgh, where he happened to be when the massing began. That town had responded in force and were overwhelmingly behind the king. Seofon was not a fighting man, he was a storyteller. He kept people entertained on long nights. He made merry with the best of them and sympathised with the rest of them. For many years he had a companion by way of a stray mutt that had just fixed himself to him and never let him out of his sight. He had long since died from old age and the wanderer had been alone for a while. As he walked to join the men he was aware of the inn keeper's young dog at his heels. He tried to shoo him away. This was not a good time to be saddled with another responsibility. The dog would not leave him. The inn keeper had scolded him once too often and so he took flight and decided on Seofon as a kinder master. He was black and lanky, with one white patch over his eye and slobber dripped from his jaw, but he would stay with his new friend and protect him. Seofon had absentmindedly fed him as he sat in the inn, the dog remembered any kindness and so the deal was done. Seofon and the dog were to become inseparable. The storyteller decided to call him Bacchus in honour of his time at the inn and the dog's fondness for a saucer of ale.

Ayken and Eldric led the village men towards their fate. Eldric was a natural leader. More so than his father for whom the role was a burden. He fell into the role alongside that of mentor and protector. More importantly he inspired others with his own bravery and they were loyal to him. Ayken was his able second and between them they led a strong team. The euphoria felt by those who had not seen battle lasted for a few days as they walked away from their predictable lives. After many miles and hearing tales from the old hands this euphoria was replaced by fearful excitement. Those who had seen war before respected their enemy and hardened their resolve. It was upon this determined band of men that Seofon came one misty summer morning as he traipsed across a field trying to find a new group with which to travel. He had tired of the men of Malmesburgh as he had been there a while before they set off and he had temporarily exhausted his audience with his oft repeated tales. Seofon recognised the large frame of Ayken before anyone else and so he hurried to catch up and fell into step beside him. He saw the look on his face, a mixture of grit and hunger for battle. It was the dichotomy of the man that his natural bent was for peaceful husbandry but this opportunity to wage war became him well and he was more than up to the task. This time he had so much more to fight for; Hild and the children and Sunny and young Borvo. Quietly he was glad, as he had never thought to be so, that Borvo was cloistered and not able to fight. He was not a killer and never would be. It would be torment for Ayken to see his brother forced to go down this path as some of the other village lads were now being driven. He and Eldric would protect as many as they could. In reality their best defence was to be strong fighting machines and so this is what they taught them as they made their way to fight for their survival.

Seofon spoke of the town and the life there; he spoke of the abbey and of Borvo. He also told Ayken that Borvo had left the abbey and was on his way to the court. Immediately Ayken worried that the one person he considered out of harms way was walking straight into it. He cast his mind back to when he had last seen his brother. He had grown taller but no fatter at the abbey. The food from the abbey kitchens was healthy enough but not generous. However he still thought of him as a young sapling in need of his protection. He could do nothing at that moment but he would be keeping a look out for him and then he would know what to do. He turned to tell Eldric of this latest news which was received in grim silence. They both knew this was no place for monks. Healers would certainly be needed. Perhaps there would be a place for him well behind the line of battle. These thoughts occupied his mind for many a mile.

After a desultory attempt at more conversation when Seofon tried to extract information from Ayken the wanderer fell back into step with the others who were straggling along behind their leaders. Any detail might be useful, if not for his survival, then for his next story to tell along the way. He was blessed with a brilliant memory for words, faces and voices. It was his talent and had saved his life more times than he could remember. He already knew that Ayken had another child, a boy named after the friend he had lost in the previous conflict. So that was still on his mind. Seofon filed that fact away. Eldric was also a family man now and had left three children and a strong wife. Weak women and childbirth did not go hand in hand. It was a fact and men chose from the strong and resilient women just as their fathers had done. Similarly the women chose men who were good providers and if they were also lusty then that was no bad thing either on a cold winter's night.

All was hectic in the household of Minister Brand. He would be with his king once more in battle, although he did not relish the idea. His bones ached now in the damp mornings and he felt that he wanted to retire to hunt and fish and enjoy what time he had left. Affairs of state would not let him and as his king needed him he made ready to go. Rimilda was indifferent to his presence; her life would be affected only by the disruption. She did not wish to contemplate losing any son to the battle but if any of them did then she hoped they would die bravely. All of her children and their families visited and all got to know Sunny to different extents. The third son was particularly taken with the new seamstress and appreciated the time that Sunny took to make Aedylpryd happier with herself. She was developing from an awkward child into a not unattractive young woman. She would never be considered beautiful but she had qualities that only Sunny, it seemed, had the time to bring out. He favoured his father in stature and looks which pleasing quality made him quite attractive to Sunny herself. She did not ever believe that he noticed her and they were never alone. She carried out her duties with her customary zeal and kept her mending heart away from any temptation. She had glimpsed Oeric only once since his offer to her, his stay was brief and business like with Brand making sure that he did not have the opportunity to meet Sunny on his own again. Sunny had seen him ride up through the trees and retreated behind the wall. She felt a pang for what might have been but was surprised that the pain was not as intense as she had feared.

They rode away, Brand and his company which included all his sons, as the sun struggled to shine through the morning fog. There was an unaccustomed chill in the air and Sunny drew her shawl round her for comfort. Aedylpryd was sensitive to her companion's state and decided to speak of the tapestries she had seen when she last went to visit the court. She knew this would enchant her friend. So it was that as they sat and sewed and spoke of fine stitches men gathered round their king to fight once more.

Chapter Twenty Five

Forces gather for one more battle

The village was quiet. People went about their daily tasks with thoughtful expressions. Life must go on. The visiting priest noticed an increase in those gathered to worship. He sensed that it was the faith of desperation rather than conviction, however not one to lose an opportunity he spoke of the scripture with added fervour and passion. He liked these people. They were honest, rough but honourable, in the main.

Malmesburgh was also quieter than usual. With so many men away the market was not so crowded, women still chatted and worked and children still ran and laughed and avoided chores if they could. The abbey prayed for a successful outcome for their king. Their ordered way was not the invaders way and they all knew what would happen to them should the king fail in his latest quest for peace. There had been news from an itinerant who had suggested that some of those for whom the east had become home embraced the church, well there was always hope. In addition came more news of slaughter and carnage. The monks prayed as hard as they might for salvation.

The settlements along the roads where the men walked were suddenly full of noise, then after a short time those left behind were bereft like a wave on the shore that leaves the rock pool abandoned in its isolation.

At court the servants left behind heaved a sigh of relief. All had been frantic for days before the main contenders in this next phase of war left. Now they could recover and if not entirely relax at least they could find some peaceful moments during the days until they returned. Even the slaves working in the fields felt a sense of relief.

Intelligence had been brought to the commanders. The enemy were fewer than they had originally thought. Discussion took place as to whether this was a trap, a decoy, misinformation or a half hearted attempt to unsettle the king and go for a stronger treaty. Skirmishes had taken place already. Forays into the hillsides to fight then withdraw. This was designed to keep the army on its toes and not let them rest. A few had suffered injury; fewer still had lost their lives. The king did not want any more fighting; he preferred treaty and peaceful coexistence. He was nonetheless nobody's fool and he knew that to show weakness was not an option. He already had the neighbouring kingdom on his side. One of his daughters had married the heir to that middle kingdom and so an alliance was inevitable. The days passed with no side gaining significant ground. Then there was a breakthrough. The king's men knew the terrain better than the enemy and so were able to take full advantage of their local knowledge. They were also filled with the fiercest desire to win and defend their country.

The village men were sidelined to begin with. There seemed to be no job for them to do. Ayken and Eldric stood apart from the others. They were battle ready and longed to go in and do the job then go home. Waiting to fight was the worst thing for them in their state. As they ate their rough spelt bread and cheese a call went up to gather and make advance along the ridge to fight and stop the enemy from making any further inroads to the west. They set off.

Now the time was here they became silent and determined. As they reached the ridge and looked down they saw a small contingent making their way round the hillside. They ran down to them and engaged them. The noise made by the shouting and clash of metal ripped through the green hills. They fought bravely, lost two of their number and routed the enemy. As they surveyed the carnage one man stood alone before them. He was familiar to Ayken. They had fought before. Konal had made his way back to his people after the rout in the woods and was even now the commander of this small fierce force. He knew he had lost the day. He wanted revenge and so he challenged Ayken. A personal challenge, a desperate challenge and one which both thought would result in death for at least one of them. Konal knew this man and knew him to be strong but without the innermost need to be a killer. But that was the old Ayken, the soft shepherd, the tiller of fields and lover of children. This new man was Ayken the avenger; Ayken the father; all to fight for and much to lose.

As they both stood their ground and summoned up their strength, swirled their swords around their heads to prepare for combat there was a shout from Ayken's group to reform and move out. He hesitated, felt rather than saw his fellow west country men at his back, and with out losing eye contact with Konal, he walked backwards and into the safety of his own men. Konal, frustrated and angry shouted in his foreign broken tongue, "It is not finished!" He turned and went back to chew on his enmity and harbour thoughts of killing the next time he met with Ayken.

The forces gathered by the king were to go in different directions as news had come that the south west near the River Exe was being threatened. It was felt that the men from the west should go and help fight for the west. So it was that the men from the village set off and once more took up the march through their own land to fight near the sea for their freedom.

Chapter Twenty Six

Elvina's journey

Elvina and Esmund had become distant from each other. They had always maintained an energetic marriage, especially emotionally. Since the departure of all of their kin they had been thrown together in a way that was to them unnatural. They needed to love, not only each other, but an extended family as well. They had both refrained from overwhelming Hild and the children. She was a good mother and her parents were there to help the tiny family as well as they. Their time was filled with tending their livestock and growing enough food to see them through the winter, as well as creating a surplus for the good of the village and the amount due to their absent, non interfering overlord. In truth they had not expected to be less than extremely busy and useful. Esmund was more cautious than previously in his proclamation about the old gods and their strengths. The new god was becoming more popular and accepted as the king's desires for education and adherence increasingly spread among his people. It was well known that he made treaties with the invaders and despite this latest set back had been successful and so it was believed that god must be on his side. In such circumstances it was difficult to remain openly hostile to the changes this brought to their everyday lives.

Elvina steadfastly refused to accept any other path than that which she had looked to all her life. She was a creature of the earth and so were her gods. She was in her mid life but her body and mind still yearned for the freedom she felt as she flung off her clothes and danced by the sacred water. Occasionally she would slip away before dawn and dance to welcome the day. She made sure no one saw her. The light in her eyes when she returned from these sallies forth gave Esmund a glimpse of the young woman he had known and instantly loved. He had tried to remonstrate with her to advise caution in such times but she would not listen. She did not understand that there were those who accepted the new religion with such fervour that any suggestion of pagan ways was anathema to them and led them to believe that all such behaviour should be outlawed.

They didn't argue, they just drew apart and spent an increasing amount of time alone. It was sad for their friends to witness but no one wished to interfere. One day Elvina decided to try to find out once and for all where Gramma had gone to live out her last days. Gramma's disappearance had caused an enormous amount of worry and added to the gradual dispersal of the family it had helped create the current rift. She came to Elvina in a dream one night; her mother was sitting on a rock by an inlet that ran from the open sea into a wide river mouth. She appeared to Elvina as though she was seen through a fog. Her arms were above her head and she was dancing with her upper body. The arrangements of the rocky cliffs to one side were distinctive enough for any stranger to recognise should they stumble across them. She went to Esmund one day and spoke softly to him, without anger but with finality; she had made up her mind, "Lover, I must go and follow my dream to find Gramma. I know she is waiting to be found; as yet I do not know why she left. There are people aplenty to help with the work.

I will be gone as long as the wind is in the west. When the cold north wind comes I will return and we will be as before." There were tears in both their eyes but they did not shed them. Life was hard and harsh decisions had to be made. Respect and care for those with age and wisdom were as important as breathing. They clasped hands and then embraced. They did not kiss. When next their lips met they would never more be parted.

Elvina left with a respectful farewell to Leofic and Cynwise. Her slim form with its burden of guilt walked slowly away with a purposeful tread. She neither looked back nor hesitated in her step. Any fear would not be shown. She must find her mother. She hoped she had not left it too long.

Leofric did not understand why she had gone but he helped Esmund find a suitable man to help with his daily labours. The fighting would soon be over and they longed then for the young men and peace to return to their village and its growing population. Since the men had left Leofric realised just how much he relied on his son Eldric for advice on the many matters that increasingly seemed to fill his time. He knew Eldric would make a far better village elder than he had. Recently he had grown weary and the pain in his legs, for many months just an irritation, had become overwhelming at times. During these bouts of pain he was irritable and cross. Cynwise, her own pains and burdens kept hidden, worried for her husband. She noticed the grey colour of his face that heralded bouts of extreme distress and could not help him. Elvina had given her a tincture of wood betony for the pain in his legs. This was to be used sparingly as it had other properties that included raising desire. Cynwise loved her husband but had long since ceased to expect or want intimacy. Age brought its own problems and they lived comfortably together in loving companionship, the eager lovemaking of their youth was a pleasant and distant memory. For the rest of the time Leofric drank nettle tea to alleviate some of his pain.

He did get some relief from these remedies but they did little to allay his fear that he would not see his eldest son again.

Borvo had noticed some of the distress of his parents before he left but was at a loss as to how to help them find a way back to each other. He had witnessed too how the village was changing. It was still a haven of quiet living but unrest reared its ugly head more than once whilst he was there. So like many before him when faced with such trials, he did nothing. This troubled him as he again took up his monk's habit and went to do the king's bidding. Soon he put the family to one side as he walked and instead tried to reason with himself about the similarities and differences between the old and the new. It had been a constant source of pleasurable debate for him since his introduction to the writings and teachings at the abbey. As he sat with the other boys, some from the town and others beholden to the brothers for their food and shelter he relished the written word as much for its form as for what it meant. As time passed he thought more of the content and how the passages of the religious teachings set off trains of thought in him that followed tortuous paths to nowhere. One such text stayed with him more than the rest.

As the brothers and lay brothers sat and ate one of the brothers would read aloud to the assembled company so that they would have guidance in their thoughts whilst they ate. One of the more regular passages from a particular brother concerned old men dreaming dreams and young men having visions. It seemed tied up with the spirit of god being given to people in years to come. He hadn't fully understood the text but it did speak to him. He had visions. The old men he had known had certainly had dreams, most especially about the past. Perhaps that is what was meant by it. Old men look to their youth and young men have visions of the future. He doubted it was that simple but no one had come forward with any deeper explanation. Well he, Borvo, had visions. Brother Mark suppressed his visions but for Borvo, his visions were profound and prophetic and instructional. At the same time he felt that he was chosen by the healing river spirit to carry out his destiny. It seemed that everyone in his life had chosen what he was to do. His parents, his god, his abbot and now his king had chosen a path for him. He wondered when it would be his turn to choose. Had he in fact chosen by acquiescing to others demands on him? Was this his fate? Could he choose to do otherwise or would it go badly for his family, or indeed for him? His thoughts turned to Alric. What horrors he must have experienced to make him pretend to be a lack wit. Borvo felt rather bitterly that he had not trusted him enough to tell him about his deception. He tried not to mind but deep down he did and it hurt. Alric's devotion to Borvo was so strong but even that was not enough to break the fool's habit. Only the sanctuary of a good village and the prospect of a new life brought the truth out of him. Borvo decided to be glad for him and waste no more time in thinking of what might have been. He had a long way to go and much to consider as he walked.

Chapter Twenty Seven

Journeys: to the sea and to deep inside the mind

As Borvo walked through the late summer countryside, making his way to do the king's bidding, he reflected on his life so far. Born to heal he had demonstrated his skill over and over again. His handling of the emergency with the king and his men, his consolidation of his art and knowledge during his time at the abbey, all this had got him to where he was now. He felt a restlessness that harkened back to his youthful freedom at the village. Why he asked himself had he acquiesced so willingly to the king's idea for his future. He had wanted an adventure and instead what he received was learning. He could now read Latin, and had been taught the scriptures. Endless days had been spent in writing out the texts given him. He was a good scribe but had not mastered the art of illumination. Brother Peter had been the abbey's talent in that direction. Borvo had felt uneasy in his presence since the first meeting. The older monk's eyes bored through him so that Borvo felt he knew all about him and his errant thoughts. One dull day as the light struggled into the scriptorium Brother Mark, his eyes tired of trying to concentrate, had put down his pen and expressed an interest in debating the scripture he was copying. Brother Peter had swiftly put him down with words of chastisement. It had not been easy keeping his ideas to himself but he had taken Brother Peter's words as a serious warning. Fundamentally he had been brought up to honour the ancient gods and to keep an open mind. He had been taught well by his parents and Gramma. The idea that Gramma had gone off on her own when she was so old caused him a pain of longing. He would have loved to say goodbye to her. It had been many months since she left. He shook his head as though to rid himself of the distraction. He walked on in the warm sun and brought his mind back to his own life.

He could understand why, in some instances the new religion had caught hold of people's imagination. They were promised eternal safety if they abided by the rules determined for them. But he could not understand or reconcile the idea of a loving god with the austerity and cruelty meted out to those who transgressed or even mildly offered other opinions. How did Brother Augustine and the abbot ever come to such differing attitudes to their beliefs and others dissention when they had access to the same teachings? It made for deep and profound thought. He let his mind wander on the vagaries of the people he had met. He was now a young man with fair experience of the world, or so he thought. He had sat beside merchants' sons during his early time at the abbey while they were introduced into the learned world by a variety of teachers. He had made friends of some of them and learnt about their life in the town, so different from the village life that he had experienced. Yet he considered that his early days were truly blessed by being free from too complex a society.

He was tired of being a monk. He had not sought it but had accepted what it had given him. Now he wanted a wider canvass for his art. He agonised about how to get out of the life without upsetting the king, and indeed Brand who had maintained an interest in his wellbeing and probably had arranged it so that he was spared some of the rigours of the abbey's strict code of penitence. He shuddered as he remembered one instance when he had been made to lie face down before the altar after foolishly challenging his teacher on the point about, 'thou shalt worship no other god but me'. In a rare lapse of concentration he had blurted out that the ancient gods were in existence long before the new one. He had paid the penalty for that for three hours, face down, to consider his opinion. After that he had a week of toil on the land rather than in the classroom. He desperately missed the life of a scholar (he thought he had become too soft for manual labour) and so he suppressed his feelings and continued to learn. As he walked he felt the urge to throw off his habit and run naked through the fields to the river overwhelming. He looked about and as there was no one on the road at that time he struck away over the field, past a small copse of trees to a small river and did just what he wanted to do. He swam and idled in the water and felt the most tremendous freedom. After this indulgence he was hungry and tired so he ate a crust of bread in his pack and settled down to sleep on the bank, he sighed with great relief as he was back where he belonged, by the water, in the sunshine and quite alone. As he slipped into sleep his mind caught on a recurring theme, 'old men dream dreams, young men have visions'. He slept and was renewed.

While Borvo slept Elvina too had made good progress down to the sea to find her mother, or her mother's remains. She knew the way south by the sun and was within half a day's walk of her destination. At the moment that Borvo temporarily shed his current life for a few hours of freedom Elvina was sitting resting on a hilltop. She felt a sudden and glorious feeling of relief. She had no idea as to why but deep down she knew that for one of her children a great change had been wrought in their lives and for this she was glad. She knew that Sunny was safe with Brand's household. She wished and hoped that Ayken would return undamaged. She longed for

Borvo to find another life without subjugation to such a strict and unforgiving god. While she sat she thought of Esmund. She loved him and always would but they must exist apart until she resolved her dilemma. She must find out what had happened to Gramma as she felt overwhelmed with guilt and grief that she had done so little to find her. In fact she had looked until she was exhausted in both mind and body. She had helped Hild with her grandchildren and Esmund with the daily grind and she had gathered herbs and made enough salves and tinctures to fend off the normal village ailments. Everyone needed a part of her and she had reached the point of screaming out to anyone who would listen that she needed time for herself. She did not sleep in the afternoon sun; she got up and walked with renewed energy to find her mother.

Esmund wished over and over again that he had gone with Elvina. He did not worry unduly about her ability to find the sea but he thought that when she did find her mother she might need him. A whole day had passed since she left and he made preparation to follow her and be there if he was wanted. He loved her as surely as the stars were in the sky so he left the running of their animals and fields to his friends and set off. His friends were willing to help, despite their own burden of work. The village without Esmund and Elvina was a poorer place and they wanted to do all they could to get things back to as they were. Hild felt as though gradually everyone was leaving her but she had two small children to feed and the daily work to do and so she gathered up her skirts, took a deep breath and got on with living and caring for her depleted family.

Godgyfu and Aescwine toddled and played and helped where they could but they were tiny and mischievous and a handful. Godgyfu looked after Aescwine in as much as she fancied, regularly rescuing him from falling in the midden or snatching him from under the feet of the goats as they foraged for food. Luckily the village had not grown so big that people were left to fend for themselves.

It still had meaning as the wider family for the inhabitants and so Hild was blessed with help from many quarters, not only for her and the children but for Ayken and his kind strength that had in the past helped out many who were built on weaker lines. As he grew in security and trust Alric helped out more and more with Hild and the children. Anyone connected to Borvo was family to him. He would give his all to both Elfgifu and Esric who had taken him in and to the family of his benefactor. As he worked and ate and slept, he grew in all his strengths and he was as happy as he could remember.

Chapter Twenty Eight

A new chapter for Borvo

While Hild and the village toiled to keep body and soul together and to prepare for the autumnal gathering in of stores, Ayken and Eldric with the rest of their overlord's men moved south and west to stop the invaders as they tried to wrong foot the king's armies by harassing Exeter. The king was determined not to fail. The six years since he came to the throne were beset by the insistent Danes and their attempts to conquer his kingdom. He had already made agreements with them and they had singularly failed to honour them either in fact or spirit. Raiding parties kept making forays into the West Saxon kingdom despite agreed borders. As he travelled the king thought of the gruelling battles of the year before he became king, unexpectedly and with a certain reluctance, after his brother died. He was mind weary with the effort. All thoughts of what he had to do swum in his head and made his anxious gut even more painful than its usual grumbling ache. He had learned to live with it and had scorned the offer of help from the old woman of the village. Her pagan ways alarmed him more than he realised and therefore he could not bring himself to accept her long honed knowledge of healing, for surely it was bound up with ritual and blessings from lesser gods than his? He steadfastly refused to consider it as a way of relief. He must harness his thoughts and concentrate so that one day, he would be able to rest and spread his desire for education through his bishops and ministers. They would do the task for him. He would offer them an incentive, but what would induce some of them to bother with educating the poor as well as the rich? He would pray and the answer would surely come to him. God would not let him down. The pope of his childhood had said as much to him. When he returned from this latest battle he hoped that Borvo would have turned up at court and he would set in motion his ideas for him and his daughter. His younger daughter was pious to a fault. Her only thought was to follow the order of daily services whenever and wherever she could. Borvo would help her to understand the ways of God's healing. But first he had to make sure that Borvo (or Brother Mark as he should now call him) was a fit companion for her. Had he accepted the church's teachings or did he harbour thoughts of his own special god? All this must be sorted but riding to battle was not the place to concentrate on such issues. He turned to the matter in hand. Fingering the hilt of his sword gave him a feeling of permanence while the touch of some of the finest Saxon workmanship gave him comfort. They all rode on with hope and fear in equal measure.

Borvo meanwhile had donned his abandoned clothing and was sitting at a wayside inn partaking of a meagre repast. At many places brothers were well looked after, sometimes because the landlord was of the church and sometimes through superstition. This latest hostelry was poorly kept, dirty and mean. The host was rough and suspicious so he offered the poorest stale bread and water to the young brother. Borvo ate speedily and moved on as quickly as possible. He was nearing a town and he felt uneasy. He felt that it would be best to get away and walk round the town keeping to the high ground so that he was able to know if anyone came near.

Winchester was a day away and he now became anxious to get there. Urgency lent speed to his steps as he put as many miles as he could between him and the inn.

The sun was setting in the overcast evening sky. After days of hot sun the clouds had rolled in to create a gloomy end to the day. Borvo stopped by a clump of trees that sat atop the largest hill which overlooked the town. As he watched he noticed that the town was laid out in a regular pattern and there, in the centre, was a large minster. Could he have miscalculated he wondered? Was this his final destination and if so where was he supposed to go? All these questions hurried through his mind as he contemplated the new town. The walls were well protected and he saw a gate to the west, guarded against intrusion by strong armed men. He would have to go carefully. Turning up at night was not a sensible option as people were usually more suspicious as darkness fell. It was a time for vagabonds, thieves and ghosts to start their eerie perambulations. Grown men crossed themselves, swore more readily through fear and the fainthearted stayed indoors with shutters firmly down against the very devil himself. Borvo decided to stay one more night in the open air where he could sit against the bole of a solid tree, wrap his cloak around him and watch the stars as they slid by in the gaps in the clouds. The menace of the open hill seemed to him less threatening than the closed dark streets of a strange town. He sat then slept fitfully against the tree for his last night before joining the bustle of the court.

A heavy morning dew covered Borvo's cloak and damp seeped into his habit. He stretched and stood up. As he had no provisions he started to make his way towards the city. After such a long and interrupted journey he was apprehensive about his reception. Westgate was open and carts had started to enter bringing in fresh food for the people and straw for the animals. Other carts dotted along the road carried any manner of goods as this was to be market day. Borvo briefly remembered his first day in Malmesburgh, that too had been market day and the bustle, colour and noise was exciting and overwhelming to the young boy. Even now he was caught up in the atmosphere of it all and hurried forward with anticipation. The guard stopped him and asked his business. Borvo showed him the piece of parchment that held the king's seal and he was allowed through the gate and given instructions as to where the minster was. He would report first to the chapter house and then speak with the abbot as to his next duties. It was not clear why the king wanted him but he thought that he might be wanted for his knowledge of healing so he went on with confidence.

Aethelgifu was a young girl of nearly thirteen summers. She had a private tutor whom she shared with her young brothers and her sisters. She was a studious girl and pious to the point of melancholy. Her father, before he had gone off to fight once again, had told her that he had sent for a young monk to help her with her desire to heal both through prayer and through the use of natural plants. There had been little time to explain fully and so she was left with scant idea of when he would arrive, what they would do and how much of her time she was to spend with him. She was kind in a distant way with her siblings and spent her days reading, composing poetry and praying. Her older sister was lively outgoing and full of mischief. Her younger sister too was more outgoing than she was and they managed to learn all the skills required of them whilst at the same time having fun, playing and laughing round the royal palace.

Borvo sought out the abbey and it's prior. He would report there first and explain his mission. Hopefully they would let him rest and eat before he withdrew to the palace to make his presentation to the court. Although he was still yet a young man he knew very well that there could be a cold welcome for him as well as a warm one. Not everyone liked to look upon a favourite of the king and jealousy sometimes set in so it was with some trepidation that he found the abbey and knocked at the door. It was now well into the morning as he had lingered by the market stalls and enjoyed the colour and bustle of the traders. One kind matron had given him bread and ale so that at least his body was nourished. After so many days on the road he welcomed some life other than that of the hedgerows. He was also relieved to be among people for whom he held no interest and who had no business but their own to consider. The unkind innkeeper had filled his tired mind with menace and nonsense. He decided to put all that behind him and concentrate on his new venture, whatever that may be.

Bishop Ealhfrith of Winchester had started to fail in health earlier in the year. He was hanging on to life by a thread. His life had been one of scholarly devotion and he was unworldly to the point of reclusive. As a scholar he had excelled in Greek and Latin but as to his pastoral abilities, they were as yet unchallenged. He would have preferred to have lived his life in calm study but had no wish to offend the king by refusing the appointment made two years previously. Despite his other worldly appearance he was astute enough to understand that his was a political appointment. The king was very keen on education and that was his forte. He had decided to spend his time, such as he had left, on forming educational ideals for boys sent to the abbey schools across the kingdom. He disagreed with the king about the employment of the vernacular; surely the only way to learn was through the classic languages. This was his strongly held view, however, he must obey the king's wishes and so he set himself the more general task of system reform. It could well occupy him for several years. He understood that the king had commissioned an incentive to the bishops but as yet there was no trace of any such prize, to date it was just a rumour. Eventually he would obey the king but for now he was tired and his bones ached and so he would rest and consider. As he lay back on his well cushioned bed he thought of the goldsmith, summoned from the street of the metalworkers on his appointment to the see, when the fellow had been asked to fashion an appropriate ring for his station the man had agreed to the commission but said it would be done after the king's commission which was urgently being finished. When pushed on the subject he clammed up and would say no more. The city goldsmith worked closely with his brother who was smith to the king. Between them they excelled in all skills with precious metals, to the envy of all.

Although the street where the smiths of the town gathered was but a short walk from the abbey the bishop did not consider it fitting for him to go delving into such areas, and so he remained in ignorance of any jewelled gift that was in the king's mind. As he contemplated this secrecy the brother in charge of the school knocked and entered advising him of the arrival of the king's monk from Malmesburgh. It was difficult to keep up with all the monks that the king had summoned. One from Wales, one from Malmesburgh and how many from whomsoever knows where. Ealhfrith said he would see the monk after his nap and to make the newcomer aware of the abbey and its daily service, which should be much the same as the one from which the young man had come. In his feeble tired voice he added, "Feed him, show him his pallet and then give him a task in your school. He is well prepared in the classics by all accounts. He will be a welcome addition." The scholar monk left with a shake of his head wondering why such an old and lacklustre man had been given the bishopric and was even now defying death by hanging onto mortal life. It was political he supposed as the greater man for the job had been more actively politically than Ealhfrith and so may have caused trouble when there was trouble enough with the invaders. He went to make Brother Mark welcome and give him his duties.

Chapter Twenty Nine

Aftermath and a death

Exeter was saved. Not only had the foot soldiers, massed bands of mixed warriors and farmers that they were, fought with bravery and much determination that they struck terror into the people on the opposing side, who were themselves awesome in battle, but the new ships, built on the command of the king had played their part to great effect. Many had died, more were maimed both physically and mentally but the strong and the lucky survived. The king turned his attention to regrouping and returning to his court, which was at that time settled in Winchester. Brand had remained at his side and had given excellent advice. He felt the signs of age weighing heavily on him and longed to return to his lands and his family. He knew his wife would not have missed him but his one remaining daughter at home, Aedylpryd, would welcome him with open arms.

An image came into Brand's head of a mature but lithe body dancing in the moonlight, the figure swayed and turned with arms raised to the dawning sky. He felt oddly disturbed and shook his head to try to get rid of the picture, but it would not go away. He had seen Elvina on one of her dawn forays into the woods when they had first stayed with the villagers. He had not been able to sleep and wandered away from the poor dwellings into the woods to think and be alone. As he had walked he had come upon the scene where Elvina had taken up her place, naked, beside the brook. He watched as she danced and prayed then quietly slipped back to the village without disturbing her vigil by the water. He had never told anyone about what he had seen but sometimes the alluring figure would reappear in his mind and cause him physical pain when he thought of her. He respected both Esmund and Elvina and so kept his feelings closely guarded deep inside where none but god himself could ever know what was in his heart.

Brand and the king rode on and spoke of what they should do to ensure peace. The Danes were ever hungry for either land or gold or both and there had to come a time when peace would be bought. The king hated to spend his time fighting when all he wanted was peace. He had inherited a fine set of laws, his ancestors had been good law makers and he had added to them as and when they became necessary. He had abbeys to found and schools to build. He was eager to see his family with the expectation that the monks sent for would be with them by now and established at court, ready to help him implement his plans for his people. Two of his daughters would make good alliances but the third; well she was always destined to be a great abbess. Her demeanour from the start was pious and perfect for the position. He daily knelt to pray and suffered long arduous bouts of pain but undeterred he kept up his prayers with the absolute faith instilled in him from Rome. Not for him the glories of a war won, he always felt dejected at the needless loss of life.

Seofon had walked with the men down to Exeter. He and Bacchus had sat with them round their camp fires, shared their food and shelters and entertained them with his stories, riddles and songs. Those who had known him of old welcomed him as a long lost brother. Others soon came to know and revel in his qualities. The exciting world of triumphant dragon slaying or successful routing of almost any enemy kept the spirits high and the laughter that rang long into the night helped many a novice fighting man, or boy, sleep more easily the night before a battle. Bacchus, who had attached himself so firmly to Seofon that they had become one, also allowed most to stroke him and thus offered his own brand of comfort in the dark days of fighting. Some considered Seofon as though he was a strong talisman that brought nothing but good fortune, others, who prayed more regularly and thought themselves less superstitious, saw him as good company. All the men prayed to god for help and success or if that was not to be they asked for a good death. Many still hedged their bets and made offerings to the old gods, arguing that it could do no harm if it did no good.

Once when upon the road, before they had joined up with the group going west, Seofon had chosen to sleep under the stars. He had enjoyed a hearty supper at the local village and had then wandered away to find rest and comfort in the straw. Bacchus slept beside him, ever vigilant, always with one eye open. Now it happened that quite a few women found Seofon and his seemingly attractive lifestyle very fetching and made it clear to him that he need not sleep alone should the fancy take him. This of course angered many husbands so that he was adept at reading most situations and avoided bodily harm, for the most part at least. This particular night he had drunk too well and allowed himself to be seduced by the comely woman who had served him his supper. They romped in the small barn at the back of the long hut much to their mutual satisfaction. Unfortunately for Seofon the husband was well endowed with brothers and friends who were keen to fight for his honour. They came looking for the traveller in the dark hours before dawn; had it not been for Bacchus they would have succeeded in ridding the land of a gifted storyteller. As it was Bacchus roused his master at the first scent of danger and harried him so that Seofon was awake and on his way before they caught up with him. He cursed the dog that had woken him from his slumber; he cursed the ale that had been so strong and delicious; he cursed the woman who had led him astray; as he walked the sun began to lighten the eastern sky and his mood improved. He washed in a river and began to feel more kindly towards his constant companion. As a young man he had been too partial to the strong ale and so had for many years he had contented himself with moderation. This one fall from the sober path had been too nearly fatal. He had finally learnt his lesson, he hoped.

His thoughts turned to recent events and the people he had encountered over the last few years. Most striking were the people of the village where the king had been looked after for a short while. Among these he was most interested in the pagan family of healers. In his line of work he kept up his store of tales by having a good memory and also by being observant. He happened to be at the village on one occasion when Minister Brand had visited to talk about the king's reward for the kindness shown him and his men. He had noticed how Brand's eyes followed Elvina whenever he thought he was not being looked at. His thoughts turned to beautiful women he had known and loved and considered that Elvina, although not classically beautiful, had a quality that was timeless and breathtaking. He wondered if Esmund knew just what she did to other men, even at her time of life. His mind then wandered on to Borvo, the young man so taken up by his spirit and his destiny that he had acquiesced too readily to the king's plans for him. Ripe and ready for adventure he had gone off to the abbey to learn and mature. He doubted that any abbey would take his essence away, his love of the river god and his complete dedication to the healing art. If that took him into conflict with some then he worried how it might affect him.

Seofon had walked for many miles and was ready to stop, as he was near a well known welcoming village he made his way there to eat, rest and continue his reveries on the people of the village. Ayken gave him concern as he remembered the haunted desperate look in his eyes when he first returned from killing. He shivered despite the warmth of the day. His would not be a good ending, but he hoped it would be swift and honourable. He had left progeny and so had done what was required to balance the population. Ayken, he felt could do no more. When he caught up with the men he would make it his business to talk with Ayken and try to soothe his troubled mind. Philosopher and counsellor were also part of his repertoire for survival.

Throughout the journey, try as he might, Seofon could not get Ayken alone long enough to talk deeply with him. The man had become even more remote from the others and was often in a world of his own choosing. Eldric kept as close an eye on his friend as he could but there were others to consider and there was a battle for which they had to prepare. As they camped under the trees for the last night before they engaged the enemy they were visited by the king's commander. He spoke with them in terms of winning the battle; losing was not an option if they were to save the kingdom of the West Saxons from the Danes. To this end they were to be put under the leadership of one of the brightest commanders, the man stepped out of the shadows and stood, strong and forbidding, grown in muscle and demeanour but instantly recognisable as Wilheard.

Eldric, being in charge of the village men stepped forward and greeted their new leader with the respect owed to such a position. He then tried to renew the acquaintance from the years before. Wilheard had not grown in sympathy with poor villagers to whom he owed a debt that to him had been and still rankled as demeaning. He acknowledged the respectful greeting then ignored any further attempts at friendly recognition. Eldric felt the dismissal keenly but for the sake of harmony in battle he returned to his men and made no more sign of friendship. Ayken could not be silent at such a public slight to his friend and spoke out; "You forget your debts too well. You needed us once and now you need us again. We stand united behind the king and our leader, Eldric. You may command us tomorrow but Eldric is our leader for the king, we follow him." His voice was even more imposing than that of Wilheard, in hand to hand fighting Ayken could easily beat him, this recklessness in publicly confronting his old enemy was not to be borne. Wilheard decided he had to deal with him or lose any respect he might have through his position. The king's man, unaware of the history between these two stood dumbfounded when he heard Wilheard say, "You, Ayken, man of oak, you will be at the forefront of any fighting. The Danes will quiver at your sight and we will not have to fight at all." He mocked the villager and therefore the villagers. No one was in any doubt as to his motive, many knew and the rest guessed that those at the forefront, on foot, had less chance of survival than many who came after. Ayken, accepted the challenge by replying, "I willingly give my strength and my life for the king." He then turned away and made no sign of obedience to his new commander. Wilheard mounted his horse and rode away into the night with the king's man. He knew he had succumbed to his seething resentment which had not lessened over the years. Instantly he saw Ayken he was back in the woods, searching for the small band of Danes, weaponless because Ayken had disarmed him. He would have his revenge.

Eldric tried to engage Ayken in conversation but his friend stood away from the rest and stared out into the gathering night. Seofon went up to him and put his hand on his shoulder. Ayken shrugged him away and stood, rocklike for a few more moments, then walked off into the trees, where he sat down, wrapped his cloak around him and slept. Seofon returned to the fire and started a tale of ancient battles won against all odds. He quieted the younger men and boys and sent them to sleep with more hope than fear in their hearts. The next day would be a defining one and they had to be fresh and alert, and god help them, they had to obey a commander who was tainted with jealousy. It was not a good sign.

The morning broke and the men were ready before dawn. They assembled as bidden and marched ready to fight as commanded. As instructed when they all banded together Ayken was at the forefront of the group. Wilheard rode up and ignored them all. He led the way and they went forward to surprise the Danes and save Wessex. The fighting lasted all day. The villagers excelled themselves in battle. Two were lost, killed by Danish swords against their battle axes. Ayken survived, wounded but slightly. He wound cloth round his wound and carried on. It was as if he were possessed of a demon. He knew no mercy and showed none. The gentle man that had nursed his children was gone, replaced by a fighting machine. Eldric fought well and was acknowledged as a good leader if not a great one. Wilheard knew he had been mistaken the night before but his feelings had taken over. He honoured Eldric and ignored Ayken. If he had hoped that Ayken would die he did not show it.

The next day the king came to lead, sword and shield in hand he rallied the men like no one else could. His energy and conviction were awesome. The men would have followed him anywhere. He recognised Eldric and Ayken, acknowledged them, turned away and on into another day of fighting. Once more the fighting was fierce, sporadic, deadly and the king victorious. As he looked around him he accepted the Danish defeated leader, he saw bodies dead and dying, he smelt fear mixed with relief from his men, most of all he felt his own relief as he thanked god for this deliverance.

Eldric looked for an hour before he found his friend. Ayken lay on his back, his eyes open, his mouth grim and his life seeping away into the ground. No more would he walk the hills with his sheep and goats. No more would he hold his daughter and son. They would not hear from his own lips how he had fought so bravely to save their future. Nor would Hild ever feel his tender nightly embrace as they kept warm and loving vigilance over their tiny domain. Eldric held his friend who looked unseeing into the sky, "Hild" he whispered, "tell her," he swallowed and tried again, "the children . . . take care of . . . the children." He died in Eldric's embrace. Battle weary, heart sore and angry Eldric stood up and shouted at the carnage. He raged against killing at the same time as wanting to kill all invaders personally. He hated Wilheard and looked round to find him so that he could remonstrate with him. As he stumbled over the bodies that lay in his way he saw Wilheard lying with other bodies where they had been dragged to be identified and their possessions collected. He had died an honourable death; fighting like one possessed as though he had something to prove. He had not killed Ayken with his own sword but he had sent him to his death. In the end he had been ashamed of this, which fact had leant a reckless edge to his own fighting which ended with his death.

It had been a victorious day but it was not a glorious battle, not with so many dead. The king would treat with the Danes; there must be no more days like this. A bought peace was essential now.

Chapter Thirty

Awakening

Borvo had been at Winchester three days before he was summoned to the palace. He went with an outward calm that he did not feel. He knew he had done no real wrong but he had taken a long time to arrive since he'd had the summons from the king. He was ready for chastisement. He was therefore happily surprised when he entered the chamber to find three young girls and a young boy waiting for him. Two of the girls were as any girls of high rank, well dressed and confident; the third was more plainly attired and held herself with a demeanour that intrigued Borvo. He was instantly smitten with her and for the first time in his life felt passion surge through his body; stirrings that greatly discomfited him. When at Malmesburgh he had noticed pretty girls in the market place. He had also taken note of young boys who were engaging, handsome and good company, but never had he felt this sudden longing. He reddened from his toes to the top of his head; he stumbled around for words that usually came tumbling over themselves to form sentences and made sense when uttered. Now his tongue stuck to his mouth and he grunted out a greeting that befitted a woman of high rank. "Greetings, Princess." His voice was so low as to be barely audible. Princess Aethelgifu turned to her personal servant who rarely left her side, the older woman nodded and so the young girl went forward and offered her hand. Brother Mark bent over in humble fealty. The girl replied with her face also of heightened colour, "We are well met Brother, my father has told me about you and your knowledge." They exchanged smiles. The bond that began in that room was forged in that moment, despite the trials of the young bodies to stay within the bounds of their calling. The two pretty sisters giggled and clapped their hands in rapturous knowledge that their plainer devout sister had just made a conquest, a most unusual occurrence.

As the moment became ever more difficult for Brother Mark there was a disturbance at the entrance to the long room at which point a young boy of about six or seven entered. He was accompanied by a male servant who obviously had charge of this boy as he was assiduous in his duties. Careless of his status as heir to the king he wandered over to Borvo and greeted him, asked him his name and business then, realising he had no reason to continue, turned away and went to play with his sisters. Edward would one day be king; he would be fair and strong and continue the fight for peace that was to be his father's greatest wish. Time was to come soon when he would leave his mother and sisters and join the men who would teach him the skills necessary to lead a kingdom. Unlike many before him his father insisted on education for all as a solid basis for decision making and understanding the high morality on which the laws were based.

As Borvo stood uncertainly to the side of the room he was approached by another monk who he had failed to see at first. "Brother Mark?" "Borvo nodded, "I am." "Welcome, we have been expecting you; I am Brother Simeon, cousin to Augustine whom I believe you know." For the first time that morning Borvo relaxed and smiled, "Yes Brother, I know him well, he has been kind to me and shown me many ways to survive a difficult beginning." Simeon continued, "Good, that is just like him, you will continue to live at the abbey but every day you will come here to teach the children what you know of plants and their uses." Borvo looked surprised but before he could say anything Simeon continued, "It does seem unusual but one daughter in particular requires the knowledge that you have. She has designs on founding an abbey with her father and you will be her inspiration. She wishes to devote her life to god and healing, just as you have done." There was no time for more discussion as the daughters came up to the two monks, told Borvo their names after which the two giggling sisters ran away to play and giggle some more. Aethelgifu smiled at him and then wandered away as though in a world of her own. He watched her go out of sight then turned once more to Simeon, "Is this what I have been summoned for, to teach my skills to . . ." he swallowed, "her?" Simeon had noted the effect she had had on Borvo and laughed, "You will get over it, she is interested only in founding her abbey and her precious plants. You will be surprised at what she already knows." Simeon ushered Borvo out of the room and as they walked down to the abbey together he spoke of generalities, about Winchester, how the Romans had been there, how it had been burnt and rebuilt, how the king loved his kingdom, about the king's longing for education for his people, about the abbot he was more reticent from which Borvo gathered he was not in favour with at least one other monk. Borvo had found him distant and indifferent. The indifference was to Borvo, a young man with fervour and passion, the worst kind of trait.

He had known, from the first acceptance of his life under the control of the king and his regime that he would take all that the life had to offer, but one day he would break free. As he walked to the abbey with Simeon, he felt an urgency about his life that had been subsumed below the desire to learn. Now it surfaced, he asked himself whether it was due to his sudden rush of feeling for the pious daughter. He wanted to run away, but to where? Where would he be fulfilled? Where was home? Was it with his parents, no of course not he had outgrown the life of the small village, he desired a larger canvass for his thoughts, his healing, his continuing learning, the abbeys were the one place where he could accept the books and the giving life that he yearned for. He was not sure at all that he wanted to spend time closeted with the object of his desire. He was sure he could push his feelings away but it would be a struggle. He tried to think of a tract that could help him. He was not in sympathy with many of the vengeful ideas that seemed to proliferate. Why he often asked himself was a god so powerful deemed to be so unforgiving, was it the thought that was the misdeed or the act, many of his fellow scholars disagreed about this although it was not encouraged to consider and debate, most asked only full and true obedience. Well that was not his way or the way of his parents who offered nothing else save the right to think, and act according to one's own conscience. His Gramma's words came to him, "Harm none and do nothing save what you believe will relieve pain and suffering." No harm should result from any act of prayer or offering to the gods, that practice hopefully had died out centuries before. No, this god he was tied to surely was not the wrathful being presented by some and feared by the many. That was not what was evident from the testament of those who walked with him. He wished Brother Augustine would happen along so that he could talk with him. He always set the young man's anxieties at rest with regards to the accepted wisdom of the day.

A month later as he sat in contemplation before the altar he wished for news of his family and especially that of Ayken. He knew his troubles and he longed to see him. He was blessed with such a brother. As he sat and let his thoughts wander, many observing him would be inclined to think how devoted was this young man to sit so long in contemplation. Not so. He was giving serious consideration to his life and to walking away even while incurring the king's displeasure and risking who knows what in terms of retribution? This time with Aethelgifu had been a difficult one. Being so close to this disturbing girl had taken all his powers of concentration not to give himself away as he had done on their first meeting. It could not go on. Once she had carelessly touched his arm to ask him to repeat a complicated mixture of herbs at which gesture he jumped as though scalded. His body was generally under control and he had formed a deep affection for her and her determination to succeed. In his mind she was the purest person he had ever met. His shame and guilt about his reaction to her filled his days and nights until he felt he could no longer be with her. It was a torment and he had no confidante to reassure him.

The time passed, he missed his meagre meal, dusk turned to night and still he sat quite still. As he sat he became part of the stones, the history, the damp wet feeling that surrounded this abbey and its church. Rivers washed under the city, in and around the buildings leaving its ever present smell wherever he went. Water was powerful; he knew that from his endless times spent at the brook. Was it possible that the god Borvo had sent him here to fulfil his destiny? Oh how he longed to go back; back to the woods and a more innocent time. He didn't want to grow old and not know once more the pleasure of the grass beneath his bare feet, the cooling clear water washing over him as though giving him new life, the hope that one day he would feel the breath of the river spirit come to him and guide him. Why must he be confined just to tell a girl all he knew? He would burst if he thought any more. He came to, disappointed that he had not had a vision, disappointed that he was still in the same damp place and also he was very hungry. He stood up and made his way to the kitchens where he was able to charm some supper out of the old monk in charge. He would sleep, he would rise and attend the midnight service then he would make his mind up as to how to proceed. On this good plan of action he slept and dreamed of woods and rivers disturbed only by a passing fancy that he was with Ayken in a place that was better than either had known before.

The first morning service was over and the monks went about their daily business, some with measured tread as though putting one sandaled foot in front of another took all the thoughts that were in their heads. Borvo walked with deliberate steps to mask any outward sign of nervous excitement. He had woken up with determined resolve to grasp his life back before he was too old to make the break. He felt an overwhelming desire to run, run as fast as he could back to the village and his family. He knew it would not be the same but he had to find out what was happening to them all. His need to feel the waters of his brook tumble over his feet was unbearable. He picked up a hoe from the store and went out of the West gate with no trouble at all. Why would the soldiers guarding the gate think twice about a monk leaving to tend the abbey's lands? It was intruders they were there to guard against not runaway monks. Borvo slipped past the thick stone walls and walked across the fields, carefully leaving his hoe leaning against the hedge that ran some way across the high downland that surrounded the city. He went west away from the rising sun so that his shadow was always in front of him. It was best to travel as a monk to begin with until he was clear of the busier roads. Only when he was near to the wilder countryside would he discard his habit, by then his already untended tonsure would be growing out.

Where were his parents? Why had Gramma disappeared? Why had he been so selfish as to accept their fate while he was indulging in his passion for reading? He must do something to right these omissions. Sunny he believed to be happy with Minister Brand's family but did he really know how she fared? Well now was the time to redress all imbalances. He would be the son and brother they deserved.

Chapter Thirty One

Sunny returns

Sunny and Aedylpryd were sitting in the shade sewing. It was late afternoon so the shadows seemed endless stretching long dark fingers across the meadows beyond the house. Sunny shivered despite the warmth of the afternoon and looked up. She saw Minister Brand walking towards them with a grave look on his face. Immediately Sunny felt alarm and dropped her sewing in a rush to stand up and move towards him. Aedylpryd too looked alarmed but rose more sedately and came up to her father with a look of expectation on her worried face. Brand held his daughter's hands and said, "All is well with our family; we have come through with no loss. The battle was won although many died; they went bravely and for our freedom, be peaceful daughter." Aedylpryd smiled weakly and turned to Sunny realising that it must be for her sake that her father held such a look of doom.

Sunny walked in a daze, staggering towards the long hall to which end she was supported by Aedylpryd and Brand. She lay on a long low settle with a woollen cover over her to try to keep her warm as she was shivering violently with shock. Ayken dead, how could that be, he was so strong and seemingly indestructible.

Poor Hild and the children they would need all the family round her to help with the daily grind of surviving. She tried to sit up but was prevented from doing so by gentle pressure on her shoulder from Aedylpryd. Sunny looked past her and asked haltingly, "Do mother and father know? Are they all right? Have they asked for me?" Brand smiled a weak attempt at a reassuring smile, none of which he felt, "They are away from home and can not be found." Alarmed Sunny went deathly pale again, "I must go home, I must go home, I must help them." Brand replied quickly and without hesitation, "Yes you must and will. We will wait until tomorrow then I will send an escort with you." Sunny lay back and drew deep ragged breaths trying to still her shaking body. This grief was like a physical shock, an actual pain suffused her whole body. She would rest then be fit to travel tomorrow. As Brand turned to leave her she asked one more question, "Did . . . did he die well?" The tears coursed down her face, "Ayken my brother, did he die well?" Brand replied in a studied voice as though he was once more back at the battle remembering the body as it lay on the bloody earth, "Yes, he died fighting bravely for the king and the kingdom. He will be remembered." Considering the family's background he added, "The earth has him back now. He will find peace with the glory tonight." With that he left her. Aedylpryd would not leave her side and tended her until she slept when she was carried to her quarters.

Pleased to have her own sons home and well, Rimilda decided to show Aedylpryd how to make an infused tea of borage to give to Sunny. It was well known as a drink that gave courage whilst also lifting the spirits which was exactly what she judged Sunny needed right now. She surprised herself by how much she had come to care for the seamstress and was equally pleased to see Aedylpryd beginning to blossom under her influence. Her own life had become empty, only now did she realise just how empty. She found that she slightly envied this young woman who lived with such passion and family love. She and Brand had long since become respectfully distant and it was many months since he had shared her bed. There was little passion left just the need for physical relief. It suited her but she wondered, for the first time, if it suited him. She knew he did not take any other woman, that was not his way. She decided that once the peace had been well established she would talk to her husband and try to reconcile their lives together. She had left it far too long. Meanwhile she would make Sunny's departure as smooth as she could. Suddenly she felt needed; it was a good feeling again. Not since the children were small and they were all struggling to survive had she felt this way.

Once she had drunk the borage tea Sunny calmed and slept deeply. When she awoke the sun was rising and she lay there for a few moments trying to remember what she had to do. Her grief came upon her swiftly and remorselessly. She rose, bathed and dressed in haste. Aedylpryd heard her moving about, came to her with grave concern on her face. "I have prepared you a drink to sustain you and then we must go. All is ready. Father has ordered your departure and you are well escorted." She let this get through Sunny's grief then added, "I am coming with you and will stay to help." Rather tentatively she then went on, "I think you will need me." Sunny held her hand, embraced her and wept on her shoulder. "Aedylpryd, you are well grown. You are a true friend."

As the horses carrying Sunny and her escort rode through the countryside, the late summer sun warmed them, despite which Sunny occasionally shivered and looked ahead with bleak eyes and a heavy heart. How would Hild be? How would she cope without Ayken? Where were her mother and father? Why had they gone off? These questions and many more swarmed through her mind until she felt dizzy. Aedylpryd who was watching Sunny closely turned to her brother, Beadmund who had insisted on leading the escort for this young woman and said that they should stop and rest. She feared that Sunny would fall from her horse. After dismounting they found a small clearing off the narrow track they had been following. The trees formed a cool green canopy against the midday sun and they sat, drank sustaining wine and ate some bread, meat and cheese that had been packed for them.

All day they had been passed by raggedy groups of fighting men returning to their villages and towns. Some were weary whilst others seemed elated with their role in the victory. Occasionally there would be news from different quarters and the escort greedily listened to any snippets that might be useful. One garrulous young man told of the last fight that had taken Ayken. Sunny looked round in alarm and the youth was quickly silenced and sent on his way. Sunny was anxious to know about Ayken but she was not ready to hear the raw details of his death.

Eager to be on her way Sunny remounted and they rode on for the rest of the afternoon until they reached the village at sunset. Even after a day's ride she needed to see Hild and the children as soon as she could so, after going to her mother's home to set down her bundle she walked to Hild's cottage on the edge of the village. As they approached the village the group had been greeted by Leofric and Cynwise with words of sorrow. They told her that Hild had refused to come back to her parent's hut so they had gone to be with her in her own place. Still Aedylpryd would not leave Sunny's side so the two of them went to find Hild. They found her sitting outside the western facing door, both children on her knee staring into the distance. Hild's mother sat on the opposite side of the door spinning. Hild's father stood alone at some distance watching the women.

When Sunny and Aedylpryd came towards them the children hesitated then recognised Sunny and ran to her, arms outstretched and hugged her so hard that she stumbled. Aedylpryd sank down on her haunches and spoke with them and introduced herself as a friend. Warily they smiled at her and then decided she was all right and hugged her too. Hild rose and embraced Sunny as though she would never let her go.

That night was long and painful. Hild had yet to cry so deep was her hurt. Sunny stayed as long as she was wanted then she and Aedylpryd went back to her family hut. Leofric had arranged quarters for the escort giving Beadmund the best room he could find. This was not only in his own honour but for his father, Brand, too for whom he had great respect.

Sunny rose the next morning with an awful ache in her leg that she had not felt for a long time. One of Brand's regular visitors was a monk with some knowledge of ailments and had studied the Arabic texts that told of their discoveries in human anatomy. He was a learned and genial man who advised Sunny to exercise in certain ways to strengthen her muscles and so reposition her walking habit. At first she had been sceptical but increasingly in her own time she had done as he suggested. It took months but she had felt the benefit and with good food she had become almost unaware of her former problem. The anxious days riding the day before had set her back and now she limped so badly every step hurt. Aedylpryd, who had spent a wakeful night in strange surroundings was determined not to be irritable and so started the fire that would warm their early meal. It took her unaccustomed hands some time but she managed it and made a sustaining breakfast for them both. Beadmund her brother joined them and teased her about her prowess but was secretly pleased to see his unprepossessing sister start to shine. He glanced unobtrusively at Sunny and was alarmed to see her limp so badly. He had an affection for her that he had known before but the feelings he had suddenly increased in intensity so that he was taken off balance for a while. He covered his feelings up with increased teasing of his sister. Sunny's bleak expression stopped this banter and they spoke of how they would organise the day and how they might help Hild. Ayken's body would be brought back with the others from the village, if such remains were complete enough for recognition and so they could prepare for the saddest homecoming. Action would help get them over the first few days of shock that sets in with profound grief.

The burden of the family was on Sunny's shoulders. Everyone was missing but she had one good thought and that was Borvo, he was at least safe in Winchester with his fellow monks. This gave her comfort as she set about the tasks of those difficult days.

Chapter Thirty Two

Borvo on the run

Borvo stumbled as he ran from whatever danger he considered himself to be in. The nights were turning chilly and damp and his poor outer garments, stolen from a dishevelled outhouse, clung hideously to his spare frame. He had abandoned his habit and his hair was growing. He thought his mind would burst with the conflicting ideas in his head. The hungrier he got the more he thought and so he got to the point where he could no longer sustain any forward movement. He sat down by a river within shade of a huge willow tree and thought. He drank the water having first given an offering of herbs and then settled to consider his position.

He had been well brought up to believe in his river god. Other gods suited other people and if no harm was wrought by this then all was well. People seemed tolerant, in the main, although he was aware of the old persecution. Suddenly, on the brink of manhood he was caught up in such a maelstrom of emotions and ideas that he was eager, or had been eager, to embrace another philosophy. He admired his king and was in awe of him. It had not been just his status but Borvo had been overwhelmed by his certainty that his faith was the true path. He was whisked away, not unwillingly, to enter a new life with a new name. The very first time he had held a stylus he was hooked. He loved the formation of letters; the brilliant illuminations by his fellow monks overwhelmed him with their beauty. When he began to read the Latin words he was struck by their awesome majesty and mystery. Just to see a page of writing filled him with a sense of wonder. Here was a world into which he was very privileged to go. As he understood the meanings of the words, the scriptures and the stories he was mesmerised by the ancient texts and for a while forgot his own thoughts and upbringing. However, as time went on he felt instinctively that this new world was very narrow. Where was there room for tolerance for others? Never had he believed that there was just one answer to any question. Like his herbs, there were many herbs that healed the same ailment, some had many properties and others just the one but it depended on the person or the time of year or the availability of the plant. There were so many variations in people too that he felt that surely one way was not sufficient to satisfy all things to all people. It began to make less sense as time went on. He respected many of the learned monks, and even his austere abbot had been fair at the very least. He had never abandoned River God Borvo, his own god, but for a while he had been less important to him. Now he was filled with rage at his own fickle heart and prayed and prayed to the god Borvo to send him a sign and a way to forge ahead. He had left the monk's habit and tonsure behind, possibly too he had left the anger of the king but he was so confused that he thought his head would burst. Thin, ragged and exhausted he lay down by the water and slept.

There were no dreams for Borvo that day, only a feeling on waking that he was not alone. The late summer light was fading and the evening mist crept along the water and over the bank. Out of this mist came a figure that seemed to the young man to materialise as if from nowhere, a huge fourlegged creature sniffed the air and cautiously came forward to greet this new companion. Slowly Borvo sat up but did not attempt to move away as he was frozen to the spot with fear. Whatever it was would perhaps go away if he stayed as still as he could. This moment seemed to last for ever but in fact it was only a matter of moments before another figure came up to him and called the large dog away.

"Well. Greetings, young man. My companion has found you asleep. May we sit together for a while? I have walked far." Seofon did not recognise Borvo at first, his appearance being so altered. Borvo however did recognise him and answered with a very relieved smile, "Seofon, you don't know me?" The storyteller looked and looked at the gaunt face and ragged hair, "Borvo? Is it really you? What are you doing here?" Many more questions formed in Seofon's mind but he left them unsaid, there was a story here that would take some time in the telling. Taking in the state of the young man he decided to make a fire and share his food with him, after which he hoped to ascertain his true condition. Seofon was alarmed by his thin frame and haunted eyes. There was serious work here for him and he would take care of the man. He knew his brother was dead but was uncertain as to whether Borvo knew of any such news. There would be time; he would be patient as he believed Borvo was not in any state to bear such distress in his current temper.

They cooked some fish that Seofon had caught and together with some rough barley bread they made a good meal; better than Borvo had eaten for some time. His spirits lifted and he prepared to listen. Seofon always spoke as though he had the right to hold the floor. People loved to hear his stories as they made their world seem rooted in something strong and permanent which gave them solid feelings of security. This night however he wanted to hear from Borvo so he sat waiting for the outpouring that he felt was very near the surface of his young companion.

As the night drew to intense darkness lit by the moon and stars when the evening mist cleared the river the silence between the two companions deepened and was comforting to both. Seofon stroked the rough coat of Bacchus who had settled between the men drawing and giving warmth, content with fish and bread that lay comforting in his belly, the scraps that had been left being eagerly devoured. Seemingly from nowhere Borvo's voice broke the stillness of the night.

"Seofon, I feel so lonely and confused I don't know which way to think. I need my family to tell me what to do, but then I am a man and need to make my own decisions." More silence followed this beginning. Again he attempted to explain, "I have run away. She made me feel things I didn't want to feel. They expected me to teach her, spend each day with her and share all my knowledge. I couldn't do it. That way of man and woman is not for me. I need nothing but the river and my learning." He stumbled on, "but then I can't have both it seems. If the king's men catch up with me, or the abbot I will be punished and I expect I shall deserve it." Seofon didn't answer although the questions were mounting up.

Borvo continued his disjointed monologue, "They said young men will have visions and old men will dream dreams. Well I have visions but it is not what they expected, they are of a former time and I find them comforting. If their god created everything as they say then he created my visions and my dreams and my river god so why is it so bad to speak of them. Why did I have to be punished? The only time I spoke of my childhood god I had to lay on the cold stone floor and beg for forgiveness. It took them hours to remember me. I was seething with anger when they released me and I have kept my counsel since then. Some of it made sense. A good and caring god. Benign and just but that doesn't fit with the cruelty of their way. Why is my river god so bad? I have never been tempted to hurt anyone just to heal them. Years ago someone called Augustine came over and then they all argued among themselves about hair and Easter and such things. It is all so confusing. Seofon, do you understand? Do you know why they have to be so cruel?" Borvo ran out of breath. He slumped back against the bank. "I just don't understand." Tempted as he was to reply, Seofon just said, "Sleep now young friend. We will speak more when the sun rises. Bacchus will keep us warm tonight." He put a woollen blanket over them both and they slept. Bacchus crept on top of their legs and wriggled down between them. He too was content.

The morning came with cloudy sky that obscured the sun. Shivering in the unaccustomed cool Borvo and Seofon woke up, stretched and yawned. They greeted each other with no self consciousness at all. Borvo stood, stripped off his clothes and waded into the cold river. He swam up the river for about ten mature tree lengths then swam back again and got out. Seofon was slower to swim but he also went into the water and refreshed his body. Tempted as he was to stare at the extreme thinness of his companion he avoided any overt eye contact, but still he was acutely aware of how wasted Borvo's body had become. This youth was in dire need of care and a few good meals. Knowing that his family was torn asunder in different ways he determined not to forsake him. He decided there and then to journey with him, hoping that Borvo meant to go back to the village to heal his troubled soul. They were only two days walking away from the village but Seofon wondered how long it would take Borvo who seemed to have so little to sustain him.

After finishing the small amount of food left from the night before they rolled up their meagre belongings and began to walk together. Borvo just accepted that Seofon was going his way and they fell into step along the hidden tracks of the woods and byways. It was not long before Borvo started to talk once more of his life at the abbey in Malmesburgh. "It was harsh you know Seofon, but I was so happy to be learning that I revelled in the teaching. There was also a good brother in the kitchen who needed my herbs and so we came to an understanding. I was not so badly off for food really. It did not seem to be a hardship at all." They walked on and the early cloud was replaced by dappled sunlight as the trees gave up their solid cover which allowed the sky and hesitant sunlight through to the travellers. Walking had warmed them and so they felt their spirits lifting with each step. "I was sent for by the king's men to go to Winchester, where he had his palace at that time. It had only just been rebuilt after the firing by the invaders." He shivered with the memory, the church there was still alive with the smell of burning, some corners still had the acrid soot finger deep, but still there were some good people there too." He smiled as he thought of the bishop, "The new bishop was lazy and did not like what the king had ordered. I overheard the prior talking one day. They took little notice of me and I went about my tasks with no interference." He stopped and looked round at Seofon who had fallen behind a pace or two, "When I had the call from the palace I had to go and it was then that I knew what the king had wanted me to do." His eyes looked into the distance, "I couldn't do it. Her presence was too disturbing. She was a princess and so devout but she made my body react such as I . . . oh it was painful and wonderful at the same time. I had to run away, I couldn't trust or believe in anything at all." He was almost shouting now, "I am meant to heal. I am not meant for other things, just to heal, it is why I was born."

Resolution suddenly suffused his face; he stood erect and lifted his shoulders. "Seofon, you have done me much good. I am in your debt."

"No debt, young Borvo. All is freely given. Go and make your life worthy of your commitment here." Now that Borvo's crisis had passed, even if it was a temporary release from his mental torment, the storyteller decided it was time the young man knew the truth about his brother. "Sit for a while and rest, we have been walking all morning." He sat and took a leathern bottle from his pack and drank some ale, he offered it to Borvo who smiled and also took a draught. They rested in the dappled sunlight while the leaves made gentle movement overhead, an idyllic scene for the breaking of horrendous news. Seofon stroked Bacchus' rough coat and pulled his ears as he fought to find the right words that would probably shatter Borvo's new found determination. "Borvo, you are struggling with your gods at the moment. Who knows whether the ancient ones are the true way or the new one? I have my feet in the past but my head in the present and my heart in the future. I believe that all things men say are true, for them, and should leave others to resolve things for themselves. With Brother Augustine I have spent many an hour talking this way and that until we are both confused and both convinced we are right." Borvo looked at him trying to make sense of this sudden discourse on gods and their meaning. He nodded his head urging him on, "Whichever god you seek and believe in, hold fast to him for now, I have bad news for you. I found you by the river as I made my way back from the west where there was a battle. Many died on both sides although the king was victorious." Borvo interrupted him with profound insight, "Ayken, he is dead isn't he?"

"Yes, he is." The silence between them deepened as the confirmation of what Borvo felt sank in. Seofon continued, "He died well and is honoured. He is being brought back to be buried as Hild would want him to be. It is not your people's way I know but Hild will have the right of his body."

There were no more words between the two men. They got up and resumed their journey. Bacchus trotted at their side and did not leave the path as he had before. He picked up the sadness in his master and friend so stayed close by in case the new emotions he sensed but did not understand meant that he would be left behind. Borvo quickened his pace and so by nightfall they had covered a good part of the way to the village. Once more they found themselves sleeping under the blanket, this time supper was burdock root, mushroom and nettle soup. To help them sleep they finished off Seofon's ale. The food was plenty to sustain life but not enough to put the flesh back on bones. One more day Seofon thought then Borvo would be among his family and they would feed him up. The village prospered now and had grown; soon it might even live up to its charter status. There was one aspect that he suddenly realised might upset this sensitive young man, the villagers had chopped down the small group of oak trees that were closest to the village. They had needed to build more houses for the growing population and the eastern end of the settlement was the most logical place in which to spread. Leofric was aware of the controversy but had no choice once the village council had met and agreed.

Seofon usually chose this village for his harvest supper and storytelling as they were welcoming and generous to a fault with their hospitality. It had been fifteen summers since he first stumbled across the isolated settlement with its hickledy houses and raw insular people. But they had been warm and comforting at a time when he needed to be sustained both in body and spirit. Because of this history between them he felt obligated to get back there each summer as they gathered in all they could for the inevitable long harsh winter ahead. This summer had been particularly warm and dry and he idly hoped as he walked along that they had enough to store as well as share. There was nothing more certain he thought than the necessity to feed not only their community but to give over a portion to their over lord as well. The old lord had been less than diligent in collecting his tythes and often gave some back if the crops were less than plentiful. The new over lord, his nephew, was more severe and much more aware of his right to the bounty, whatever it cost the villagers in going hungry or cold.

Seofon trusted that Leofric was still alive for under his reluctant leadership things were fairly apportioned and the community either loosened or tightened their belts together. Without some of their youngest and strongest men the harvest would be hard fought for those that had been left behind but still he had high hopes for this particular village. He travelled hopefully.

Borvo meanwhile blundered on, hardly knowing which way he went but just instinctively going home, back to his village, his trees and his brook. He would be needed by his family now; of this one thing he was certain. He would trust to any god that would listen to help him survive so that he might help rear his nephew and niece with Hild and the rest of the family. He wondered why his mother and father had not sent for him but that thought went to the back of his restless mind. He would deal with that when he was established in his safe sanctuary among his own kind. He prayed that he would find little changed.

Chapter Thirty Three

Bitter sweet reunion

Elvina knew she was on a wild goose chase. She was following a dream, albeit a vivid dream such as might be prophetic, but she had left her mother too long alone. Why she had suddenly gone off could only be because her medication for her pains was too strong and she had become muddled. Sometimes, when Gramma told her daughter of her waking nightmares she shivered as she re lived them. Clearly they had been disturbing but what with Hild and the babies she had taken her mind away from her own mother and left her to sink into unimaginable pain. Esmund too had been busy with the work on the land, the livestock, going to market, worrying about his sons and daughter, and revelling in his growing family. He also had been too busy to attend closely to Gramma's pain ridden life. She had disappeared one summer evening and despite months of searching had not been found. Elvina knew that Gramma's father had suffered so badly with his bones that he had wandered off one day when it all became too much to bear, fallen down a hillside and broken his neck. He had been set adrift with his treasured possessions and sent with honour to the next world. Elvina knew that if she found any trace of her mother she would give her the same, belated, honouring farewell.

Once Esmund had caught up with his wife they had travelled together and after the second day had sat above a sweeping vista of the sea. A small coastal settlement nestled by the river outlet as it met the ocean; it lay below them as if in miniature. They smelt the salty air as the afternoon on shore air brought with it a taste of another world too fabulous and too mighty ever to be conquered. They saw small fishing boats far out to sea bobbing with the tide as the men endeavoured to make their living from this fish rich but dangerous element. More importantly for Elvina she saw that there was at the mouth of the river opening to the sea a pattern of rocks such as had come to her in her dream.

Knowing that the hospitality of the fisher folk was legendary they carefully made their weary way down the cliffs to the tiny settlement. As they neared the poor dwellings they became aware that they were being followed. They slowly turned to find two heavy set men behind them, threatening cudgels in hand but for the moment, passive. This matched the sour look upon the wind ravaged faces of the men. One of them softened his attitude when he took note of Elvina's fine mature form. Esmund spread his arms to show that there was no threat from them and indicated a sheathed knife, firmly wrapped in leather strapping attached to his belt. Elvina smiled and also indicated that she was armed in a similar way, as befits one who would use a knife to survive but not to cause trouble. The two men let their arms fall beside them and asked roughly who they were and what they wanted.

Esmund spoke, "We are well met today, we seek my wife's mother who wandered from us in agony of pain with confused wits. My wife had a dream that we had to make for the shore. We ask only shelter from you, a bowl of soup and news of our kinswoman."

He bowed his head very slightly to indicate respect but not too low as to indicate weakness. The men responded with wary kindness.

"Come with us and we will meet with our elders. We will decide what to do." As this response was ambiguous Esmund and Elvina knew that they had not yet won them over completely and so were still on their guard. Cautiously they followed the leading man while the second brought up the rear and so closely penned on the narrow cliff walk they entered the fishing village.

The village elders sat round the central fire in the meeting house, which compared to that in Esmund's village was a poor cramped place that smelt of the sea and fish. A broadly built older woman brought them thin ale. While they drank they answered the many questions put to them by the fishing elders. After an hour they seemed satisfied with the travellers and gave them fish soup and rough bread. The hostile reception had unnerved the two but as the atmosphere began to warm they found the right words to ask why they had been treated with such suspicion. The main man answered; his grizzled, plaited hair framed a face that had seen many harsh winters, "We are well hidden here but we keep a lookout on the headland. We have seen too many foreign boats passing lately and have to be cautious. News came along the coast that the Danes were invading again. Can you add anything?"

Esmund again answered, "When we left our village for this quest our eldest son was away fighting with the king. We have no more news than you have except that you are wise to be so protective. We seek only our kin then we will return to our village."

The group of men and women looked at them for some time then asked them to leave the building, "Go and watch the fish being landed. We will send you away well serviced. Fish are plentiful now and we are happy to share. We may have news for you. Go and wait."

Elvina went to speak but Esmund took her arm and led her out of the dark into the bright glare of the light over the water. They made their way down to the small jetty that had boats bobbing on the tide, nets strewn beside them and barrels of fish being salted. "Why would you not let me speak?" Her fear gave her voice a harsh edge that Esmund recognised. "I think they have news and are wondering if we are who we say. Give them time. They are cautious and for that we should be grateful."

They spoke no more but relaxed as they sat on a wooden barrel and watched the busy men and women as they performed their tasks. A small gang of children came over to them and asked them who they were and where they were from. Esmund smiling told them of the woods and the hills, the trees and the goats. He explained how they kept sheep and how the wool was spun and made into cloth. He had such a way of speaking that he captured their attention and so passed another hour before they were summoned back to the hall and away from the sunlight and the children.

The grizzled elder rose and asked them to accompany him, "Before the harsh winter had finally left us we found an old lady wandering on the cliffs. She had no memory of who she was or where she had come from. She was thin, cold and in much pain. My wife has been caring for her." He led them to a cottage on the far side of the village, under the cliff and well protected from the prevailing westerly winds. "She had a bag of herbs with her, tied to her belt, but her fingers were too crooked to get them out. We brewed them and gave them to her which seemed to ease her."

Elvina whispered, "Gramma!" As they entered the small room they saw a tiny figure, wrapped in blankets sitting in a corner. She was asleep by the fire. The elderwife had lit the fire, despite the warmth of the day, to warm the old woman's bones. Elvina rushed up to her mother, stroked her hand and woke her with soft caressing words, "Gramma, Gramma, we have come for you.

Gramma." Gramma woke up and smiled. It was a vacant smile but some distant memory stirred and she recognised this kind face that looked upon her with delight.

It was decided that the next morning two strong men from the fishing village would help Esmund and Elvina carry Gramma up the cliff and back to their village. It would take several days and they hoped the old lady was fit enough but it was only right that she should be restored to her family for her last days. Elvina's bitter sweet delight in finding her mother touched the elderwife who asked Elvina to send word back of their safe arrival. She also asked about the herb that had helped ease the painful joints. Elvina promised to send that back too as the older woman was prone to pain when the wind blew and the rain relentlessly hammered at their shutters.

Only one donkey could be spared to help them on their journey so that was packed with salt fish for the village, and provisions for the time on the road, while the men helped Esmund carry his much lighter kinswoman up the steep cliff path and off over the heathland that was strewn with gorse and heather. Gramma was wrapped in several blankets which were roughly made but warm enough. Elvina determined to send the elderwife a fine blanket from their own wool as well as the comphrey for her aches and pains. The villagers had a tough existence but nothing compared to the poor fishing life she had witnessed. Her joy at finding her mother was marred only by the lack of true recognition in her mother's face. Elvina had known she was failing but had not been prepared for this lack of understanding. Perhaps she would re awaken to her family when she was back in familiar surroundings. Elvina cheered at the thought and concentrated on getting her mother home safely.

Chapter Thirty Four

Restoration

Sunny woke up from a feverish nightmare. All the family were dead, she was left alone on a windswept hillside. She tried to walk but her legs were stuck in mire and she was sinking ever quicker into the earth. As she came to and her day senses returned to her she sat up and shivered in the cool morning air. The summer was passing and autumn would soon be upon them. Harvest had been slowly gathered in as the reduced population tried to get on with their lives without the dead or absent members of their village. Sunny unhappily remembered the loss of Ayken, the disappearance of her mother and father and the unknown whereabouts of Borvo. Surely he, of all of them, was safe and well and content. She had asked Minister Brand to get word to Borvo about Ayken but had heard nothing from him since she left to come home.

Leofric wandered through the days carrying out his duties as elder as well as maintaining his own crops and livestock at the same time as making sure Esmund's crops were well harvested. He was getting older and his frame was no longer that of a virile man but one of age when the strength slowly dies. Everyone helped everyone else, even the incomers had settled into the community and now were firmly part of the village family. It had been a struggle to accept them as the influx had been rather too much for a time but slowly they had integrated and the new larger village was more self sufficient as a result.

Leofric felt the loss of Ayken keenly as he was such an asset to the village in so many ways. He mourned the loss of his friend, Esmund, off on a hopeless chase after Elvina and her mother. His was a pragmatic approach and he felt that the old lady had lost her wits and thus fallen to her death somewhere in her confusion. There was nothing to be done. He would console Elvina and Esmund when they returned and help them by talking to them in the tiny church that had become much more of a meeting place since the village had grown. He had long believed what Brother Augustine had told him but he knew it was a struggle for the others sometimes. When the village council had decided to cut down the old, and previously sacred, oak trees by the edge of the forest he had spoken against such action. Even he knew how important the trees had been and still were to so many. Besides which he knew that they afforded the village much needed protection. However he had been overruled and so the mighty gnarled trees had been felled. At least the king had been successful and perhaps now they would live in peace for a while. It seemed all his adult life they had lived with danger from one quarter or another. He gave himself a mental shake and concentrated on the present. Harvest would be celebrated in a few days and he hoped that Seofon would join them as usual. It would be good to hear his stories again and talk with him about this and that and drink some good ale. One more harvest would be well done and the long winter months maybe would seem a little shorter for the hope that good news may bring.

Leofric walked towards the farthest part of the southern most field. He needed to check the boundary and spend some time looking towards the south where he knew his friend had gone. He did this most days as he pretended to check one thing or another. No one was fooled but they let him be. This day he scanned the horizon and saw what he wanted to see. He thought he saw two people crest the far hill following an old drovers' route, but then his eyesight wasn't what it was and so he shook his head, rubbed his eyes and looked again. There were definitely two people, but then there were two more and a donkey. He hurried back to the village to collect more men in case there was danger in the group. They set off and met the ragged bunch as they crested one last hill before the village. Two strangers carried a litter with a body on it. Elvina and Esmund walked beside the donkey, Esmund had the rope in his hand that went round the animal's head. They all looked weary. Elvina and Esmund had lost a lot of weight but the two strangers were robust and hearty. The villagers took the burden from the fishermen, introductions were made and they reached the village where they were properly welcomed and Gramma quickly despatched to her house where she could rest and hopefully recover. Sunny had risen from her nightmarish sleep and immediately gone to help Hild. She had got into the habit of spending all day helping with the children and the daily chores while leaving Aedylpryd to keep the family hut in good order. So it was that Elvina arrived at her own home to find a stranger there stirring Elvina's pot with Elvina's food and wearing Sunny's shawl tied round her shoulders and back down to her waist. Tired and anxious and so too swift to judge Elvina curtly asked the young woman what she thought she was doing in her home. She told her to leave as she had to make way for her sick mother. Aedylpryd tried to explain but Elvina cut her short and dismissed her with a fierce look. Aedylpryd immediately left the cooking as she was rather in awe of this older woman and ran to Hild's cottage to summon Sunny back to help her explain.

Esmund bumped into the fleeing young woman as he entered his home. The question as to her identity died on his lips as he saw the determined look on his wife's face. It was closed to all reasoned thought and he knew of old that to try to talk anything through at the onset of this stony mood would bring nothing but anger. All would be clear in time. He set about bringing in their scant travelling belongings and putting them away.

The village entertained the fishermen with food and songs. They spoke of their different lives and they formed a bond of friendship between their two communities. After a good night's sleep the two indefatigable men took off for home with their donkey laden with gifts, among which were a bundle of herbs for the goodwife and her pains.

Chapter Thirty Five

Difficult homecoming

Most of the work for harvest was done. Once more the village felt the passing of the year and its inhabitants were apt to idle a little more, spend time gossiping and meeting with other villagers. Daily chores were ever present but the great burden of work was over. Soon there would be feasting, stories, celebrations for the drawing in of the summer and welcoming the autumn. Their usual visitors would be welcomed with great generosity as when the winter weather blew there would be few who travelled the roads and woods until the thaw came. Seofon had not missed many years and his legend caused great excitement among the young and impressionable. Brother Augustine did not get to the village as much as he would like. There was a new Brother who saw to their spiritual needs and so he felt less able to come and go as before. This year was somehow different from the few previous years. Augustine felt a strong urgency about being with the villagers and so he heaved his heavy frame onto an abbey pony and made his way south to his favourite village to join in their harvest excesses. He had heard about Ayken's death, and that of the other young village men, and wanted to be there to help with any melancholy which might result. As he rode slowly down the well worn tracks he wondered if Seofon would make it this year. He hoped that he would be there as he made good company and an exchange of views was always welcome.

Seofon and Borvo had spent their few short days travelling together but had covered such a range of topics that they had squeezed a lifetime of discussion into those hours. Since he had revealed the news of Ayken's death Borvo had at first been so quiet that Seofon became alarmed for his sanity. Gradually as they travelled Borvo opened up once more and spoke of death, heaven, glory, and his brother's good heart and bravery. Seofon did not show that he noticed how Borvo spoke the beginning words of the Lord's Prayer and then immediately prayed to Borvo the river god. In chanting both he seemed to find comfort and so Seofon did not challenge him as he might have done in other circumstances. He was travelling with a very confused young man and did not wish to push him to any rash action.

The two weary travellers finally made it to the edge of the well trodden paths of Borvo's home territory. Suddenly Borvo turned to Seofon and said in tones of great sadness, "I do not feel ready to face the village yet; I am a runaway and do not yet know my fate should the king or his men catch up with me. Seofon, will you leave me here to spend one last night on my own in my woods? I promise I will not run away but will enter the village as the sun sets on the day. If I am to be taken back I want to have the feel of the water between my toes one more time."

The storyteller turned an anxious face to his companion and thought for a long time. He knew he had to trust him, but in the event that he ran away again, he would not blame himself. For after all, he wanted no slave, and would not condemn any other to a life of forced servitude. He understood much and he had debated long into the night with many a monk about the king and his chosen church and how they reconciled the loving god with the keeping of slaves. Many of the people were also in another kind of bondage too, that of their overlord, who had rights over their persons and their lives that could also be enslavement. In his mind it did not tally but he was careful to whom he expressed these thoughts.

"Borvo," he said his name deliberately slowly, "I speak to Brovo, not Brother Mark; spend your night in your woods and river. Make me one promise only, and that is to fulfil your destiny of a healing man, whichever path you choose." Borvo clasped him in a fond embrace, such as he would have given Ayken and then answered simply, "I will."

Seofon left him then and walked purposefully on towards the village and his many friends who still welcomed him and his dramatic gifts.

Seofon and Bacchus strolled into the village unnoticed at first as it was dusk. He made his way to Leofric's hut where he was welcomed with pleasure. He spoke only of the battles, he did not speak of Borvo, he commiserated about the loss of the villagers who had died, and was encouraged to go to the small wooden church to pray with Leofric. Seofon felt this would be the circumspect thing to do and so he walked with his host to the modest place which the village had made its spiritual centre. There was little of value as might be found in the abbeys but the table with the wooden cross on it still dominated the interior. It had been made ready for the celebrations on the next day and so there were offerings of many kinds that spelt out the villagers desire to thank god for their plentiful harvest. Seofon took note of the increased organisation of the church compared to a few years previously when things were more haphazard and free. He knew it was an inevitable consequence of the king's desire for order in such matters.

Leofric spoke at length to Seofon about the village and all that had occurred since last they met. Some of the news Seofon already knew but there were details that Leofric and Cynwise added that put flesh on the bones of the story. They were seated round the outside of the main hut, night had fallen but there was no hurry to sleep. Leofric told the traveller of the return of Sunny and her young companion, of the very recent return of Esmund and Elvina just the day before and of the hoped for return of the survivors from the battle. There were many arrangements to be made for their honouring and burial. He spoke with undisguised relief when he mentioned Eldric, his son, and how he was still alive. He related the dreadful scene that had occurred when Elvina had been told of Ayken's death. Sunny had rushed back from helping Hild to see her mother and father and explain what had happened. Shock and disbelief had given way to intense mourning and an outpouring of grief such that those who heard the painful sounds wondered if they would ever cease.

Elvina and Esmund, without words passing between them, hugged, wept and then turned to tend to Gramma. They found solace in practical tasks and in making their hut the warm and generous place it had always been. Sunny and Aedylpryd (the latter now fully accepted even if still a little afraid of Elvina) proved invaluable in their help and presence. Beadmund was still around and was delaying his departure for many reasons. He spent time with the men of the village and was treated as an honoured guest. The truth was that he couldn't bear to leave the company of such a sweet person as Sunny. He wanted to take her as his second wife and he thought that she was not indifferent to him. However, with the death of her brother and the absence of her family the time was not auspicious for such dealings. He knew he had to go home to see to his own household but decided to stay for the harvest celebrations and then he would depart.

Celebrations started in late afternoon and continued until the dark sky revealed its panoply of stars well into the night. Those that were close to Ayken and the others who had lost their lives found it difficult to celebrate but in the end Elvina, Esmund, Sunny and Hild put in an appearance and stayed to hear Seofon's entertainment, after which time they slipped away to hug their grief to them in the quiet of their own place. Seofon had chosen his story carefully this year as he led up to it he threw in riddles and tricks then quietly sat and began to speak. His voice was soft and low and people began to listen so that within a minute of beginning he held the floor spellbound. He spoke of a time, long gone when the invaders from across the sea had taken the islands and driven the elite, the learned and spiritual leaders off the northern shore by the land of the Celt and there they slaughtered them. The moral in his tale was difficult to find as the aggressor seemed to win and hold all the cards. As he began he told of how the native peoples had been driven to the extremities of the islands, of how some had embraced the newcomers and settled down with them as their masters, of how some had been sold into slavery and taken to lands far away, of how many teachers had been killed, for by killing the leaders the rest would have no one else to follow and so conquest would be easy. He continued as he had begun with his words put to a rhythmic, almost mesmeric chanting:

They chased them over the mountains 'til they brushed against the sea
They hounded all before them 'til there was no one left but thee
Their robes they flowed around and out behind them billowing free

As they crowded on the stormy shore they needs must face the tide
For all behind was danger, death from the fabled men that tried
To take or break for empire those that would not stand aside

Women and their children, aged folk too were swept along
By the anguished need of the elders, the hitherto ruling throng
Battled hardened foe relentless went and marched to a bitter song

Those hunted down and harried, those who fled from soldiers bold
Kept up their faith, believed in what they preached from songs of old
That the ancient ones had handed down along with torques of gold

As the sea grew dark and the storm whipped wild over the straits they went
To the island where they hoped and prayed that their lives would then be spent
They were welcomed in with fires and broth though the signs spoke ill portent

But the sea stopped still and the army saw that the natives now were near
Legions crossed the narrow tract and swarmed with sword, dagger, spear
They showed no pity as the blood lust rose with their corralled foe in fear

Carnage it was that bitter day when druids all slain where're they stood
Cries of the children, dying mothers, elders' pleading did no good
Limbs and heads and torsos stained the oak trees with their blood

One only lived to tell the tale, a small boy of ragged frame
He saw and smelt the killing 'til all bodies looked the same
He wandered on as story man building myth and hence his fame

It was not long before the bloody soldiers sailed for home
For pagan hoards had swept along and south and into Rome
Sad irony that killing always means there's ever more to come

To further shores they went to save their own beleaguered races
Their families were dying on their knees in sacred places
All that met them as they journeyed home were haunted deathly faces

'Tis quiet now as wind and rain sweep over tracks of ancient land
Weak summer light plays tricks so maybe where they took their stand
Their ghosts still walk and wail until the world can understand

Seofon stopped suddenly as the rhyme ended. He did not stand or sit with a flourish as he might have done but he put out his hand, took up his ale and drank a deep draught. Elvina rose gracefully then with soft tread she went to Seofon, stroked his head and smiled at him. As she looked straight into his eyes she seemed to see deep into his very soul as if she understood that it might have well been Seofon himself who had been that small boy who saw such horror. The story had been about her and her people, Esmund's people and Borvo's people. She was grateful to him for such a story but she had had enough of other people so she went back and gathered up her family and they left in silence. Seofon leant down and stroked Bacchus's ears. The silence of Esmund and Elvina's departure lasted but a few seconds then people started to talk and eat and drink and gradually laughter could be heard by anyone who was unlucky enough to be left out in the cooling darkness on such a night.

A thin figure sat hunched up behind the northern wall of the hall. Borvo had crept in to the village unnoticed to seek some solace in his desperate state. He had been able to grab some food and drink as it passed by on its way into the hall. Barely enough to sustain him but it was all he could manage. He listened to Seofon's tale and was moved beyond words by the story. Was it another of Seofon's fantasies or was it true? Had his druid ancestors been hounded and slaughtered in such a fashion? Where was this island that had given them shelter? He thought that the story might have a grain of truth because he had been brought up to know of previous generations and their persecution. What to do? He longed to go to his mother and father. He ached to see his nephew and niece and he felt physical pain at the thought that no more would he see Ayken. Where was Sunny? Had she been informed? Not knowing how to proceed he crept away into the nearby woods and settled down for yet another night in the open. The morning would decide his fate, he was too tired to run any more yet he had no strength to decide to stay either. He slept.

Chapter Thirty Six

Return to rest

On the day following the revelry a runner panted into the village and shouted for an audience. Leofric and Cynwise were late abed that morning but they tumbled out into the morning adjusting their dress to find out what the commotion was about. The noise was from a youth who had followed the men to battle and now was used as a herald to announce the sad party that returned and were even now an hour away from the village. By the time the solemn group came to the village over the track way used by generations of drovers there was a welcoming mournful reception waiting for them. They bore with them a grisly reminder of the cost of victory. Ayken and his companions were coming home to be honoured and buried. Hild and Elvina had fallen out over the way that Ayken should go. Hild won and declared that he would be buried with Christian words said over him but she had given in to Elvina in that he would have his grave goods too. Eldric was in charge of the homecoming and he acted with authority and resolution. He was determined that these men would be spoken of and never forgotten. They were all to be buried on the day they returned as the corpses were not in a good way having travelled in boxes on a cart in warm weather.

The boxes were opened briefly for the families to see their loved ones one last time and to put personal crosses in with them. Only Ayken was given his sword and pots of herbs to see him into the next world.

All the village made ready to turn out and walk through the dwellings to the hill on which they were to find their final resting place. As the people gathered it was noticeable that some were still in poor fettle from the excesses of the previous night. Hild, Elvina and Esmund, accompanied by Sunny who held the hands of Godgyfu and Aescwine with Beadmund protectively behind them, were all aware of the tragic sense of loss but at the same time knowing that sacrifice had been the only way to keep their freedom. So it was with desperate mixed feelings that the bereaved families took the head of the procession while the rest gathered to form the tail as it wound its sorrowful way to the hill beyond. As the people walked in quiet procession, some burning torches of herbs to rid the air of any evil or contagious smell a ragged figure joined the very last person at the rear. Borvo had decided to come out and face his fate, then when he realised what was happening he rushed to join in the honouring of his brother and comrades. Realising who had joined the throng a murmur went out and up the line of mourners until it reached Esmund's ears. He stopped and turned then with slow dignity held up his hand to stop everyone until Borvo had reached his side. Shocked at his son's appearance he made no sign that anything untoward had happened just held his hand out and grasped Borvo tightly, then turned him to walk beside him and Elvina. Elvina's face gave nothing away although she too held Borvo's arm, briefly, then continued to walk to honour her eldest son.

Brother Augustine said the appropriate words over the graves and then the three rectangular holes were filled in with fresh soil. Eldric stepped forward and spoke in a voice so loud and clear they may have heard him at court, "Good people, here lie three most valiant men who died honourably to save the rest of us from the blasted Danes. The most beloved of friends, Ayken, sent before his time for he dared to challenge a king's man, did not turn away but strode ahead to meet his fate. I pray that wherever he goes now he will find honour and peace. We will do most to honour him, and the others, by keeping his family dear to us from now until we too find our way to peace beyond." He did not cry as he was beyond that emotion; he stood and beat the air with his clenched fist. "We must not forget. They died well."

Most of the villagers chorused the sentiment; they too raised their fists and beat an unseen rhythm on the peaceful hillside air. After a while they then drifted away to get on with their lives. Hild and the children threw flowers on Ayken's grave. Elvina and Esmund threw their arms to the wind and summoned the gods to take care of their son as he made his next journey. Borvo knelt and prayed to whomsoever would listen. He prayed for Ayken, he prayed for Hild and the children and finally he prayed for himself as he knew that he needed whatever help was on offer. It was over and the family went back to Elvina's hut to talk and remember. They were also desperately anxious about Borvo's current dishevelled and gaunt state.

Aedylpryd had stayed with Gramma who, showing little sign of remembering much from her former life lay on her pallet, warm and cared for with enough to eat, and stared vacantly into the flickering flames of the fire that was never left to go out. The minister's daughter had become inexhaustible in her devotion to the young family of Hild and she was always willing to help Sunny in whatever way she could. For the first time in her life she was not only wanted and loved but she was useful and needed. She grew daily in the affections of all the family and blossomed. Gramma liked her as well as any of the rest so she took her turn in being there to notice any little thing that would ease Gramma's daily routine of pain and sleep. She knew her brother would want her to come away with him but she was confident enough now to tell him that she would stay and return at another time more convenient for the family.

The family gathered and sat around the central fire while Elvina put some soup into a wooden bowl and gave it to Borvo with the instruction to eat and then talk. He was grateful for the moment in which to gather his thoughts. While he ate the soup he noticed Gramma in the corner and went to her and gathered her in his arms. No one had told him she was returned to them and his joy overwhelmed him. Gramma took this embrace as any other, then she raised her old head and smiled at him. She held out her hand and stroked his sunken cheek, her lips moved and she uttered the one word which held them all enthralled, "Borvo." It was quietly said in a very weak croaky voice but she recognised him. All assembled hoped beyond hoping that she might now recover some of her wits.

Elvina looked at her son and asked directly how he had come to be in so poor a circumstance that he was unfed, unwashed and not in his monastery.

"I have run away. I left without permission and I fear that I will be brought back to be punished. I am so confused. They read to us at all mealtimes from the bishop of Hippo who seemed to have pronounced on all things holy and unholy. It just went on and on until I felt that I wanted to shout out, enough, stop, let our minds rest. I felt such relief when I was entrusted to take to the roads with Alric. Freedom of the open was magic to me. Then as you know I brought Alric here and felt that I had done my duty by him. He is content?"

Esmund answered after a while as the stream of words seemed to be never ending so that no one quite realised that a question had been asked. "He fares better than you at the moment. Esric and Elfgifu have not known such peace for many years. They revel in his company. He has grown a little but, yes, he is well."

"Good." Borvo was tired from speaking. He had said little enough but he was weary beyond any measuring and wanted to sleep. "I will regain my strength and then go back to face the wrath of the king and the bishop." With that he went back to kiss Gramma's forehead, bowed to everyone else and went to his bed to sleep. Sunny covered him with a bright woollen blanket and soothed his brow. "Poor Borvo, what trials."

As the family slept, some fitful others deeply, one person sat upright with no hint of sleep about her. Elvina had regained some of her family, lost a precious part of it, not only had Ayken gone on to the next world but Borvo was a cause of great concern. She longed to help but this was way outside her experience and she wondered if his dilemma was partly caused by his loyalty to her and her stubborn refusal to change. Esmund, her dear husband whom she had pushed away so often he had stopped trying to comfort her, was caught between the old and new worlds so that he looked back with softness but forward with hope. Why could she not see it? Borvo had such gifts and was perhaps too thoughtful. He examined every minute detail until he fully understood all and that seemed to have been his undoing. Although there must be more to his current distress than that because he had always challenged Brother Augustine after which he was neither angry nor confused but determined to unpick the truth. No, she would wait for more of the story before she decided how to help him. She stretched and got up to stir the dying fire, Gramma must not be allowed to chill.

The morning saw much activity in the hut as those with urgent chores got up to see to them and others made ready for the first meal of the day. Borvo woke and felt enormously hungry but in the end could only manage a small portion of bread as his stomach was not used to much food of late. He seemed cheerier and went out to feel the morning air on his face and decide how to proceed with his story. He would have to tell them the truth. What was the truth? After all he had been given a task and because of feeling lust or was it love for the king's daughter, which did not abate for the month that he was thrust into her company, he had fled and given up all hope of keeping the king's favour and even Minister Brand might shun him and would that upset Sunny's future too? He would be honest and let them decide. The family council would help him. He knew he had to go back or run away permanently and be lost to all he knew and loved.

When the sun was higher in the sky and was making shorter shadows on the earthen floor Borvo asked to speak to everyone. Hild had resumed her own hut and was with her parents. Sunny had remained with Elvina as Gramma was now a little more lively and thus needed more attention. That morning she had called Elvina, "Daughter." The pain was still etched on her by now crooked face, one side seemed to have dropped, not allowing her mouth to control the dribble from her lips. Through this she smiled. The family gathered and Borvo told his tale. He left nothing out even to the point of beginning to describe his talks with Seofon in great detail. Esmund cut him short and told him that they were for another time. The matter of the moment was what to do about deflecting the potential anger of the king and the abbey. Word would have to be sent to Winchester and if the court had moved on to winter at one of the other sites favoured by the king then the messenger would keep trying until he was heard. He knew what had to be done and he knew that he had to do it. As he looked across at Elvina he saw renewed love for him in her eyes and was glad. When he returned they would be reunited as before and work together until the end.

"Borvo, you stay here until you have regained your strength. Your mother will feed you and you will help her. Gramma may not have long and they will all need you. Sunny will continue to help Hild and we will have to seek advice about Aedylpryd. Beadmund will advise us and take care of her now. Minister Brand will have to be consulted and told the truth, well almost all the truth. Borvo, before I set out you and I will walk to the far field and we will talk together about your feelings for the girl. There are things that we can do." Sunny stood up and pronounced, "Firstly brother you will wash and change your tunic. You smell worse than a midden in high summer. I will go with you to the brook to make sure you don't run away again. You are a man now; no man should smell as you do. Come." She held out her hand and beckoned him. Borvo followed her and for the first time in many months he laughed.

Chapter Thirty Seven

Borvo needs to face his temptor

Autumn was well and truly set in at the village. Frosty mornings gave way to weak sunshine or windy dull days that lowered over the huts as they appeared to nestle together for warmth. The main track that ran through the village was muddy most of the time as this autumn seemed to have been wetter than many could remember in their lifetime. The brook was nearly full to bursting its banks and as it swelled and splashed its way over its long course to the sea it carried with it brown, red and golden leaves from the woods.

Borvo had filled out once more to his normal size which meant that his face no longer appeared gaunt and ragged. The dark circles under his eyes were gone and he seemed more at peace than in many a long month. He had two saviours to thank for his recovery. One had been Sunny as she mothered him and smoothed his mind with practical talk about the family and where they had come from and indeed where they were likely to go. This she did with her gentle speech that in itself soothed any worry lines from his brow. Alric was the other friend who came to him, unbidden but as welcome as any. He had stayed with his former protector as often as his work allowed. Alric coaxed him and walked with him for hours in silence if that is what Borvo needed or just talked about the days in the abbey when they had been on less equal terms. Now it seemed to Borvo that he was the pupil and Alric was teaching him how to live with whatever was inside him that was desperate to get out. His friend reminded him of the patience needed and how philosophers had sometimes to take years to come to an understanding of the wider theological issues. He was a true help and Borvo was glad of him. One day when they were sitting by the torrent that the brook had become and Alric was plaiting Borvo's hair, he suddenly said, "Brother Mark, when will you go back to face them?" Borvo spun round startled, "Why? You call me by that name as though it is who I am." "Yes, I do because it is how I knew and respected you from the first. You will always be that to me." After a considered pause Alric continued, "There are two worlds for you and you chose to let them take you to one from the other. It is in your hands what you do. I believe in you and your destiny. You told me that you need a wider world in which to practise. You will not find it here. Your gifts are for sharing." Borvo knew he was right. "How did you become so wise so quickly?" Expecting a quick joke as a response Borvo was taken aback when the younger man continued in reflective mood, quietly he answered, "It was my father first told me that I was without wits. He wanted to make money from me as a healer, just as my grandmother had been. But I had none of the skills and so he decided he could beat me into it. When that failed he sold me to a passing merchant. He continued in my father's ways and so I ran away and ended up with the monks." Borvo stood up and started to walk back to the village, "Of course I am going back, I won't let you, or anyone else down. I'll take my punishment and go on from there." He took a deep breath of courage, "It won't be so bad."

Before they arrived back at the village proper Alric turned aside and asked Borvo to follow him. He had, in his tunic, some things that he knew would make amends for some of the thoughtless destruction of the oak trees whose demise had greatly saddened his champion. They went to a clearing where nature had taken its toll leaving a large scar in the woods. Alric knelt down and, using a piece of wood, dug a hole. As he stood up he took the objects from the fold in his tunic and handed Borvo three acorns. Now Borvo smiled as though his face would crack in half, what better way to start afresh than to plant such a mighty group of trees for the future? He gladly performed the task, insisting that Alric plant one and he the other two, one for Gramma and one for Ayken. He would have liked to know that he would be immortalised in such a magnificent way. After this quietly enacted devotion during which they stood and silently prayed for the unhindered growth and protection of the trees and by association also that of the people they went back to the village. Borvo realised in a blinding flash how lucky he was to have such a thoughtful friend. He became much more hopeful for the future knowing such a man was in it.

Elvina had withdrawn to her own place as she spent each day looking after Gramma and encouraging her rekindled understanding. Esmund spent more time each day with Leofic and Eldric as the daylight hours in which to complete their chores were cut short by the gathering night. Leofric showed signs of distress when he walked and his jerkin no longer fitted him hanging loose across his former rounded belly. Cynwise looked daily at the blood in their bed where he bled as he slept. She knew he could not go on for long but even so sought the advice of Elvina. As Cynwise described the symptoms Elvina's face betrayed her understanding that the cause was lost before she even began. She held out her hand to the anxious wife and said plainly but kindly, "I can ease only the pain for a while. He will not be cured." Cynwise looked beyond the kind face into a bleak future without her kind companion. "I understand." She left to go and prepare for whatever time she had left with him.

Esmund was talking to Leofric at the same time while Aescwine played about his knees with a handful of rounded stones and an old cracked wooden bowl. "Borvo is ready now. If he doesn't set out soon the roads will be impassable. He is easier in his mind now and knows he has to face the wrath and any punishment. He is sorry if he had brought any disgrace on the village. Beadmund promised to speak to Minister Brand for us and let us know Borvo's fate but so far we have heard nothing. He has been gone over three weeks now."

Leofric replied with some difficulty as his gut ached as though the devil himself was deep inside making mischief, "Borvo had to come here. It is his home. Your family has given much. We will be well." As another spasm of pain hit him he added, "I will not be here long myself, Edmund. Look out for Cynwise and Eldric too. He is strong and wise but may yet need your counsel." Esmund looked at his friend and knew his time was near. He did not dissemble and reassure where there was no hope; he merely nodded and said, "You need have no fear. You have our respect. Cynwise will never go hungry or cold while we are here. I doubt though that Eldric will have need of us. He is strong and has his own family now, but if it eases your mind you may tell him that we are his as well for any advice or comfort he may need." A thoughtful silence followed. Esmund swooped up Aescwine in his still muscular arms and swung him onto his shoulders. The little boy laughed and hugged his Grandfather's neck. Esmund smiled and said in parting to Leofric, "I must get the boy back to his mother. Your son will be a fine leader. You have done well." Leofric watched him walk away with an ache in his heart to match that of his belly.

Hild had rallied her spirits as the days passed by and she could now look at her children and be glad that she had them. There were others who could teach Aescwine all he needed to know and she had the comfort of knowing that Ayken had died honourably.

She was proud of him and the village had all helped her and the other bereaved families. The visiting Brother had been helpful too and she found solace in the words he spoke to her. Esmund was wonderful with the children but Elvina had withdrawn from her. She tried to understand that she had her own mother for whom she took full responsibility but Hild had noticed that even Borvo gave the older woman little pleasure at the moment. Sunny still came and helped when she could but she had an idea that her sister in law may well be away by next spring. The young thegn Beadmund had shown great interest in her and she had responded to any sisterly enquiry with blushes and confusion. Aedylpryd had gone back to her own mother when her brother had taken off after the late summer celebrations. She had been a nice young woman and fitted in despite her high born status. These thoughts flowed through Hild's mind as she prepared her evening meal with the help of Godgyfu, her little helpmeet.

Borvo appeared at the entrance to the hut and cast a long shadow over the floor, "I must go soon Hild. I will be back one day." He made a face and added, "It may be painful for a while if they judge me harshly." He knelt down to hug Godgyfu and said, "Don't let them forget me." Hild's surprise showed in her face as she spoke, "Do you go now then? Is it wise? The paths will be dangerous." As she looked into his eyes she realised that this was a very hard thing for him so she just added, "Take care. Come back when you are ready. We will be here." They embraced then Borvo stroked his niece's cheek and conjured up a silver penny seemingly from nowhere and gave it to her. "Use it wisely it was given to me by Brother Augustine in harsher times when he thought I might need it. Where I am going I doubt I will have use for it for a while anyway." He turned and left to go back to his hut and make ready to depart. He knew what he had to do and was willing and ready to face whatever may come his way. His crisis was passed and he was strong again. His parting from his mother would be the most difficult as she seemed determined not to engage with him in anything other than mundane practicalities.

Esmund had agreed to go with him as the village council had asked that the young runaway was accompanied to make sure that he did go back to face his abbey's (or the king's) displeasure and abide by their decision as to his future and whilst some considered the father might be lenient with his son most agreed that Esmund was honourable and would not let any disgrace fall on the village. They were favoured by the king and wanted it to remain that way. These were hard and uncertain times when all good men and women fought to keep favour with those that had the power to protect and enhance them. However fond the people were of Borvo he must not be allowed to bring them poor fortune. It was decided; he and his father would set out on the next morning. The weather was set fair for a few days and that would see them over the pathways and byways to better wider tracks to the town. They would go back to Malmesburgh as the court had probably moved on to another favoured setting by now and the abbot there would know what to do.

Esmund and Borvo set off having made their farewells. Borvo's leave taking of Gramma was tender but that of Elvina was less than he had hoped. As they made their way to the edge of the wood Esmund put his hand on Borvo's shoulder and spoke softly and with sadness, "Your mother has retreated to a dark place. It is how Ayken was after the first battle. They are very much alike. She will return to us but she must have time. For now remember and honour her as she is and was for she will be whole again. Gramma must come first; when she has gone Mother will be well again. Trust me." Borvo squared his shoulders and simply replied, "I do." No more needed to be said and they continued their journey. They had hardly begun through the woods when they met two Brothers on ponies riding towards them. In great delight Borvo recognised Brother Simeon from Winchester. After greeting and introductions Simeon told the pair that he had been sent to fetch the truant monk and take him to Winchester. The court had moved to Wantage but he was to stay at Winchester and do penance for his waywardness. As Simeon spoke he smiled at the young man, "Don't worry, it will be harsh but not unbearable and then you will work with me until such time as the king sends for you again." He looked long and hard at Borvo then said, "You seem to be a mission with the king. You are lucky that he decided to let the church law prevail in this matter. Secular law would be less tolerant." The lay Brother who accompanied Simeon was shocked at Borvo's hair and said as much. Borvo put his hand to his plaits and agreed that it must go before Winchester but he would like to keep them for a while. Simeon agreed although he was rather disturbed by this portrayal of wilfulness when the man was in such bother. However, the four journeyed together to Winchester as Esmund was determined to see his son back to the arms of the abbey before returning home. He had been given this task and he would not let the village down for much depended on them keeping their good name with the king.

The journey passed with the company in good spirits so that when they reached their destination Esmund stayed for a few days at the abbey as a guest and was able to explore the market and the many streets. He thought it might be a good new venue for their sheep as one of the hills that over looked the city was known as St Giles' Hill where they held an enormous fair every year. People from many miles around came to it, even from across the water where it was known that the West Saxon wool was among the best in the world. Esmund knew that the sheep from the village could stand among the best so he thought they might get a better price here than their usual market. He would report back to the village to let them decide. He left to return home without seeing Borvo again as the errant monk, newly tonsured, was not allowed such a luxury. Esmund took his leave of Simeon and asked him to look out for his son. Simeon said that he would and blessed his journey home as the rains had come again in ever increasing ferocity. He hoped and prayed that Esmund would make it back home before the roads became impassable.

End of part two

Part Three

Borvo's journey is interrupted while he pays the price for his time at bay. He finds the patience to wait for the king's bidding and when it comes he knows he will be ready to meet the challenge. Not yet abandoned by his former guardian he finds the wit to accommodate everyone's demands, but whether it is enough to satisfy the inner turmoil remains to be seen.

Words meant to convey the spirit of the cross came to him from an old poem and set him free to wait and think:

> *"Grieving in spirit for a long, long while,*
> *Until I heard it utter sounds, the best*
> *Of woods began to speak these words to me"*

Dramatis Personae Part Three

Bishop Tunbeorht	New Bishop of Winchester
Welsh monk	An important aide to the king
Cedric	Beadmund's freed slave
Gwynne	Cedric's woman

Chapter Thirty Eight

Borvo's gift

The winter had been hard and long. Brother Mark was well and truly back in the cloisters. It seemed to the man of the woods and brook that he would die in the dank cold of the abbey and never see his beloved forest again. His penance had been a harsh one and as he swept the dung from the floors of the abbey stables his mind had wandered to and fro ranging over each and every step of his life which had brought him to this point where he was at that moment. Memories of his freedom among the woods and villagers of home to the exciting world of Malmesburgh Abbey mingled with his journey to Winchester and the regrettable feelings that sent him into an internal torture resulting in flight and the state of a fugitive. Without intellectual stimulation he had wallowed in his thoughts and while his body had filled out a little with regular abbey fare still his eyes shone out with misery whenever he considered his foolishness. The king had not sent any word of his eventual fate but Minister Brand had been to see him. The kindly elder man had expressed his sympathy over Ayken's loss but did not dwell on the subject for too long. Theirs was a harsh life and the strength of society was paramount, loss of life was part of that survival and must be borne. His visit had been brief but he left Borvo with the hope that he would find favour with the king again and be allowed to heal once more. A new bishop had been appointed after the expected death of the long failing Eahlfrith. Bishop Tunbeorht was just but dealt swiftly with any sign of dissent. One day when the frost was on the ground the bishop's 'shadow' had seen Brother Mark idling at his duties (what he actually was doing was calling on his river god to help him understand) so in an effort to redirect errant thoughts the bishop had issued an order for Brother Mark to wash the feet of all the brothers in the abbey. Brother Mark did not feel any humiliation at this and accepted the duty. It was during this act of penance that Brother Mark was suffused with an inner light that allowed him to understand some things that had been troubling him of late.

It had started with the horses in the abbey's stables. One of the beasts had a sore flank and the young healer had quieted the animal by putting his hand over the area of pain. With soothing words and eyes closed in humble entreaty for the animal's welfare he felt a cool wind blow around him and within minutes the horse was still and stood without pain. At first he thought that his river god was upon him once more then he realised that the manifestation was subtly different with no song or words to lead him along any particular path just a cooling breath of wind that took him and the animal up within its healing presence. For the rest of that day he had been full of energy and smiled as he worked. It mystified him but he accepted that he had a newfound talent to hide away from the prying eyes of his brothers. Most would not understand how he was so blessed and in a closed society such as theirs jealousy could take hold and cause mayhem. This had been brought home to him all those long months ago when he defended Alric at Malmesburgh. It had taken a long time for some of the brothers to accept he was completely innocent of any wrong doing; some had never reached that conclusion preferring to think of him as a dangerous influence. Perhaps the only one here who would listen to his rambling thoughts was Brother Simeon but as the errant runaway had been banned from the library for the duration of his punishment he rarely saw the kindly monk. So the time of washing the feet was upon him and as he knelt to minister to his fellow monks he came upon one old fellow who had such painful feet he could hardly shuffle along to the offices of the day. As Brother Mark held his feet in his hands he prayed over the old man, his hands became hot and once more the cooling wind wound itself round the tired feet and gave relief. The elderly brother looked down and saw such a look of entreaty in the young monk's face that he said nothing but he smiled at him as a way of thanks and relaxed without pain for the first time in many a long day.

"So," Borvo thought, "this is my way also. I have the gift of knowledge for healing and now the gift of healing touch. What am I to do with it in this narrow place?" He knew then that he must leave the abbey, but not without permission. He did not like the idea of being a fugitive once more and recoiled when he remembered the state he had fallen into. He would find a way to talk with Simeon and ask his advice. Meanwhile he would do all that was asked of him and be an exemplary brother. Surely the king would, must, decide soon. The long winter months were nearly at an end and spring would be waving its magic touch over the land once more. He would hate to miss its glory.

As the leaves unfurled their bright green promise and shoots of all kinds wound their way up out of the brown soil Mark received a message from an abbey servant that he was to present himself to the Bishop after the midday office was completed. Duly the young contrite monk went as bidden and waited, within the cool inner sanctum, to be summoned. He waited for some time and was beginning to think he was to be dismissed without audience when he was ushered into the bishop's quarters. Minister Brand was within and he beckoned Mark forward. Hesitantly he went forward and waited upon his fate. "Well Brother Mark, the bishop tells me you have served well and made no complaint about your long penance. It is well done. You have missed the books?" Immediately Brother Mark held out his hands in a gesture of hopelessness, "I have." Wondering if he should say more he added, "So much, there are still so many things to learn and understand." Brand smiled and said, "You are not forgotten but the king had to be sure. There has been much to do this winter, it has not been restful." The minister's eyes became distant as he remembered the wanton carnage. "So many raids but we are triumphant and seek a permanent end to these troubles. You are to be allowed back into the library where you will be appointed to help Brother Simeon," here the older man smiled and added, "in particular you will scribe the Herbal. Also you will be allowed back to the infirmary. Be obedient young Brother and in a while you will set out once more on the king's business. Be patient for you will not be disappointed at your journey's end." With those words he was dismissed and went back to his daily tasks so that he might go to the library the next day having a clear conscience that nothing was left undone. Inside he felt such joy at the thought of being with Simeon and talking when they could and smelling the vellum and inks and paints and the dust and absolutely everything about the books that drew him in and gave him peace. Of course the words were baffling and made him think and question, in particular he become angry or mystified at the difference between the old and new testament god. Jesus was just and he could live with that but the vengeful wrath of the god of Moses was anathema to him and he could not reconcile it however much he tried. For the moment he was content to believe that all would be well once he was again lost within the pages. Of equal import was his desire, which went beyond his ability to express it, to be back and able to help with healing the sick.

As Minister Brand continued his conversation with Bishop Tunbeorht his mind raced with desire for, seeing the face of the young monk had jolted his senses. Shining out of the young man's face were the eyes that startlingly reminded him of Elvina, the eyes and face and body that tormented his dreams. His was a hopeless case; he honoured his wife but could not rid himself of the bewitching pagan woman. He idly wondered if perhaps she had put a spell on him, then as quickly dismissed such a thought, his god was greater, he would pray and all would be well.

In the village changes had taken place that were hard to live with. Leofric had died a painful death with only mild relief given from the myrtle boiled up as a tincture from Elvina. Cynwise was sad as she became part of her son's household. She missed Leofric more than she could bear and hoped her days would be numbered. It was time for the next generation to take over the reins of leadership. She was tired, body and soul. Eldric was actually a better leader than his father. He was a dutiful son but was so busy that he had little time to dwell with her on the past and relive the memories that were stored so clearly in her mind.

Gramma too had gone on her next journey into the unknown. Elvina had not left her side during those long last weeks. Gramma had gradually faded from them. Her awakening in remembering her grandson brought joy to them all but it was short lived. Esmund saw the pain in Elvina's face as she contemplated the future without her mother, whom she had in effect lost already. She was lost to them when her mind first went and she had wandered away finally ending up with the harsh life of the fisher community. Finding her but a shell of her former vibrant acerbic self was a double blow and Elvina took it hard. She tried all the concoctions she knew and some she experimented with but nothing brought her mother back to her. After recognising Borvo Gramma held her daughter's hand and whispered 'Daughter' to her. The moment lasted but seconds but it was enough. She knew she was home and there she was to stay until the final journey. Finally, days before the mid winter celebrations when the Christs' mass was kept and much was made of the feasting, Gramma drew her last laboured breath and died. The moon had risen and the night was well set. A fire kept the glow in the hut up to soft amber and as the shadows played around the walls the old woman turned her face to the wall and died. Her dying face was serene and her tiny bony, aching body seemed to melt into the blanket until she was as a wraith with no substance.

Elvina clung to her mother's lifeless body as though there were more to it than the passing of one generation. Elvina felt that this departure meant more than the loss of her dear mother, more she thought of it as the beginning of the end of another chapter in the annuls of 'the old ways'. There were so few of them left now with the conviction or the courage to stand up and be counted amongst the fervour of the king's religion. Even her beloved second son was taken into it and cloistered until he believed enough to be let out. She felt so alone and was inconsolable. It was not possible to let her mother depart in fire so she had to be content to bury her with all the grave goods that she could muster to help her across the river to the next life. Prized among the possessions were an amber bead, a pot with her comphrey mixture and an acorn from the oldest oak that had been cut down by the village. She thanked her moon goddess that her mother never realised what had happened to the sacred oaks. At least she could bury part of them with her. There, it was done and she must get on with the living. Godgyfu and Aescwine were a delight. She had neglected them whilst caring for Gramma but now she was free again she would devote her time to them, then guiltily she thought that Esmund might want some of her time as well. There was much to mend there so she must resolve to be his helpmeet once more.

His too had been an uncomfortable winter. The desolate wet journey home from delivering Borvo to the abbey at Winchester had taken its toll on his health. He had developed lung fever and was critically ill on his return. Elvina, Hild and Sunny had been run ragged tending the sick. Each day they thanked god that the children were fit and healthy. Villagers stepped up to help look after the benighted family until their own kin fell foul of the season and its bitter fruit. Esmund was born of indestructible mettle as he gradually got better from the fever and rose to help once more with others. He was left with a rasping cough that only warm spring sun and good food would cure, with that he was content to be up and almost back to his old strength. The death of Leofric hit him harder than many as they had grown very close and would talk whilst walking for miles around the village taking in nature, the ways of the invaders, the king's strategy and their gods. Their friendship had strengthened daily and so it was with an enormous sense of loss that he watched his friend lowered into his grave with his polished wooden cross round his neck and a penny in his hand.

Midwinter came and the festivities were held with as much gusto as any other year. The dead were celebrated too but the living felt that part of the respect due was to carry on and honour them in stories and wine. It was a good time. It was a cleansing time. The weather was harsh and all needed to hunker down and survive the long winter days and nights which were borne with the usual intrepid spirit that had fashioned them and made them a race of survivors.

Chapter Thirty Nine

Borvo's patience is rewarded

During the main meal of the day for the monks an appointed Reader would sit aside and read enlightening words of wisdom to the assembled brothers. The king had long since been an admirer of the Bishop of Hippo and so, Brother Mark remembered, the text of the City of God being repeated endlessly at Malmesburgh until the words either washed over the simpleton or burned into the brain of the interested searcher after truth. It seemed to Borvo the pagan healer that the argument for one god was a seductive idea that gave men hope for eternal salvation when the world around them seemed to be so full of doubt and uncertainty. But then his gods too had held out hope for an exciting journey on the far side of death that told of adventure and a search for the elusive final rest in peace and happiness. The idea of dual belief one in good and the other in evil as a life balance also seemed to be how things were ordered. He had not encountered true evil in his life just, on reflection, minor difficulties that required his decision as to which way his life would go. Brother Mark on the other hand found solace in the word of the gospels and there he discovered a feeling of hope beyond all that he had ever experienced. How he longed to discuss all this with Brother Simeon. He would find a way through because he was convinced that the answer was there if only he could just reach that tantalising truth that was always just beyond his mental reach.

Borvo felt that to fully embrace the teachings of the church would be a betrayal of his beloved Gramma. He had not gone to her funeral as the roads were impassable at the time and he would have arrived too late. He had had to content himself with praying to both Jesus and Borvo the river god for her safe deliverance to whichever final rest she was headed. He knew she would be all right because if there was any spiritual justice of any kind she would be cared for just as she had cared for others throughout her whole life. He liked to think of her on her next journey finding Ayken and walking hand in hand with him towards the happiest place of all. Ayken too would have thrown off the mantle of gloom that had been embedded in his heart from the first time he had killed another man. During this latest sad time he had sought refuge from the daily offices and his daily grind whenever he could on the bank of the river that ran thought the city. He had heard tell that in ancient times it had been dedicated to the goddess Kasto who in the pantheon of gods was known for her swift running and listening ways. Perhaps he should listen and wait for inspiration. It was often shrouded in mist or thick fog which gave him a sense of isolation that for him at these times was a great comfort. On one such occasion as he sat wrapped in his warm but roughly woven woollen cloak by the river he had once more felt the stirring of another presence and had heard again the familiar voice that sang to him of his next journey. Strangely he had been praying to Jesus when Borvo the river god came to him. Perhaps they were one and the same but with a different name. Perhaps it was the Holy Spirit in another guise, whatever or whomsoever it was it spoke to him and led him back to where he actually thought he wanted to be.

The Third Song of Borvo

Borvo Borvo hear my song
This is not where you belong
You are meant to live life free
Making well where none can see

Making well with healing art
Making all things glad at heart
Borvo Borvo take the road
Yours is such a precious load

It was not for you to dwell
In a dank and lightless cell
Praying all the hours of night
You were meant to live in light

Throw off your mantle of despair
Walk away and breathe the air
Healings gifts are many now
Borvo take another vow

Borvo Borvo hear my song
This is not where you belong
Go to where the ancients' bled
Fill your soul with those long dead

One good companion by your side
With his shadow four feet astride
Black his coat but not his heart
He will bless your healing art

That visitation had come to him after the Christmas mid winter service at the darkest time of year. Now spring was beckoning and it still sat inside his heart as his goal. First though he must do the king's bidding, he was stronger now and could face the young princess with equanimity and friendship. She was often in his thoughts but only as a true and loving friend, no more, no less. It had been a great relief to him to feel the uncomplicated love, at last he felt free to help her. He had learned patience through necessity which quality he saw as essential for survival. Soon, he thought, soon he would be summoned and he would be ready.

Meanwhile he was enjoying being back with Simeon and his books and helping at the infirmary. If there were some monks who viewed him with suspicion he was unaware of them and so he passed his days in better spirits than he had over the previous winter. As the pale sunshine struggled through the cloisters he walked with a lighter tread as he considered that this was probably the last time he would spend within the walls of this particular abbey. He did not regret anything as he went about his daily routine. He was here at this moment because of all that had gone before. He was healing people again, helping them with their sores and aches and anxieties. The old monk that had suffered with bad feet for years, he had actually accepted the pain as a punishment for past crimes, was a regular visitor to the infirmary when Brother Mark was there. He always waited until there was a lull in proceedings then asked quietly and with reverence if the younger monk would hold his feet as before. Each time there was such intense heat from the healing hands and a period of profound relief for the sufferer. Neither one spoke of it and so it remained their secret. Brother Mark had asked to be allowed to help with the leper settlement outside the city walls which up to now was served by others but he had not been allowed to go there. He was not quite sure why but thought, rightly as it turned out, that the king would not want anyone near his precious family who had been in contact with such contagion.

It was a day when the morning had broken clear and sweet and the smell of spring pushed through the city smells and brought a smile to the hitherto pinched winter faces of the people. Two riders came early to the city walls and demanded to be allowed entry via the heavily fortified west gate. Once the guardians of the gate had seen the royal insignia they were permitted access without delay. One of the men was Beadmund, son of Brand, who was accompanied by a younger man in his service. They made their greetings to the elders who had come out to start the day's business and then they rode straight away to the abbey. Here they were offered sustenance consisting of ale and bread and thick porridge flavoured with the honey from the abbey gardens. While they ate they spoke little of their task but idled their time with Brother Simeon talking of the state of the road, the latest news from the borders and what likely fate would come to any who crossed into the West Saxon land while the king was in power and thus they spent a pleasant hour and waited upon the bishop.

Beadmund wore his voluminous cloak, fastened at the shoulder, just as was his father's habit, with a round broach made of gold set with enamel highlighting the geometric design which incorporated the four ways of the compass and an elaborate cross. These identical broaches were a gift from the king to both father and son in recognition of their loyalty and bravery. The chambers of the bishop were scarcely warm so the emissary kept his cloak fastened around him to ward off the chill air. All formalities over Beadmund spoke of the young, one time errant monk, and how the king wished for him to accompany him back to the king's quarters, currently in the north of the kingdom. They would spend but one night at the abbey then take their leave at first light. It was a hard day's ride and they were anxious to be back at the hub of the kingdom. Peace was occasionally brought and then broken so trouble could break out at any moment, Beadmund knew his place was at the head of his men and revelled in his duty to the king. He had chosen to fetch Brother Mark for Sunny's sake. She filled his head as he lay alone at night and considered when her family duties would relieve her to follow her own life, with him; for this is what he had determined would be her lot. His young son needed another mother and he loved Sunny, it was the best solution. Brother Mark greeted the news of his departure with admirable restraint when in fact he wanted to leap for joy. His two attempts to tell Simeon of his hopes had been dashed both times by the intrusion of the bishop's man whose sole purpose, it seemed to Mark, was to prevent him from free discourse. The arrival of Beadmund rendered this confidence unnecessary, which was just as well because although Simeon was a good man he was an even better monk and would have recoiled at the inclusion of Borvo the pagan god's influence over his young friend. Brother Mark collected his meagre pack for the journey which included his staple plants in a leather pouch and a poor abbey cloak. He was off and one step nearer to being free. He must contain his spirits, just a while longer.

Chapter Forty

Beadmund makes up his mind

Seofon and Bacchus had wintered well by being taken under the protection of Minister Brand and Rimilda. Each evening their long hall held many of their fighting men and their families, alongside the many visitors who sought his counsel because of his closeness to the king. The assembled company, well served by the servants or slaves required for such a vast household, needed to relieve the boredom of the winter months which were less active than the rest of the year and so Seofon's storytelling was a welcome addition to the inevitable singing that helped while away the darkest of nights. The talk round the central hearth was mostly of victory and peace. There were some among the number for whom the excitement of war was always uppermost in their thoughts. They would never be free from the desire to fight. It was bred in them. For the rest their hopes were of husbanding the soil and rearing the finest wool in the land. They would go to market and get the best price for their fleece or their women would make up the wool into the softest cloth. Then they would wear fine clothes, eat well, sport the best swords and gold adornments. Their wives would order the servants and their children would learn to read and so please their over lord mightily.

All knew of his plans for his people to grow through education. Few were aware of what this actually meant and some considered that education was wasted on the many but they honoured their king and so decided he might know what was best for them. Meanwhile they feasted well during the warm months and tightened their belts during the harsher times; they were well served by their king and they trusted him.

Beadmund's small son played with the other children of the household. They crowded round the men who played chess with roughly worked bone chessmen; they played round the skirts of the women who spun the oily fleeces and the others who weaved the thread into fine cloth. These winter activities stopped hands from being idle while the tongues ran on stories, adventure and myth. Beadmund had ceased to keep a separate place when the invasions became more frequent so as he needed to fight alongside his father and over lord he had decided that his mother was best served to keep his infant safe. Aedylpryd took her nephew under her wing and saw to it that he was well friended, well fed and brought up in the manner her brother would wish. She also taught him some letters that she had learnt. Rimilda could read and, whatever else she may have been she wanted the best for her daughter, despite her unprepossessing appearance, perhaps she thought Aedylpryd would make a good sister at the nearby abbey. Under this king abbeys were springing up all over the kingdom and there were plenty of spaces for well born girls. If Aedylpryd did not find a husband then that was to be her fate. All would be well and her sewing talent, greatly enhanced under the tutelage of Sunny, was outstanding and would grace any establishment that took her in.

Sunny had not returned to help with the household of her benefactor. There had been so much to do at the village. Gramma needed care, her father needed care, Hild needed less help with the children as her parents increased their participation in their daughter's life. The more they did the less suspicious of the healers they became and went about with a newly found confidence in their presence. Esmund had been so ill that the ultimate plant used sparingly for its addictive properties had been employed by Elvina to quieten and sooth him. Sunny had been afraid to use it but her mother insisted it was the only way to still his shaking so that his body could then heal itself. The old name for the plant was framynd and grew in warmer climes than theirs so it was quite rare and only bought at fairs when the darker merchants from the south made their way to the larger gatherings. Seofon had brought some with him on his last journey to the village. Where he got it from nobody knew or asked, it was welcome in extremis. Esmund had been so eager to tell Leofric and Eldric about the great fair at Winchester but his illness had come upon him on his desperate way home those long months ago and he had not been strong enough to tell his story but as he regained some strength his friend lost his and died. His story would have to keep.

Sunny mourned her Gramma, more so because she was alone without Ayken or Borvo to share the grief. Elvina continued her lonely struggle for inner peace and reconciliation with Esmund which meant that she also pushed her daughter away at the time when each would have comforted the other. As her father needed her less and less her thoughts turned to Aedylpryd and her friend's strong handsome brother. She had enjoyed her time with Minister Brand's household and she had been well treated. Now she began to long once more for the freedom the distance from home had given her. She wanted to be a wife and she yearned for Beadmund. Her dreams turned to how they might be together and how it might feel to lie with him in the long dark nights of winter under a fur rug, in the soft summer nights under the stars or cosily in their hut as the frost nipped at the grass outside on the turn of the season. Her face took on a faraway look while she wandered more idly than ever before in her life. She finished her work then found she had wandered to the woods or to the brook where she sat and thought and daydreamed.

As she sat and pondered the object of her thoughts was busy escorting her brother to the spring palace of the king. His daughter had expressed a desire to see the young monk again and discuss with him, as they had begun to do, all aspects of herbs and their healing properties. She knew she was destined to be an abbess and nothing pleased her more than the idea of running her own establishment for the good of other pious young women in the service of god. Brother Mark would give her good counsel in the ways of healing and this she prized among his many gifts. She was haughty as befitted her status but this mien did not blind her to the simple truths about others whom she studied from beneath her heavy lidded deep blue eyes whilst she tried to assess their character. In this she was well practised and was rarely wrong in her judgement. She had not been blind to the attraction from Brother Mark but she felt only intellectual harmony and friendship with him and hoped that by now he would be of the same mind. In fact she was convinced that he was destined to be a great healer and advocate for Jesus, who was the greatest healer of all time. This she firmly and fervently believed to be so and would do all in her considerable power to make it happen. Thus she begged her father and prayed with her father to set the ball rolling to bring Mark to her and the process could begin. She had much to learn before she could set up her abbey and a few more years of maturity would be better for her own respect and bearing among the pious.

Beadmund delivered his charge and asked the king's permission to depart on his pressing business. There had been negotiations with the Danes and hope was widespread that there would be a peaceful bargain brought by the emissaries. In this mood of optimism the king felt that he could spare Beadmund for a short journey to the village and back. He gave Beadmund his blessing for his union with Sunny. As he rode away to the south and west he took with him his trusty servant and felt that he needed no other. The weather was getting warmer and there was to be peace, after so long there were to be no more raids and fear, and so he felt the joyous freedom that comes with the cessation of war. His heart was light and he was careless.

Despite there being agreement for peace on the horizon there were still bands of raiders who took an opportunistic view of life and used hostages to enhance their leader's powerful position. One such band of soldiers came upon Beadmund and his servant by surprise as the two carefree men entered a deep cutting that led to the steep hills of the central region. Swiftly and without fuss three Danes jumped onto the two men and pulled them from their horses. Beadmund's servant was despatched without thought for his life as his clothes marked him out as low born and as such not valuable. It would have taken food to keep him alive and he was not worth the cost of such treatment, his throat was cut and his body tossed to one side being of no further significance. Beadmund put up a struggle and fought bravely but the surprise was such that he hardly had time to draw his sword before he was trussed up and flung over his own steed. His servant's mount was used to carry one of the attackers and the others sprang onto their own and rode away as fast as they could back to the border country where they knew they would be well paid for such a prize. Beadmund was tied to his own saddle, unconscious and bleeding from a wound in his arm. It was not a deep wound but would be troublesome if not treated. The blood that fell from his wound onto the path was copious thus indicating his direction of capture. It was not until later that day that a shepherd was moving his flock to a new spring pasture that the local man found the body of Beadmund's companion and noticed the trail of blood leading north and east. Having safely corralled his sheep he went to find the elder of his village who would send word to the reeve who would in turn ride to the king's court. So it was that as nightfall came upon the optimistic court one of the king's reeves entered and sought an audience with the king.

The king was furious with the duplicity of the Danish leader. He had fought so hard to bring about peace for his people. He longed to settle the borders and live alongside the invaders with confidence. Many of their number had exchanged the sword for the hoe and farmed the conquered land for themselves. They married local women and showed every indication of desiring an end to hostilities as much as he did himself. He despaired for Beadmund and mourned his servant for he was certain that it was the young man they had taken. Brand was still his finest minister and he honoured his family with position and gifts. Beadmund was a rich young man and worthy of a fine ransom. He could not ignore Beadmund's family's entreaty on his behalf but longed to stop this trade in flesh. The weary king thought long and hard on this fresh dilemma so he withdrew to his chapel with his priest to pray and there he stayed until the morning when he fell into his bed exhausted but calm.

Meanwhile the object of Beadmund's desire was blissfully unaware of any disaster and continued to mope about the village longing for what she considered unattainable. Every day that passed without word from him or his kin strengthened her belief that she would die unwed and alone. The passion in her heart made her thoughts uncharacteristically melodramatic.

Chapter Forty One

Bargain

Borvo fell into his regained life as Brother Mark, confidante to the pious princess, with renewed fervour. He was grateful to be once more in a less rigid life where he was able to wander at will during certain times of the day. There was about the court a growing number of eminent scholars brought there from all corners of the known world for whom the king had a particular spiritual or scholarly need. These men were mosty of the cloth and so they kept up the offices of a sort in the king's chapel in which Brother Mark was expected to join them in offering their prayers and contemplations. He was sometimes privy to their discussions and from these he learnt that even the most learned of men disagreed about the scripture and whether or not it was one big allegory or factual history. He found these devotions welcome as there was a lot of time for silent thought and this he used to good effect. He mused upon his favourite gospel for it was written by Luke, a doctor, for whom the healer in him felt a distinct empathy. He loved the stories of Jesus the healer, again he felt so in tune with the message behind these tales that he made a long distance connection through the centuries to the man who had walked and healed and suffered for his people. Since he had discovered the gift of laying on hands to heal certain ailments he had grown apart from those who might have claimed friendship with him at the abbey. He did not want anyone to know of these latest occurrences because he feared being denounced as a magician or, worse still, as a fake. The former accusation would be serious but the latter disastrous to his ability to offer healing to those who needed him.

The time he spent with Aethelgifu was easier with every passing day. The first overwhelming feelings he had experienced, all those months ago, had been replaced by a genuine platonic love and meeting of minds. She had grown in maturity, as had he, and they spent many a long hour discussing the bible, plants, healing and closed communities. Not once did he drop his guard or mention his favourite river god. He had decided to trust no one but Seofon with that secret part of his daily considerations. The Princess longed for the order of an abbey and he longed for the freedom of the open road and meeting adventure face to face. He harboured his secret desire, spelt out to him by Borvo the river god, to find the Druids' place of slaughter but knew he must bide his time until the conditions were favourable. He had a lot of ground to make up in the king's eyes. The king had greeted him warmly but was so distracted by external events he had no time to spend discussing points of spiritual interest with an errant monk. The news of Beadmund's capture weighed heavy on the court, he was a popular figure who treated people with kindness mixed with just the right amount of authority so that people felt gently stroked whilst they ran off to do his bidding. Mark obviously knew Sunny loved the man and he had hoped that they would be together although he realised that Beadmund's station was far above their own. He thought of Gramma and her words tumbled into his head, "Borvo, there are those who put themselves above the rest, and leaders are needed, but across the river all are equal, we are given a fresh start in the next life. That is what I believe." Jesus had said that those who were humble would inherit the earth but this did not seem the Saxon way, humility was in short supply, except perhaps for the king himself who prayed and prayed for humility. He spent so long on his knees some nights that he could scarce get up in the morning he was so stiff. Coupled with his ongoing problem of the gut that his Gramma had offered to cure the king was in almost constant pain, a burden he bore with great equanimity. Instead of making him bad tempered with others it seemed to open him up to their pain as well. The longer Mark was around the king, even distantly, the more he admired and respected him.

The spring sun grew in warmth although tempered by a bitter wind that blew from the east while the people on the land who worked tirelessly to sow their crops and husband their animals pulled their meagre cloth shawls around them to keep out the cold. One day when Mark walked down to the local river he wandered further than he realised as he was lost in thought. His attention was caught by an early bee that drank from each foxglove trumpet and came out each time covered with golden pollen. As he contemplated such a sight he considered how even such tiny things as bees were made for the balancing of nature. He could not believe that nature was not part of god's plan and so his ancient belief in nature as a mother goddess fitted nicely into his trust in Jesus the healer. If god made all things then he obviously approved of man's desire to honour his creation in whatever way that was a power and source for good. These thoughts weighed him down then lifted his spirits again, into this ever present dilemma a large black shadow crossed in front of his vision. Startled he leapt to his feet to defend himself and then laughed out loud as he was bowled over by Bacchus with Seofon languidly leaning against the bole of a large willow watching him. The multitude of long branches that bent over the river trailed their ends in the clear water creating ripples and soft plopping sounds as the water eddied around them. The scene was tranquil in the extreme or had been until Bacchus bounded up and made his noisy welcome. He did not know how long Seofon had been there but it seemed to Mark that he was well met and the intrusion welcome and timely.

Such was their friendship that they spent the next hours walking and talking about any manner of subjects. They fell into an easy pattern of joking and story telling as old friends do who do not need to meet every day to keep such a relationship alive but instead, so solid is the grounding one or a hundred days might pass between meeting yet each time it is as if they had but just finished a conversation and were continuing with the subject as before. Seofon spoke of his time with Brand's household over the winter and how that family spoke of Sunny with great warmth. He then told his young friend about the plans Beadmund had for her and how he had probably been taken by the Danes distracted as he was for love of Sunny. This bitter sweet information gave Mark hope that his sister would eventually find happiness, if only Beadmund could be ransomed and freed unharmed. He would offer to go as an envoy and exchange himself for Beadmund, at least then Sunny would have a chance of a good life with the man she loved. Oeric had long since faded from her thoughts; if she thought of him at all it was with a smile at how young and foolish she had been. He had been her first love but he would not be her last. Brother Mark became Borvo once more, hot headed and determined to be of use to his family. He did not consider that he was of little use to the enemy as his ransom price was as nought. He told his plan to Seofon who said nothing as his words would have put out the light in his young friend's eyes. The king and his ministers would soon do that for him. It was a hapless plan.

It so happened that on his return to the king's spring palace that Brother Mark was summoned to the presence of the king and his ministers, chief amongst whom was Minister Brand. He had visibly aged since the abduction of his son and wore an anxious air of such intensity that most turned away knowing not how to offer comfort so they did what they did best and prepared for practical action to retrieve one of their own. Brother Mark stood with his hands folded in front of him in an act of assumed humility waiting to be told what he was wanted for in this august company. In the end it was the king himself who bade him come forward with a simple gesture, "Borvo," the king always forgot his abbey name and referred to him thus, "we need your help in a grave and dangerous matter." He searched the young man's face for signs of fear or weakness, what he saw was only light calm confidence, "We require you to venture within the house of the enemy and bring back your future brother under the law." Borvo smiled, "My Lord, I thought this very thought as I sat and prayed under the willow. Your service is my honour." It was settled. The plans would be drawn up for the monk to go, accompanied only by an armed servant, to the meeting place agreed between the defending and the offending kings. It was to be an act of true bravery and one which would, in time, help turn the pagan king into a Christian one. To see the light of faith enacted so was an inspiration to many more than would instantly admit such feelings. These rough and ever ready fighting men normally found their grit in the glint of steel and protection of shield with the blood curdling cries that enraged and fortified them. Few would show such courage with only belief to sustain and protect them. Some thought that their king was sacrificing the younger man for his own arrogance but those who knew him best were convinced of his infallibility and trusted him as well as they trusted in god.

All was set for the ransom to be taken by Brother Mark and his soldier servant companion. The Danish king had agreed to the terms and knew he pushed his opponent to the very limits of his tolerance. This was the last time such an arrangement would be agreed upon. There would be agreed boundaries and trade agreements between the increasingly settled east and the Saxon west. Even so it was a gamble for the Saxon king. His judgement had been influenced by his fondness for his trusted minister and his family. Borvo would be tested to the endurance of his mettle but the king knew he was up to the task. Sometimes even he did not know quite why he wanted this young healer to be around him and his daughter. The young man had a quality of spirit that was beyond the norm, almost the king believed, as if he was touched by the holy spirit. Perhaps even his pagan god had invested some of his godlike spirit into him. Whatever if was it made him shine out from the common man as special.

Borvo was well served by his companion who himself had a younger brother and felt this young man needed him as well as his own might have done. They had to travel for one day and a half to get to the meeting place. It was here that the ancient ones had built a ring of stones from which to worship whatever deity they sought. The site was visible for some distance and so no one could sneak up on the waiting emissaries with their captive. The exchange was simple and involved some considerable gold adornments as well as gold coin. In with the torcs and amulets the king had put a gold cross to remind the Danish king of his promise to convert at some stage. Before the meeting Borvo had decided to take this out and hold it above his head as he approached the enemy. His servant held his own arm beneath his cloak with his hand on the hilt of his sword. If they were to die they would take some of the enemy with them. The two brave men walked up the hill to the massive stone circle, both of them were sweating with fear and anticipation, Borvo prayed to both Jesus and Borvo the river god, he held the cross aloft and considered that at such times there was no such thing as too many gods on your side. At first there were no others to be seen but as they came within shouting distance one man came from behind the largest upright stone and stood watching and waiting. Within minutes there were a dozen men emerging from the stones, one was bound and bloody but upright and walking unaided. Borvo heaved a sigh of relief but carried on as though he had not seen them. He walked past the first man, past the second, who watched with sheathed swords, knowing that they could easily take the two men if commanded. With head held high in a manner too bold for a monk Borvo went up to the man he considered to be the one in charge and stood, silent before him, still holding the gold cross before him. The spring sun weakly warmed the place while the wind whipped up the cloaks of the assembled men which frenetic movement made Borvo's stillness more powerful.

The silence held for some minutes until Konal, newly appointed Danish emissary, broke it by greeting the two in their own tongue. Borvo bowed in recognition and held out his hand which contained the gold cross, then he brought his other up to join it from under his cloak and there within his grasp was the leather pouch of gold that was to buy Beadmund his freedom. All assembled wondered whether the Danes would honour their pact. They were not best known for keeping to treaties if it so suited them to break them. The tension was almost unbearable. Konal was impressed by the courage of these men, weighed the bag and held the cross which he threw to another. If they thought to upset the monk with their game they were mistaken, Borvo held his nerve and waited with dignity and patience. Beadmund was finally brought before the Danish leader and made to kneel; the Dane brought up his sword and held it above the captive. He swung it above his head and brought it flat side down on Beadmund's shoulder, severing the leather bonds that held his arms high behind his back. If he drew a little blood at the same time, well the young man would heal in time. Borvo started forward to help Beadmund up while the Danish soldiers laughed at their discomfort. They knew this was a deal not to be broken but they still wanted their sport. If truth be told they were disappointed that things had gone so well. A skirmish would have lightened their trek back to the border and been another tale to tell at the evening supper. However their sport was short lived and three men returned where two had come. As they walked away to where they had left their horses they tried not to turn round and look at what was happening behind them. Showing weakness was not an option and so with weary anxious tread the three assorted men, two helping the third who was weak from his capture, made their horses and comparative safety.

As they mounted and rode away they heard horses behind them, they all turned thinking their end had come. Two of the Danes rode up to them with great speed; they held the three men in their gaze and waved to them to stop. Borvo's heart sank. It had all gone so well, now he would offer himself as hostage and let Beadmund go back. He turned his horse in readiness to accompany them back as hostage when one of the Danes smiled at him, made a sign of the cross on his chest and gave him a silver cross made in a circle with runes round the outside. He had been so impressed with the other's courage that he decided to give him the cross that his wife had given him as he left for battle. She had converted but he remained unmoved, until that very afternoon when he witnessed the power of faith. Little did he know that Borvo was never less certain of anything than when he walked up the hill to the awesomely impressive ancient stones with their spirit of the past deep within them.

Chapter Forty Two

Borvo's family begin one more special journey

Esmund was asked to join the elders as they sat round on benches which were placed outside in the cool spring sun. They had chosen a sheltered spot for their discussion which let in the sunlight but stopped the chill wind which could freeze even the sturdiest heart. As Esmund approached with his slow gait, never more than an amble since his debilitating illness of the previous year, he sensed a lightness about the group that went beyond the norm. Rarely morose nevertheless the elders often chewed over weighty topics, as any peoples under siege might do. This morning was different in that when they saw Esmund approach Eldric spoke and they all laughed, not unkindly, and waited with suppressed mirth for him to sit and make himself comfortable. Eldric spoke first, "Greetings friend, you are fit now I see. The sun will soon chase away any lingering sore." Esmund looked around the group wondering if the laughter was with him or against him. He decided that he had done nothing to engender such hilarity and so thought there was a joke about to be shared. "Well enough Eldric." Eldric smiled and asked after Sunny. "She mopes still for her lost companion?" As this could have been a reference to Aedylpryd, Esmund answered that she would return to help Aedylpryd when the weather was more settled and travelling a joy not a curse. Eldric could contain himself no longer, "Esmund, dear friend of my father, a rider came in the night and asked for Sunny to go on a journey with him. You and Elvina are to go as well. It is the king's wish. The soldier rode all night and even now is asleep in my hut. When you are ready, make good preparations as I doubt Sunny will return for many a long while." Esmund was alarmed so blurted out, "Enough games Eldric, speak plain truth."

"You have more than one son of which to be proud in courage. Ayken died well but Borvo did well and went into the enemy's camp to offer as hostage instead of Beadmund. All is well now. He held his nerve and brought his future brother in law back safe to his family. It is his, Brand's and the king's dearest wish for him to marry Sunny." Esmund stood up and beamed. "Is this true? There must be more to the story than that. How did Borvo end up as emissary?" He sat down again and buried his face in his hands. After composing himself and standing once more he asked, "When are we to start out?" Eldric stood up also, clasped his hand and said, "Tomorrow. You will ride with your wife and daughter to the spring palace in the north and from there they will be married. The village gives you all blessing." He stopped then added, "God bless you. Come back to rest and be well. The village needs you both."

Esmund went to tell Elvina and Sunny what had occurred. Before he got to his hut Sunny rushed out and hugged him asking, "Is it true?" over and over again. Elvina came out into the light more slowly but she smiled and reached out for her husband, as she had not for many a month. They clung to each other in silent bond each knowing that this was the start of the healing. Sunny hugged them both then ran around in circles not knowing how to take the news. Never had she felt this happy and apprehensive. Her time was coming and she longed to see Beadmund again, feel his arms round her waist and gaze into his eyes. Esmund decided that there was a place they must go to, as a family, he took them out of the village, past the site of the old oaks, and down to the brook. Here the water sparkled with fresh energy and the apparent excitement of the water matched their own state. Elvina made an offer to the river god and spoke to Borvo through his own personal protector. They then sat, as a threesome, for possibly the last time, on the bank of their beloved water and each reflected on the times past and of those to come. The moment was special and spiritually sustaining. It was what they all needed. There were so many questions and no answers, yet, so they must be content to busy themselves with the preparations for their departure the following day.

Sunny had a wooden box in which she kept fine garments that she had made for her future. There were two fine undershifts from the best flaxen linen, given to her by Rimilda, someone from such a village would not have aspired to such finery, she had been lucky in her patron. There was a green woollen dress with a cowl that would protect her head in inclement weather and a fine spun shawl of yellow and brown. She had lovingly worked at these and occasionally looked at them in the hope of making a marriage, latterly with Beadmund. Philosophically she considered that if she never made a match then she could exchange the fine clothes for essentials come the hard times. However she kept them with lavender strewn on them to avoid them taking up the smell of the beasts that pervaded all in winter when the animals were brought in from the fields.

Now the time had come and it was understood that Beadmund had chosen her she emptied the box into a leather bag with her other scant belongings and made ready for whatever lay before her. Elvina secretly took with her an amulet of her own Gramma which she had always hoped to give to her daughter on her wedding day. The amulet was silver with crossed chain markings around the rim.

It had been kept, secret for the most part, hidden among Elvina's own box of herbs and ointments. Now was the time to pass it on and trust that its presence would seal a happy future for her daughter, with whom she found it increasingly rare to share a confidence. Elvina knew it was her dark mood that had formed the barrier and she was now willing to meet her family with fresh energy to make amends for the hurt she knew she had caused them. Esmund was the first and she had already begun to talk with him and show him she still loved him. She felt that she was emerging from the deepest mire and could see the light again. Esmund had been patient but it would take a while to renew their easy bond. The journey in the company of the king's man and their daughter might help draw a line under the recent past and rekindle some old personal magic.

It was a misty morning as the four travellers set out on their happy journey. Elvina had been up at dawn and had gone to the brook to make an offering and to dance for joy and prosperity as the sun came up for her daughter, Sunniva. The sun stayed away hidden from her by the early mist so she performed a special naked dance to make sure the power of her offering would bring good fortune to the young bride. It was all she could do and now she must give up her own way of worshipping until she returned. There was increasing intolerance abroad and she knew she had to be circumspect. Even Esmund had embraced the Christian way, much as a tribute to his friend Leofric rather than from any strong conviction. It was one way and theirs had been another. If he added a prayer to his former deities then there was no one to know this or chastise him for it. He did not believe that god knew everything that was in his head and heart at all times as they were told. Goodness was the key to his belief and if any god showed goodness and strength for the safety of his family then he was content. Ayken had been unsure when he went to battle just who his god was because Hild had been converted and so Ayken was on the verge of it too. He died and so whatever he believed had gone unspoken to the grave, a grave that looked both ways, forwards and to the past. Wherever he was he would be honoured for his courage and loving heart. Of this Esmund had no doubt at all.

By midday the mist had cleared and the spring day melted into one of cool sunshine where the clouds on the far horizon began to form with their threat of unsettled weather to follow. The next day would be stormy with spring gales to whip up the winter debris and clear it away. These times were uncomfortable to say the least but there was nothing to be done but to endure. Their journey would be over by the next evening and so they rode on as fast as they could.

Chapter Forty Three

Beadmund restored

Borvo rode at the rear of the party that made its triumphant way back to the spring palace at Wantage. Beadmund was in shock but tried hard not to show the pain he suffered from where his shackles had cut into him. His wrists were bloody and raw and he felt acute pain in his right shoulder where he had been bladed. However, given what could have been the outcome he was jubilant. He thanked god for Borvo's bravery and wondered why he had been sent as emissary rather than a minister or Ceorl. He had acted with brave subtlety instinctively understanding the mood of the Danes. He would be proud to call him brother in law. The soldiers were alert when the raggedy group neared the palace and sent word that the homecoming was a cause for celebration. They had been joined on their return by mounted soldiers on the look out for them and towards the end of their journey Seofon had also fallen in step with them accompanied by Bacchus who whined with pleasure when he smelt Borvo. The dog had grown especially fond of him during their many amblings by the river for Borvo always absentmindedly shared his food with him.

All was ready for feasting and celebration, the huge iron pot that hung from the rafters was full to over flowing with meat, wine and ale were flowing while the musicians made ready to entertain the night away. Brand and the king were waiting with ill concealed delight to embrace the son and subject. All was happy confusion which made it easy for Borvo to slip away without notice to find a quiet corner in which to regain his shattered senses. It was not until later that Aethelgifu sought him out and made him go to the king to receive his public commendation. It was at this stage that the welsh monk on whom the king relied heavily for matters of religion and conscience, stepped forward and held his hands over the young monk's head and prayed for him. He gave thanks to god for the safe deliverance of the party and looked deep into the eyes of the young man, searching for who knew what, but whatever it was he seemed to find it because his naturally solemn face broke into a smile and as he patted Borvo on the shoulder he spoke directly, "It was well done. God was with you." Borvo hesitated, not knowing if he should respond, then just bowed his head and turned to go. The king stepped up and said, "You may go for now Borvo but tomorrow you and I will talk. It is time." As Borvo looked alarmed he added, "It will be well. Go now, eat and rest. Today was well done. Beadmund will be forever in your debt. As will I."

Rimilda came up to him, she was the happiest of women, one of her beloved sons was returned to her, she held Borvo's hand and thanked him without flowery speech, but the words were heartfelt. Then it was the turn of Aedylpryd who had no such reserve, feeling she knew all the family because of her friendship with Sunny. The slightly ungainly young woman flung her arms round the young monk and kissed his cheek. Neither was embarrassed, it was natural to feel such joy and relief. Borvo felt nothing but brotherly monkish love for his sister's friend. All was well. He went off to eat, pray and sleep. All the feasting and merriment in the world would not have woken him that night; he slept as though he was making up for all the disturbed nights the years at the different abbeys had caused him. Just for that night he was accompanied by a warm furry body that snuggled up to him and would not leave his side. Seofon looked down at them contentedly then returned to his own merrymaking.

The next day saw the coming of a spring storm that broke early with a severity such as many could not recall. Trees were uprooted, some roofs were blown off, carts over turned and the rain hammered down until not one person was left untouched by the ferocity of nature. Beadmund had his ills tended by the infirmerer and took the time to regain his strength. He knew that Sunny and her family were on their way, he feared for them in the storm. After all the waiting and fighting, he could not contemplate losing her at this last stage of their journey. The day was long and full of frustration as people tried to protect their homes and livestock from the gales. The king sent Borvo a message that he was to put off their talk until the weather calmed as all hands were needed to survive that storm. Borvo sighed with relief then set about helping with injuries that occurred throughout the day. He knew it was merely putting off the inevitable but the respite would give him more time to think about what the king might have to say to him. He had thought that to get an audience with him would take all his pleading, but it was now clear the he was wanted for another mission. He decided that he was to just speak plain sense and ask for his freedom.

While the storm raged the travellers were undecided as to which way to go. At first it seemed that they might out run the worst of it but soon they realised the error of their judgement and so sought shelter in the middle of a thick copse of trees that appeared to be their safest option. Elvina was concerned, not only for Sunny but for Esmund as his chest was weak from the illness of the previous winter and she feared this might bring it all back with extra force. The king's man was made of sensible stock and decided that they would rest and keep as dry as they could under the thick canopy.

Quickly he made shelter for them using what he could find but the trees were as yet not fully leafed and so their shelter was not in any way watertight. They did their best and sat it out. The horses helped to shelter them and so they waited while the winds howled and raged around them. Sunny was concerned for her father but her mind kept wandering to Beadmund and how he fared. She longed to meet him again and have him confirm his regard for her. They were only a few hours ride from the palace, but they might as well have been oceans away for she was in dramatic mood and everything seemed exaggerated. For her the intensity of the storm was greater than for the rest, the dark sky appeared lower and more menacing and her father seemed to lose his health and she wondered if he would recover. Her mother, practical as always, used her cloak to help keep off the worst of the rain from her husband's vulnerable and so precious head. And so they waited. The soldier lit a fire in an attempt to keep warm but the wind was so great that most of the heat dissipated without giving much comfort.

Beadmund paced and worried. He threw himself into helping where he could but his weakened wrists hampered his progress in that direction. His mother tried to sooth him by bringing his son, Godric, to him for comfort. This was always a welcome distraction but deep down his thoughts were elsewhere.

There was little more any one could do, they just had to let the gale blow itself out then assess and make good the damage. The king decided that he would see his ministers and then have that long awaited conversation with his protégé. Borvo was duly sent for and he joined the king in his private room which was strewn with parchment and writing materials. Clearly the king was engaged on some new venture. Everyone close to him knew and understood his love of learning and his scholarly ways. He was known to be writing in their tongue to give more people the chance to read and understand. Brand and the Welsh monk were also present but they sat a little apart and listened without interrupting while they were locked in a solemn game of chess. This was the king's mission and he would play it his way.

"Borvo, you have caused me much distress. We will talk and one of us will be clearer, if all goes well we may both be clearer in our minds. Are you ready?" Borvo answered simply, "Yes my Lord, I am."

"First then I ask you why you ran away. Do you fear me?" As there was no immediate answer he asked, "Well?"

Borvo became bold, "Yes I did at first but then I realised that it was myself I feared. I was confused. I have grown since then."

"What confused you?" The king's voice flowed like water round his senses so that he felt that every part of his mind was invaded. Borvo's mouth was dry, perhaps he was frightened, he had not felt it until now, this very moment. This man before him, questioning him had power of life and death over him. It was a moment of pure clarity. Borvo decided that from here on he would not be afraid because whichever spiritual path he chose there was salvation at the end of each road. It was just the journey that would be different, different words but in essence they spoke of similar needs and desires. They spoke of the protection of the strong for the weak, respect for the wisdom of the ages and to care for the sick. This last he was so bound up with it would be impossible to separate the body and soul. Healing now flowed through him and from him so that when he was engaged on its purpose he almost shone with his own light.

"My Lord, you threw me into confusion when I was sent to be a monk. I learned the word and wonder of the written and spoken word of the ancient tongue. I revelled in its beauty but questioned, always questioned its purity. I knew my god so well." Borvo looked to his patron with honest eyes and did not find the expected loathing for his god that he expected. "Did you never wonder, Borvo, why I never called you by your abbey name?"

"Well, I thought that you had so much to think about that you simply forgot what it was. You knew me first as Borvo and that is who I am."

The tension in the room was less now. Brand and the Welsh monk seemed to have broken their deadlock and were moving the pieces more swiftly and were almost at the end of their game.

"It was because, Borvo, that I considered your name to be part of you and your river spirit was and is actually more your guardian angel. It would be wrong to deprive you of his comfort and guidance. It does not diminish my faith or my god. Do you understand what I am saying?"

"Last winter I sat by the river in Winchester and heard my river god again. It was then that my confusion started to clear. I felt what Brother Simeon called the holy spirit and there was Borvo again telling me my destiny. I felt that they were one and the same, or," here he hesitated, how would the king receive this latest revelation, was this a step too far, "at least they might be, could be."

"There are many pagan converts to Christianity Borvo who take their gods with them and integrate, it is not uncommon." The king then became more severe as his own faith burned in him bringing him down in tormented humility. "There is but one true way but you must come to it by your own path." He searched into the young man's eyes and added quietly, "You may not yet be truly ready."

Wishing to divert the melancholy that seemed to have pervaded the room Borvo continued, "Your pious daughter sir, also confused me," he continued more hesitantly now as he was on thinner ground with this, "But we are friends now and I have grown up. We talk daily and learn much together. She almost knows as much about the plants and their properties as my family." The king found this rather disarming in its honesty. "So you are friends are you?"

"Only with the greatest respect for her position and with nothing more than," again a pause and then hurriedly he concluded, "monkish affection sir. Nothing more." He finished and grinned shyly glad to have accomplished this revelation with the right words.

"That's all right Borvo. I know. I also talk daily with my daughter. We will found her an abbey soon. When the time is right. It was why she was born. Perhaps even you may help in some way. If you are available."

"If I can my lord, I will."

The king changed tack and asked Borvo if he knew what he was working on; he indicated the piles of parchment around the room. He then showed him a piece of writing which was unfamiliar to Borvo as he could read and write Latin but not his own tongue. The king helped him through the passage. It was by a man called Boethius who, the king explained, wrote about man's dilemma and put it in the form of a conversation or dialogue between the author and Lady Philosophy.

"You see Borvo, the words are there to make us think and decide for ourselves. She poses questions to which we must find the moral answer. Do you understand me?"

"I do." Borvo's mind was in excited turmoil. The king was actually discussing philosophy with him. Him, Borvo, sometime Brother Mark, a lowly humble healer who he had determined would be educated and live for a while as a monk. Now he understood. It all became clear. The king wanted him to have the learning, the understanding and the discipline to think for himself. That is why he had encouraged and allowed his children to be individuals. They were all educated but free to follow their own talents. This was almost overwhelming but Borvo needed to answer the king in a considered way. He felt that this was his test. If he passed this test he would be set up in both his and more importantly the king's estimation. He continued, "I would like to know more my Lord. What questions arose between them?" The king beamed with pleasure. He had not been mistaken in this young man, or the boy as he had first known him, he had an agile mind and would do very well. The game of chess had drawn to a close, the Welsh monk beating Minister Brand who took it all with good grace. After discussing the moves and how and why the game had the outcome it had the two wise men settled more comfortably in their seats and waited. They were silent and had turned to look at the two, potential adversaries, discussing philosophy as both were keen to hear how Borvo fared in this latest of his hurdles.

"I will tell you of Boethius and you will then tell me why you think he wrote as he did."

Borvo took a deep breath and prepared to listen with all his wits honed as never before. He felt as though he was in a contest for reclaiming his life, whatever the outcome he instinctively knew it was of the highest importance.

Chapter Forty Four

Beadmund's anxiety is matched by that of

Elvina and Sunny

The raggedy group of travellers forced themselves to get up before daybreak the next morning and start out once more for the palace. Having spent the wettest night any of them could remember they were remarkably reluctant to get going again. Sore, wet cold and hungry they were none of them in the best of moods. One overriding emotion though for both Elvina and Sunny was concern for Esmund as his cough had returned with a vengeance and he could hardly find the strength to mount his sodden horse. With the practise of long years Elvina mixed some meadow sweet with some wine and forced her husband to drink it. He had no time to dissemble and was soon feeling some relief although it would take more than one dose to rid him of so troublesome an ailment.

The storm had broken its strength and now only left a straggly occasional wind and some few drops of rain. The horses slipped and stumbled their way over the rough pathways the mile it took them to find a more well kept byway. They were still half a day from their destination and longed for dry clothes and a warm meal inside them. Sullen and silent they rode on with purpose and determination brightening at any sign in the early spring sky that the sun may appear through any tiny break in the clouds. As they rode they dried out and became a little more lively although still painfully aware of the rasping cough that accompanied almost every step.

Beadmund meanwhile walked through the day anxious and distressed. He had spoken with his father but the older man had not found the words to comfort his son. The wounds were still highly visible on his wrists but what other physical pain he suffered he kept well hidden. His anxiety he could not hide. He looked for Borvo to seek his help but the young monk could not be found, it was a concerned servant who told him that the person he sought had been closeted with the king for several hours. Even though he was in favour with the king Beadmund would never interrupt a closed session unless the situation was a dire emergency. So it was that the loveworn man continued his pacing uncomforted with the burning heat of his wounds as nothing to his fear for Sunny's safety. No riders had been sent out to look for the overdue party as all available people were busy making everything secure after the storm.

The object of his desire and every thought was riding with her party only hours away from the best of reunions. Her leg ached with the damp, her heart ached for her father, and her whole body, mind and spirit ached for Beadmund. She rode on in discomfort but determined to make it before another nightfall. The group encountered many obstacles to their smooth passage as trees had been uprooted and lay across their path, debris from unsound buildings also barred some of the narrower ways. They stopped to help some people in distress, each one of the travellers torn between helping their fellow sufferers and knowing that they should not try to survive another night out in the open with Esmund in so precarious a condition and so must press on with their journey.

258

By late noon the storm seemed to have lost its power and the sky cleared. It was with a heavy heart that Beadmund looked at the horizon as another day was drawing to a close without his bride in sight. He turned to go and find his son, whom he had neglected of late. The small boy was growing fast and was getting to the age when he must leave the confines and comfort of his kinswomen and look to develop skills that would make him a protector and defender although his mother had told him in no uncertain terms that his son showed great promise as a scholar. Well, a decision would have to be made but he was loath to do so until his marriage was settled. No other thought took priority with him but now he might find solace in the affection of his son. He was feeling sorry for himself although he had every blessing.

As Beadmund sat with Godric by his side before the fire he was aware of fresh arrivals but such was his self absorbed melancholy he continued to sit and stare at the flames as they licked the base of the huge iron pot that hung over them. This honest pot was held to the rafters by a long iron chain that was black with soot and the grease of many a meal. Its permanence gave the onlookers comfort. Into this reverie came a blast of cold air as the visitors swept in bringing the damp evening sir with them. Beadmund turned and looked to see who had disturbed his thoughts; he leapt from the bench and ran to embrace the slight worried figure that stood staring at him. He had forgotten that he had made no declaration to Sunny and such were his emotions that he sidestepped all normal protestations and hugged her, looked down into her pale tired face and gently kissed her. She felt that she had waited for this all her life and after maidenly reticence kissed him back. She then withdrew and smiled at him, stooped and hugged his son and the three of them stood and swayed together in a unit of pure joy. This moment was broken by the rasping cough that came from behind Sunny and the magic was gone. Instead room was made by the fire for Esmund and Elvina to warm themselves and start to attend to Esmund's desperate state. Before they parted Sunny squeezed Beadmund's hand and planted a chaste kiss on his cheek, which she had to stand on tip toe to reach. Beadmund called for a servant to take his son to his bed and then was all attention to his future father under the law. Despite the deep cough that accompanied nearly every breath the atmosphere in the room had changed from despair to one of hope and light. Beadmund noticed everything, the wind had dropped, the rain had ceased, the night had come, Sunny's face had a glow that warmed his heart, Elvina was attending to Esmund, Sunny's figure was perfection, Rimilda had arrived and brought a servant with her with refreshments, Sunny's demeanour was warm and loving and he loved her with his whole being. He pulled himself together, he was after all a highly born king's man who fought with honour and led his men with great bravery. He held their respect and loyalty and needed to be seen to be strong but oh how he loved Sunny who made him melt with her softness and her devotion and her love for his son and her friendship for his poor plain sister. He stood tall and brought back his shoulders and decided that he could be both a good and loving husband as well as a strong soldier. This was his way and his men would cheer at his wedding and sing him into battle. Beadmund would brook no argument, this would be his command and that was that. He walked with renewed energy and a spring to his step. A man in love is magnificent to behold in his grinning happiness.

The next morning people woke to the quiet of a usual spring day with early morning mist giving way to weak sunshine. The early risers started clearing up the debris from the storm alongside their normal chores that kept the palace running and the crops and livestock on their annual course to feed and clothe the population. Work would be never ending now until the harvest was in and secure. Each one hoped for peace to hold and allow them to get on with the humdrum rather than be away fighting and losing members of their family groups. Nature took enough people away with disease and accidents, war took too many strong men who were needed in the fields. Those that wanted to prayed as they worked that this year would be the start of a new phase of peace and consolidation. In a few days there would be feasting and fun as the minister's son married the young woman from the remote village. Some thought she was not good enough for him, after all what was her father but a jumped up churl who had prospered only by association with those who were high born, others thought that she would bring a freshness to the family and that her late brother's heroism justly enhanced the family status to its rightful place and she was taking their honour to an appropriate level. For the rest they were just glad to have another excuse to eat and drink their fill, get so heady with mead that the realities of this harsh life could be forgotten in an evening of revelry.

Preparations were well under way for the wedding of the much respected Beadmund. The king had ordered his huntsmen to kill several of his hinds to augment the yet meagre supply of spring meat for the feast. Mead, honey cakes and bread all in abundance were prepared by the king's servants. The service was to be performed by the Welsh priest whom the king so favoured. All was honour for the happy couple. There was but one problem and that was Beadmund's continuing pain from his capture. He felt acute pain still in his arm and shoulder. He tried to bear it but occasionally he could be seen wincing with the severity of the burden. On the eve of the wedding day Borvo happened across his future brother under the law. While they were conversing Borvo decided to trust him with his secret and offered to help him by passing his hands over his shoulder, back and arm. Beadmund listened to him and asked how he had discovered this talent. The thegn was well aware of his future family and their aptitude for healing but this was something outside the norm even for such a family. Beadmund considered and asked Borvo if he acted with god's grace. Carefully he answered, "Beadmund, you will marry Sunny tomorrow and I know you love her and will care for her. We are to be kin and so I will not lie to you. I have recently finished a long discourse with the king who put me through a gruelling process. I will answer thus, god made all things and so all of his world should be acceptable to those who believe in him, is that not so?" Beadmund, not unintelligent but not really a deep thinker, felt a trap but could not see any harm so agreed with Borvo that this was the case.

"Good then whatever I do is in god's hands is that not so also?"

"Yes young brother."

"So I offer you healing in that respect, will you accept?"

For answer Beadmund took off his mantle and sat, meekly accepting. Borvo held his hands together to pray to all who would listen and then offered his healing to the now recumbent man. His hands grew hot, all the while Beadmund watched him but as the process continued he felt the healing heat sear through his tormented muscles and he relaxed. Almost he fell asleep as his eyes became heavy and he breathed long deep breaths of cooling air. After the length of time it took to burn half a candle to its wick it was over. Beadmund slept where he lay on a cushioned settle in the dark recess of the long room. Borvo sat with him and when he woke Beadmund looked in wonder as he felt no pain in his shoulder or arm. It felt tender to the touch but the debilitating pain had gone. Borvo smiled and said, "Just say a prayer to whomsoever you like and all will be well. Sunny will have a whole husband tomorrow. Sleep well tonight and wake up tomorrow to start the rest of your life." As the young man turned to go he said over his shoulder, "Tell none but Sunny what I have done. Many will not understand." With that he left him to recover and be whole once more.

Brand and Rimilda watched as their son took his bride to him in faith and with the blessing of the king and all assembled high born and those who supported them. Chief among the other ranks were of course Elvina and Esmund, the latter had rallied sufficiently to see his only daughter wed to a good man. Elvina had given her husband a strong syrup of meadow sweet to stifle the cough that still racked his failing body. They were to return to their village as soon as he was fit to travel. They needed to get back to their lives and begin the process of healing both his body and their marriage. Beadmund had insisted that they have a proper escort as his experience of capture had made him much more wary when any of his kinfolk should venture abroad. He embraced their kindness and thought little of their lowly status. If they were honoured by the king then that was more than enough for him. He knew they were good people and as such were worthy of his attention even before they became part of his family. Even Rimilda had welcomed them to her and had found Elvina as good a companion as she had Sunny. She looked forward to welcoming Elvina to her own home and estates when they returned there after the festivities. Her daughter in law pleased her and she felt that she had renewed purpose in life and maybe, just maybe, the emptiness she felt from her own marriage would be filled with an affection for this latest addition to the household. In her view Beadmund's first wife had been a scold and shrewish and not worthy of her time or particularity. This would be different; she smiled and hugged the thought to her.

Sunny had looked magnificent in a beautiful fine spun cream woollen dress and cloak that had threads of silver running through it. The light caught the thread and sparkled as she moved with her usual grace. The dress had been a wedding present from her groom and the elaborate brooches that held the cloak to her slender shoulders were made of silver studded with amethysts, a gift from Brand and his wife. Her hair was braided and woven into the nape of her neck from which hung her grandmother's simple silver moon. Where her Gramma had obtained this treasure nobody asked but it held such memories of a loving, nurturing influence in her life that Sunny refused any other adornment for her throat.

Beadmund was torn for love of her when he saw her come to him to be his bride. He stood tall and without pain, still wondering if the healing wrought by Borvo was magic or faith. He had decided to keep his trust with Borvo and not tell what had occurred between them. He would discuss it all with Sunny in due course but for now he had other things to occupy him. Would he set up his own establishment again or continue to live within his father's household? Beadmund of course had land of his own as befitted his status as thegn for the king but he was reluctant to take his new bride to the house where his first had held reign. He knew she was unpopular and thought that Sunny would have an uphill task to gain control of the servants and slaves that tended his lands. Then he reasoned that Sunny was so wonderful and loving that no one who met her could but love her so he decided that, given an appropriate interval when his mother would entertain the ennobling of Sunny and teach her how to run a household, he would take his bride to a refurbished house and there live his own life with his new family. Aedylpryd would go with them and be companion to Sunny until such times as she wed or entered a convent. Aedylpryd held no particular view as to which she would prefer, thinking that she could be happy with either prospect.

It was with such thoughts that Beadmund led the revels on his wedding night and so started his life with Sunny with an enormous mead induced headache and great hopes for their future.

Chapter Forty Five

Seofon and Borvo make plans

Seofon had wintered very well. Bacchus had enjoyed less welcoming company from the deer hounds that slept about Brand's household. Usually he got on well with all creatures but one pack leader of the resident hounds had taken exception to Bacchus taking food from under the long table with the result of a torn ear for Bacchus and triumph and victory for the deer hound, one of the master's favourites. Subsequently Bacchus had slunk about keeping well out of harm's way and so reminded Seofon that perhaps the time had come to go on his way to keep abreast of the comings and goings from both the court and the insurgents on the borders. All news was grist to his way of life of collecting songs and spreading the news far and wide. He could not expect to be welcomed in important homes if he was ill informed. He decided that he would enjoy the wedding of Beadmund and Sunny, catch up with Borvo's news then go on his way. The freedom of his way of life gave him great pleasure but he knew that if he showed disloyalty to the king or his ministers he would not fare so well. Bacchus' ear had almost healed, albeit with a piece missing, by the judicious application of some honey, well known as having great healing properties. He was left with just an irritating sore that lingered.

He managed to avoid the worst of the drinking and stay relatively sober. He knew that his old demon would take hold if he gave it a chance. After the revels Seofon sat in a corner watching and taking mental notes about who fitted in with whom and who the king favoured. It was well to know. The following morning when Beadmund and Sunny had ridden off to set up their new lives together he sought out Borvo. The monk was with his parents as they prepared to leave for home. Well saddled and with an escort they left the court with more pomp than they arrived. Esmund was still coughing and Elvina wore a worried look under her brave worldly face. Brand saw them off alongside Borvo and Seofon spoke some words of comfort and then retreated into the background as the family made their farewells. Borvo suddenly ran up to his father and took his hand in his; he held it without speaking searching deep into his eyes. He knew, his father understood, finally he truly did understand what Borvo was about. It took no words just a holding of hands and a long mutual embrace. They both turned away without need for more. Esmund and his younger son tacitly agreed that this would be their last meeting on this side of the great river. Their mutual love and respect was too profound for speech and so they parted. It was done. Borvo moved away.

The king had gone hunting and the palace was in a state of disarray as the slaves and servants worked hard, with their own sore heads throbbing fit to burst, to make all as the king and queen liked it. Borvo skipped the morning offices and was bursting to get to the river and sit beneath his willow tree and read. The queen had favoured him with a book of psalms and he longed to reacquaint himself with the songs. His pious princess had left the revels early and gone with her companion to her own dower where she felt able to be quiet and read. Since his closeting with the king and the discussion, that carried on through the night, about Boethius and his Lady Philosophy Borvo had seen little of the princess and less of the king. The latter seemed satisfied with his demeanour that night and his answers must have been acceptable to him or Borvo thought that he would be subject to another session. It had been a strain but he had enjoyed it all the same. He longed to tell someone about what he had learnt but knew not who to completely trust. Seofon was his conscience companion and it was to him that he now turned for some debate.

Borvo walked to the river with concern for his father in his heart. He knew he would not see him this side of the great divide. He had looked so grey and weary. The journey would sap some of his strength but he would be much better in his own village surrounded by the familiar. He could not worry, he had tried to heal him but his mother would not listen in her anxiety for her husband she had inadvertently pushed Borvo away so he'd not had any chance to lay his hands on his father. He was beginning to realise that he was not a miracle worker and could only heal where he was welcomed. As he pondered on this he decided that not everyone was meant to be healed.

He sat under the willow with his cloak around him pulled tight as the spring wind was cold and blustery with as yet little of the promised warmth. The beautifully crafted book had fallen open where someone had left a small piece of fine cloth to mark the page. He had started to read the psalm numbered 139 that spoke of how the holy lord knew him inside out and wherever and whatever he thought or did. He found that concept frightening as his thoughts did not always turn as he had been told they should. He loved the passage that told of King David riding on the wings of the dawn. What a picture it conjured up and what a wonderful sense of freedom. If god created it and meant it to be so be it but Borvo longed to ride on the morning and see just how far he could go. Perhaps the wings of the dawn would take him all the way to the Isle of the Druids about which the river god had spoken. He put down his book and stared into the future and there he saw a narrow strip of sea, which could be the uttermost part of the seas as the psalm went on to describe. As once before his reverie was broken by the arrival of Seofon and Bacchus; Borvo absentmindedly stretched out his hand to stroke the loving dog Bacchus who winced under the pressure on his ear. It was taking a time to heal properly. Without thinking Borvo covered the damaged ear with both hands and sought guidance from his healing gods and for good measure from the holy spirit too. Bacchus became very still, his ears went back and he lay down next to Borvo and his eyes looked directly into those of the man.

Seofon's greeting died on his lips as he realised that this was no ordinary caress. After a short while both dog and man noticed the storyteller so Borvo slipped his hand away from the dog's head and stood up to greet his friend. Bacchus ran to the river and jumped in and swam up and down as though he were on fire. When cool enough he got out, shook himself until he was almost dry then slept a deep and healing sleep. When he awoke he would have no more trouble with his ear. The two men sat down against the bole of the willow and spoke together. First Borvo told him of his discovery about his healing hands and the cool wind that accompanied each session. Seofon passed no opinion; he merely listened although he did ask, "Is that what you have just done for Bacchus?" Borvo nodded, "Do you understand? It happens almost without me. I am like a tool for a greater spirit."

They spent some time in silence after this revelation. Seofon got up and walked a way along the river bank then came back and sat beside his companion once more. Borvo realised that what he had told him was unusual to say the least and was giving his friend time to take it in. Then Borvo told him of the prophesy from

Borvo the river god about the Isle of the Druids. In this Seofon had an opinion he was willing to share and he told Borvo of the time when the Romans had harried the Druids, including the learned ones and the teachers and the women and children, to an island where they were slaughtered. One only lived to tell the tale, it so happened that the family of Seofon considered that they were the sole descendants left from that time. This Seofon decided to share with his friend. They had each other's ultimate trust. "Do you remember Borvo, when you were a fugitive in the village and I sang that song about the people who were chased and slaughtered, well that song was for you." It was Borvo's turn to be silent and digest what he heard. It seemed that this was a life changing moment for both of them. They had been drawn together and soon may make a journey to fulfil their destiny. Only one problem remained and that was the king. Would he let Borvo go? Had Borvo convinced him of his loyalty?

"Tell me about your time with the king. There are rumours about the court that your life hung in the balance, was the king pleased or displeased? Did the Welsh monk join in or leave the king to make the arguments? He loves to debate, and usually wins. How did you fare?"

Borvo laughed and said, "I will tell you but I had no idea of my life being in danger, some gossip I suppose." He settled more easily against the tree and began.

As he related the tale the scene came back to him with great clarity. The king's chamber was festooned with vellum, parchment, inks, books and soft cushions on the chairs and tapestries hung from the wall. He had at first stood before the king but when offered sat reluctantly on the edge of a bench. The first verbal exchanges were over and now the king had to probe deeper into this young man's soul. He felt inextricably linked to this fine mind and needed to understand his complex thoughts.

"I tell you of this martyr, Borvo. He lived hundreds of years since and lost his life by doing the right things by others. He acted according to his conscience. His name was Boethius and he wrote while imprisoned for charity to the oppressed. The pagan king relented his death but as you know, only Christ can raise people from that state." Here the king stopped and smiled, "I know of your healing gifts, Borvo, but even you are not able to enact that final miracle." His teasing tone alarmed Borvo as well as the revelation that he had known about his latest talent. He sat bolt upright and shifted uneasily on the settle.

"Be not alarmed. I feel it is god's gift not your pagan demigod." He stared hard into Borvo's face, "What you believe it to be I cannot yet tell." He waited for a reaction but Borvo, wisely kept his counsel.

"We need to understand the writings of Boethius and his words of capture. Understanding will release us from the chains of doubt and aid our study of the scriptures. You need to know that Boethius wrote in no specific Christian terms rather he wrote philosophically to embrace all who think and search for truth. One passage I want to discuss is that of free will. We have not time to go through all his work. I must be a king as well as tutor." The king looked to his Welsh monk and advisor. "It is well begun?" The Welsh monk nodded and carried on with his game against Brand.

"In his anguished state he writes of a visitation of a Lady he calls Philosophy or Wisdom. He discourses with her and she asks him questions that make him think clearly and without need to dissemble. One such question raises our thoughts to whether we have free will or has god ordained each breath and step we take. It is that on which I would like your thoughts young man. Consider and let me have your answer." The king rose and made a gesture to Brand who summoned a servant to bring wine and bread. This indication of a long session was not lost on Borvo. His mind was racing and he knew what he wanted to answer as this was not the first time he had considered the question although he had been unaware of the greatness of the thought.

"My lord I have pondered this at times. I have listened to the learned monks debating this but was never asked my opinion. Before I answer may I know what Boethius said on the subject?"

"No Borvo, I want your thoughts. We are given access to the great philosophers, not as a fetter with which to burden our instincts but as a guide that lets us grow."

Borvo took the wine that was offered him and sipped but lightly. He did not want his mind befuddled. "My whole being cries out for freedom. Freedom from bad deeds and freedom from the yoke of expectation." He gulped as this came out rather more strongly than he had thought the words in his head. He sat before a powerful man and he must needs be mindful of that. But the king had asked him and now he was set on a course he must follow that through. "If we are but things to be moved," he indicated the game that was being played in the corner, "moved to the ultimate will then we need have no minds of our own. We would be as the soldier pieces and moved without conscious effort. If we have to allow freewill then we acknowledge the gods gave us the tools to do and think and take the path we choose." He warmed to his theme unaware that he had slipped back to the plurality of god. "My lord, if you believed in the ultimate order then why would you fight the wars, you may as well sit and quaff or give in to bodily pleasures for that would be all that was within your grasp." He wondered if he had gone too far but he ploughed on, "surely we are given the mind so that we think and seek the wisdom of the world and the one that comes after this. What would be the point of learning and education for we would make no use of it? Should we think to take one path through the forest but god wanted us to take another then we would merely end up doing god's predetermined will and wondering what it would be like to have freewill." Borvo stopped as he felt a pit opening up in front of him and sought to consider more before he went on. If indeed the king had not tired of seeking his opinion.

"Borvo," the king's voice had gone very low as though seeking to bring the conversation to a more intimate level, "what do you consider to be point of ultimate freedom? Should man be left to make evil where he may? Does god look down upon us and shrug his shoulders leaving us to the black arts? Is there no divine intervention?"

Borvo sat and thought for some time before answering. No one in the room seemed at all in a hurry to hasten his reply. Eventually, after draining his goblet, Borvo looked directly at his interrogator, "My lord, here on this earth I obey the laws of the land, we have good laws I think. They protect and they compensate for wrong doing according to a man's worth and status. God's laws, if such they can be called, are guidance to live a good life and seek fulfilment in another. We have the mind to think and the spirit to look after for we hold it for this life only in such a body. After that our," he stumbled for the right word, "our essence goes on to cross the great river and learn more in the next life. If we made no mistakes we would have nothing to learn, I feel that god wants us to live good lives and hurt none that does no harm to us or our kin. We are offered guidance and must make our own choices. The pagan way is this also of worship and harming none. Men do harm, perhaps, because they have not sought guidance from the gods. We listen and act and thank the gods for their gifts. Jesus was a gift. There may have been no need for such suffering if we had no choices." He ran out of steam and sank back in his softly cushioned seat.

The king got up and walked around his quarters. The Welsh monk and Brand were silent and listening to this discourse. They made no sound. Borvo wondered if his mention of the pagan gods was his undoing. He could not let it go. Why could others not see that there was more to harness them together than there was to split them asunder. Even the pagan celebrations were being celebrated in the church but with a different name. One of Borvo's favourite days was the lighting of candles in the second month of the year. It lit the way into the new time, leaving the darkness behind. Now the church celebrated the virgin's renewal after the birth of Jesus at the same time. That too was a lighting of the darkness after being hidden away from society.

"Borvo, you give me cause for reflection. When I noticed you in your village all those years ago I felt that you had spirit. How much was not evident then. Now you shine. Do you regret the times at the monastery?"

"My lord, I have to thank you for that time as I was unschooled and now know that my head needed to learn. I loved the books and the scripts. The healing with Brother Andrew. So many tormented bodies that we were able to help. My gift of the hands was not sought by me, it just happened. Does your Boethius have words for how I use that?"

"Here is my gift to you." The Welsh monk stood up and with his own ink stained fingers gave Borvo a beautiful book, it was not illuminated but it was the translation by the king of the words of Boethius, the martyr in whom the king seemed to have an abiding interest. There was a palpable lessening of tension in the chamber, the silent servant moved among the four unequal men and filled their goblets with deep red wine. Borvo was being treated with respect but he was painfully aware of his monk's habit and what that meant to the assembled company. He did not touch his newly charged drink. The three older men drank and then as one turned to Borvo and smiled; the king spoke, "My daughter has learnt much from you. She will soon be her own abbess. I plan a great building for her." He paused, looked at the Welsh monk and shrugged his large shoulders, "it was my intention that you should be her herbal

273

healer. Now I think that must wait. You have other journeys to make. Go Borvo, read my book and then we will talk again before you have to go. Worry not that I will keep you for ever. Yours is a different path, I see that now. God has guided me and in his hands I will place your life. It is for you to decide in whom you trust. You need to read. Leave us now, your day will come."

Borvo bowed low and left the chamber, he had entered with a beating heart, now he departed with reluctance. He was under the spell of a mighty and great man.

All this he told to Seofon as they sat under the willow. The story had taken a long time in the telling and as Borvo came back from his reverie he turned to a gently snoring teller of tales and his sleeping fourlegged companion. Well, he thought I could obviously not make my living by my wits and my stories. He too then pulled his cloak more tightly round him and slept in the cool spring afternoon.

Chapter Forty Six

Esmund and Elvina re-united

It was high summer. The spring storms had led the kingdom into unsettled capricious weather patterns that made the work on the land even more onerous than usual. Some crops had been washed away and others failed through lack of warmth. Herdsmen found their flocks suffering from footrot and other pestilences. It was a hard time. Peace had been secured and held so that the people could start to rebuild their lives in the certainty that, at least for now, they would not be called upon to fight for their overlords. The people of the village fared no better than any other. After the celebrations for one of their own marrying into the higher echelons all had been dull drudgery of survival against the odds. All knew, even the small children knew, that summer was usually the time of plenty but if there was not enough surplus to pay in kind to their local lord and set by for winter then many would starve. By the next spring their numbers would be uncommonly depleted and not enough strong young men and women left to work in the fields.

Sunny had visited her family once since being wed. She had been alarmed at her father's emaciated body and the look of transparency about his skin told of great pain and wasting. Her mother looked after him with great care and tenderness but even her skills were useless against the ravaging of the disease which gripped him. He may last till autumn but no further. He would certainly not be able to survive the onset of the cold wet seasons without sufficient food and comfort. It would soon be his time to cross the river and go to meet all who had gone before. What and where he was going to exercised his mind daily. He knew of Borvo's dilemma. Some words came back to him that Borvo had told him. It was from one of the holy books that his son had helped scribe when he first went to Malmesburgh. It had been written by an ancient healer called Luke. The lines flashed into his head and stayed, 'there was a fig tree that knew when it was summer and fruited. Just so a man knew when he was to give no more fruit and go to heaven.' This he thought was his time to stop fruiting. Esmund remembered the last embrace from his younger son. It had been a farewell. They both knew it although no words were spoken. He had no need to tell him that he was proud of him. It was understood. The dying man also considered Elvina's constancy in her ancient and colourful gods. He spoke often with Hild about her and Leofric's faith in the king's god. His daughter in law had been adamant that Ayken was with Jesus and she regularly could be seen with her children by her side kneeling in the wooden hut that served as a church. He almost envied her the certainty that she carried with her in her heart. As he sat beside the ever present fire in his cottage with Elvina stirring their meal in the iron pot he asked her for a last favour when his time came, "Elvie, dear wife, when I go, it will not be long now, we both know. You have been considering for weeks how to ask me and I have decided to put you out of your uncertainty. I have made up my mind." Here he stopped to catch his breath and cough up the blood that formed the most part of his phlegm. He continued "A proper burial with an oak cross and a penny for the ferryman. It is my wish." Elvina stopped her stirring and came to him, held his thin face in her loving hands and her tears washed his cheeks as she replied, "I will do it. You have been patient with me during my dreadful moods. They are gone now and I can't regret the wasted time. What is, is. Your wish will be as you desire. Just tell Ayken and Gramma that we are all coming and to be ready for that great reunion." She leant down and kissed him, full on the mouth and then his dear eyes and forehead. "You have been my life and I yours. We have created wonderful kinder. Borvo will heal many more. He will never have children but his gift will heal many that do. This I know. It is your legacy. One day Sunny too will tell her boys what you were like. You will live on." She turned to stir the dinner once more and they both relaxed into companionable quiet. All that had to be said was done with. They both knew and sighed with relief that it was over. Whatever time left they would spend in loving gestures and everyday caring touches in between the necessities of the daily grind. Alric helped them out with their fields and livestock. He had proven himself worthy of Borvo's friendship and between his own adopted parents and Borvo's family he worked hard and made people glad of him. One day he would inherit Esric's land and become lauded for his sense and judgement. For now he was a strong young man who gave all that he could to those who loved him.

Sunny's first weeks as a wife were alarming for her. She was daily schooled in her duties as a lady by her mother in law who had decided that she would make an ally of this pleasant young woman. It was however the nights for which she was unprepared. Elvina had told her of love and the joining of two bodies in making both love and babies. Beadmund was many things but a sensitive lover he was not. Sunny was taken and taken again without thought for her pleasure, pain or enjoyment. He was both tender and seemingly indifferent. He truly loved her but knew not how to show this in the marriage bed. By day he was all attention and encouragement but by night, Sunny thought he was the very devil himself. She was sensible enough to know that he did not mean to hurt but she also realised that she could not put up with this nightly terror. It was two weeks since they were wed and they were still getting used to knowing and understanding each other. Sunny had seen what a good marriage was, despite the difficulties with both her parents and those of Ayken and Hild, she looked and observed the mutual love and respect that got them through the differences. Dear gentle Sunny decided on a course of action that would save their marriage and make their lives altogether happier and more fulfilled but she needed her courage.

One evening she retired to their own chamber earlier than was usual. The evening meal was still in full swing and she was expected to stay and be hostess. She quietly got up, indicated to Beadmund that she was leaving and then head high she left the long hall. He was astonished but indulgent thinking she was eager for their nightly lovemaking. So not long after Sunny's departure he too left the hall and went in search of his willing wife. He entered their quarters in a rush to be stopped in his tracks by the sight of Sunny sitting at a writing table and scribing on a parchment. "Sunny, this is no time for lessons. We have babies to make." She turned a tearstained face to him and begged him to sit and listen to her. "My dear husband. I have loved you since I saw you when I was first taken up by your parents. As I helped Aedylpryd get to know her own person I watched you and your precious son. I ached for you and thought how it might be between us." Here she stood up and walked tentatively round the bed so that it was between them, as indeed it was, she took a deep breath not knowing how he might take what she had to say, "I must submit to you but I have been led to think that there is more to lovemaking that possession." She watched intently as a mask came down over his features and he carefully sat down. "I ask you as your loving wife, can we start again with more patience and take our time. I think we might both be glad of it." Beadmund was upset and stood up quivering with embarrassment. He was about to reply then storm out when he thought again how his first wife had turned from him and used every device to avoid coupling with him. Was he such a monster that he did not know himself? He loved Sunny so much, indeed so much more than his first wife for whom the joining had been political and estate enhancing. How had he not seen what he was? "You will sleep alone tonight Sunny, tomorrow, we will see what happens, tomorrow." He turned on his heel and left her. Sunny collapsed on her bed and wept until morning. She had gambled and lost. Her beloved Beadmund had spurned her entreaty and left her, probably for a plump slave or servant who would have no qualms about being taken by the master.

Beadmund did not go to any other woman, he wanted no other woman, but he was shocked by his wife's stand. He had a right to his marriage bed, he was her lord he would provide for her and she would give him sons. That was the way. He made his way out of the courtyard and beyond to the stables where a sleeping groom was awakened and made to saddle his horse and he rode off into the night. He knew not where he was bound and he had no servant with him. He had no thought of his earlier capture; his whole being was suffused with anger, shame and humility. He burned with love of Sunny and he had treated her as a chattel. How could he have got it so wrong? He was a monster. It was nearly dawn when he turned for home having decided that he would start afresh and make Sunny pleased and proud to be his wife.

Beadmund rode in front of the stockade and dismounted. He was tired and saddle sore longing for refreshment and to talk with Sunny. As he walked across the courtyard he was stopped by his mother who met him in great distress. Rimilda recounted how his young son had been playing with his friend and climbed up a tree. It was his misfortune that the large smooth barked walnut tree's main branch had been weakened by the recent storms and even his small weight was the final catalyst for disaster. It broke and took the youngster with it. He lay in a tangled heap as the servants ran to help and release him. He had lost consciousness and was bleeding from his temple. By the time Beadmund returned his son was in his sleeping quarters surrounded by love and anxiety. Beadmund ran to where his son lay, Sunny was with the boy and she barely looked up as her husband entered the room. The early light from the awakening sun lit the crowded room. The weak rays lighted on such pale cheeks his heart almost stopped with fear as his son lay there, as if already dead. He drank in the pallor of his face, the heavy eyes of his wife and the bloodied cloth that she held to his soft young head. Swiftly he ordered that the physician be fetched and that all must be kept quiet around his son. He knelt and held the little hand in his large one and unashamedly wept for fear of losing him. "Dearest Sunny, make my boy well. I have wronged you and will make amends. I've been riding all . . ." "Ssh, dear one. I will care for him." He turned and planted a kiss on the top of her head and his tears coursed down her forehead and mingled with her own.

The next weeks proved difficult for the whole household. The child was much loved as much by the people for whom he was a daily nuisance with his antics as by those who bore him familial love.

As the days passed with unbearable slowness Godric seemed to gain in strength and after ten days he had regained consciousness and those that cared for him renewed their prayers with thanks for his awakening. It was soon clear however that some of his wits were lost in the fall and his speech was slower and his eyesight less keen. His grandmother took turn and turn about with Sunny to be by his side at all times so that he was never alone for an instant. By the end of the month they were exhausted but indefatigable. Beadmund took a decision seeing the two women looking pale and anxious; he ordered them to rest and let the servants take over. Godric's old wetnurse was to be the main carer and organise the others. She was formidable and effective, she ordered everyone about with an authority that would have sat well on the shoulders of the king, she was in her element at being needed once more and proceeded with determination that her young charge would have every opportunity to recover all his faculties to their former exuberance.

No more could have been done for the child and now it was down to providence and prayer.

Sunny was released from her daily vigil and immediately went for a long walk in the hills with her personal servant and one of Beadmund's favourite hounds. She drank in the clear air and breathed deeply of her beloved countryside. Her lameness which had been so much better in recent years had come back to her, days of sitting had not been good. As she walked she felt increasing pain from her hip and was so unusually tired that she feared she was contracting some dread disease. Her servant helped her to a sheltered spot and ran off back to her lord's hall to get help for her mistress. Within an hour she returned with a group of men, led by Beadmund himself, carrying a litter on which to transport their precious cargo. As she was carried with great care down the hillside to her chamber she passed out and did not come round until she was safely lying on her bed covered with soft woollen blankets. When they were alone her mother in law came to her bedside and smiled at her, "Have you bled recently?" Sunny looked at her bewildered so the older woman continued, "Is your bleeding regular daughter?" After a short pause Sunny looked startled and shook her head, "I have been so tired with our vigil that it slipped my mind. I have had none over two moons now." Mother in law leant down and kissed this naive young woman on her cheek, "You will be a mother yourself. I will bring your husband to you and you can tell him." She swept out of the room with renewed lightness of tread leaving Sunny with her personal woman attendant.

Beadmund entered and dismissed the servant with a gesture. He knelt by Sunny's side and took her in his arms as he had not done since their falling out. "Mother could not help herself; she beamed from ear to ear with not telling me. Forgive me dear wife. I make you a promise. Come through this with child and good health and we will love as you wish it to be. I have learnt consideration with my passion. I never meant to hurt you." He smiled tentatively at her and added, "No one had told me." As he considered his words he continued, "perhaps they didn't have your courage." He kissed her tenderly and longingly on her smiling mouth. "I am blessed." Sunny was not only content she knew happiness now as she had never dared to hope.

The weeks passed and Godric walked unsteadily about never being alone for an instant in case he fell. The more he did the more he could do and so he gradually got better. The legacy of the fall was threefold in that his speech had a slight stammer and his left eye was dimmer than the right. His wits returned but his reckoning was slower than before. All in all they were thankful for his survival. He could continue his riding lessons and would, eventually become as good a horseman as his father and grandfather. He would wield a sword and hold his own in the hunting field. Reading would always be a trial but the perseverance of his grandmother would prevail and he would know his letters at the very least.

Chapter Forty Seven

Borvo and Boethius

Borvo had another summons from the king. He was to go to his chamber the next morning after the early offices of the day. It was summer now and the population looked everywhere for the promises of good weather but the auspices were not good. The spring storms had left uncertainty in the countryside and although people toiled as always there seemed to be an air of hopelessness about. Blackthorn was late, birds had fewer eggs and bees were in short supply. Borvo had been busy looking for herbs and plants to supplement the curative pastes and infusions that were necessary for his art. Many more than usual came to him with sores, fevers and even pestilence in their livestock. He did his best and many were cured but the feeling of 'bad luck' persisted. Borvo kept his laying on of hands to a minimum so as to avoid ignorant or malicious talk. Some were still suspicious of his gift.

Before entering the king's writing chamber Borvo spoke with Seofon about his desire to go north through the land of the Celts. Seofon had been away for some weeks and had only just returned. Bacchus' ear was almost as good as new and gave him no trouble at all. Seofon said as much to Borvo whilst joking with him about the pagan arts. Borvo hushed him and asked him to be careful. "There are some who would do me harm, I feel it although have no proof. Be close lipped when you speak of me. I am to go to talk with the king; it is about the book he gave me. It is my next trial. I think I am prepared as I have been reading the words of Boethius over and over to get their meaning." Seofon appeared distracted, "Do you know the whole story?" Borvo nodded, "When I first heard of it it put me in mind of my own father's position. He was imprisoned without cause and then summarily killed. We all fled to safety, and that is how we came to the land of the West Saxon's for here we found safety if not always acceptance. I took to the road shortly after that, I was only a lad but my mother had enough mouths to feed without mine. She found a new man who took her in so she was not abandoned but he did not want me. I annoyed him. So I left." Borvo touched his friend's arm in sympathy, "I must even now go into the king where I think we may talk of kings and riches on this earth and perhaps fame and perhaps god and who knows what but, my friend, I wish to ask the king for permission to go, will you agree to come with me? It was sung to me as you may remember. I told you of it by the willow."

"Go into your king Borvo and we will talk when you emerge." He laughed and said, "If you take my advice take all your gods in there with you, you may need them." Borvo looked sternly at him trying to rid himself of the fear of failure. "I must be free." "Then go and be yourself and honest. The king will respect you the more for being so." Seofon kept the news he had to impart about Sunny and Beadmund and Godric until after his ordeal. He had passed by their enclave and offered to fetch Borvo to see if he could advance the youngster's full recovery.

The king was seated at his writing table, the Welsh monk was with him and the morning sun streamed in and lit up where the king's parchments lay. As Borvo entered the king spoke while indicating a chair by the table, "There is your chair Borvo, we are well met today. This may be our last meeting. Are you prepared?" "Greetings my lord, I have read your book many times over and have given much thought to its meaning." "Good, then we will discuss the fate of kings to begin with. What were your thoughts on that?"

"My lord, he particularly talks of unjust kings so I may justifiably speak without fear of offence." At this the Welsh monk unusually for him, smiled and nodded at the king. It was clear that the man before them had grown, not only in stature, but in wisdom and diplomacy. The king also nodded for him to continue. "I have sought greater knowledge than mine for the history of the story and understand that the old empire was often ruled by despots or madmen. Albeit if we take away any trappings of wealth we may find that we are all one under the skin. Our mettle surely is proven by our actions and not by our gold and silver. We must have laws and people to enforce them and those to obey. If we were all kings or lords then who must do the work? If we were all servants then who must command? It is the order that keeps the kingdom strong but it must be just and any king or lord who ill uses his power should indeed meet the wrath and justice of the law." He felt that he had run on too much so he stopped abruptly. "Good, Borvo you have read well. The laws must be obeyed by all, even those that make them. Does this also apply to god do you think?" "If you believe in a loving god then the answer must be yes but the god of the old book is full of retribution and not at all loving it seems. Even he made a sacrifice of his own son, was this therefore his own punishment perhaps?" "I cannot answer for that Borvo; all I can say is that I do not believe it to be so. It was the ultimate sacrifice, goodness for evil and goodness won."

Borvo became brave, "My Lord, there is another passage that caught my attention. May I speak of it?" The king, having been somewhat concerned by the reference to the old testament, lightened in spirit again as his capable protégé begged for more discourse and so he nodded whilst saying, "Which part is that you wish to speak of?"

"My lord it is about shining lights and hiding your light away and if you shine then you shine and whether there are clouds in the way then you are still shining and needs must move out so that you may be seen. Is it about god or about all of us? If it is about god and all of us then I need to beg for your permission." Had he gone too soon to the point of his argument? Had the king guessed what was in his mind? Would the Welsh monk interject and say he had overstepped his mark as a humble monk? He waited for the reply and did not realise he held his breath. The king stood up and paced around the room. He stood over Borvo as he too tried to stand as he could not sit whilst the king stood. The king put his hand on Borvo's shoulder and very quietly answered him, "You have proven your good intent and you have made my daughter a good companion. She speaks highly of you and wishes you to help her set up her abbey. I have however told her, this very morning, that you are to be released from your life as a monk, which you never sought, and go to find your future as a healer." "How did my lady princess take the news?" "As you know her as well as any by now, she was philosophical. She does understand however that you and she have a shared destiny. She believes, as do I, that you will meet and benefit each other in the future, when you have settled your mind and your past." Borvo looked impatient now and made as if to rise but he must wait for the king to dismiss him. There was one more surprise for Borvo however for, as he waited for his dismissal the king looked at the Welsh monk who nodded, rose and reached into a small wooden, beautifully carved and inlaid box from whence he took a silver cross and a gold brooch studded with garnets. These he gave to Borvo, "These are from your king. Keep them well and wear them with pride. You have been well taught by the monks of

Malmesburgh and Winchester. Do not let them down as you go on your journey. The king has faith in you, as do I. Keep faith with him and those you serve. Your path will cross by this family once more to the benefit of the most precious." It was unusual to be so noticed by one of such high esteem in the church but Borvo was mindful of the honour and made suitable obeisance but he was also careful to make his fealty to the king even more obvious. "Go now, find my pious daughter and make your farewells. You will discover her in reflective mood at your going. I give you leave to make an application to me for a servant to accompany you. Make your choice and let Minister Brand know. He will arrange all. Farewell young healer, come back to us with your heart quiet for your past." The king smiled and as he turned away to continue with affairs of state, his manuscripts and translations and his worry about keeping the state of peace which was dearly bought he added, "To my mind Boethius was meaning a rather higher light than we humble mortals but on reflection it may be that some of us shine with god's light and so must not be hidden behind the clouds of darkness and ignorance." His words were soft and meant not to chastise but to soothe. Also on his mind was the question of how to educate his people without oppression. His trial with Borvo had taught him much, in terms of forcing opinions onto those who had thoughts of their own, and he had used the young man's skill with argument to determine his policy. He would distribute the bejewelled gold manuscript pointers that his Winchester goldsmith had fashioned at his command, to the leaders of the church schools. His bishops would be thus encouraged to join with him in his quest. Yes, Borvo had indeed been very useful to him.

Aethelgifu was sitting at her table surrounded by pots and bowls with potions and herbs in abundance. She had her own herbal beside her, opened at a random page; she was staring into the distance unaware of her surroundings. She had dismissed her

287

constant companion to go and work elsewhere as she wished to be quite alone. This life she had chosen had never once given her cause for doubt. She knew and felt that god wanted her to found an abbey for women and to heal as many of her father's people as she may. To this end she had demanded that she be given the chance to learn all about the healing plants of her kingdom. She had not taken into account that the teacher would be no more than a youth when he first came to her and that he would be charming and disarming in his manners. He had brought light to her existence and she would miss his company very much. She knew when they first met that he was attracted to her but realised that this would pass. Neither of them wanted the carnal kind of relationship but she loved him as a brother and now he was going to leave her. She must bear the parting and grow in her own way. As she steeled herself to say farewell she heard noises outside and knew that the time had come.

Borvo entered and bent low over the proffered hand. Their usual greeting over he looked into her eyes and smiled. Her eyes were moist as were his and they both turned away to stifle the emotions they felt. "My lady princess, you know that I must go. I have to find my destiny and satisfy my longing for seeking out the truth in another land. We have learned together and you know as much as you need for your abbey." Her haughty ability to cope with any situation had temporarily deserted her so he continued to give her time to recover, "I hear that the site has been found at Shaftesbury and that even now the masons are despatched to view it and start work. It will be a fine site for you and your women." He abruptly came to a halt breathless and uncertain how to pacify her. Through her freely falling tears she answered, "Yes, I have not been there yet but may go soon when the ways and by ways have dried from the rains. Borvo," she took her father's stance on calling him by his first name, "Borvo, when you return come to my abbey and help me for a while there. I would value your advice above all others where the infirmary is concerned." She held out her hand and laid it upon his sleeve, "Promise me you will come, however long it is to be before we meet again? Promise me?" He had realised some time before how vulnerable she was behind her regal stance but now he felt a twinge of guilt that he must leave her. "I have loved our time together and have learnt as you have learnt. I will come to you and be glad to see that you might just need me one more time. I promise you, if I am alive I will come to you." Before he left her he bowed low over her hand once more and this time kissed it lingering over the act rather longer than was necessary. She did not take her hand away but turned it over and gently squeezed his hand in return. It was the most intimate they had been and gave them both much comfort. He left her then and thought that he may not see her again for years, if at all. As he walked away he felt bereft and a little scared. Now that the time was near he knew he would need all his courage to take that first step. Hopefully he would not be alone.

Minister Brand had dismounted and had washed the dirt from his face and hands when Borvo requested an audience with him. Brand went straight into the story of his grandson's accident and how he was left with slow wits and poor sight. "Borvo will you go to them to help if you can as you set off on your journey. Lay your hands upon him and heal him if you can. Beadmund will be ever in your debt." His careworn face showed signs of his great age, he was well past fifty and had lived an active life and it was beginning to take its toll. Beadmund's kidnap, his marriage and now this latest strain all etched more lines upon his troubled soul. He was running out of energy. His unrequited passion for Elvina had also contributed to the stress of life. Now her son may be the only means for his grandson to regain his former health. What spells this family weaved and how he longed to be able to fulfil his desires. He was an old man what right had he to think such thoughts? Borvo was replying to him, " . . . and so I will ride by Beadmund's home and do what I can. The king also said that I could choose a servant to come with me. I am hoping that Seofon will accompany me but may I also have the company of the slave that Beadmund freed in honour of his marriage to Sunny. His name is Cedric. I would want him to be willing." Brand would have agreed this young man anything at that moment, his whole mind being on his ailing family. "It will be done, when he returns he will have the gift of 5 hides to set himself up. I think you will find him willing enough." Borvo thanked him and they discussed when he might leave. "I will have all my plants gathered and ready by tomorrow, I have been working hard to make ready. It will be time to go at dawn the day after that. Will Cedric have enough time to prepare?" "He will have help to do so. So be it. I wish you god speed young man. We will welcome you home when your travels are over. The king has ordered that you come back to Shaftesbury Abbey to his daughter who will be abbess by then. In whatever guise you decide to remain, monk or freed man, the choice will be yours." "I am grateful and leave you now with assurance of my loyalty." His speech was stilted as he had never felt entirely at ease with this man for whom he felt an underlying trouble that was never expressed. He left to go and find Seofon to tell him of the day of departure.

Chapter Forty Eight

Endings and beginnings, happy or wistful

Dawn broke scarcely noticed by the three adventurers. The weather was overcast and there was slight spitting of rain in the keen wind. All three were mounted on horses gifted from the king's stables. They wore their cloaks pulled tightly round them, even so they, to a man, felt the chill seep into their bones. Why had the king been so generous; even he didn't know. Bacchus trotted along beside them as they left the fortified palace and set off on their journey. Before they could strike north and west which is where their path would take them they had to go west to visit Sunny and Beadmund to see if Borvo could help with their troubles.

It took them until the sun was showing blood red signs that it was dying away to see the boarded walls of Beadmund's stockade. They had stopped briefly for refreshment on the top of an escarpment. They were able to see the path they had taken and the path yet to come. Borvo found the significance of the resting place overwhelming and wandered away from the others to consider this momentous watershed in his life. Midday saw the clouds break and the sun appear to warm the air. Cedric was pleased to be with the two uncommon characters and had already made a firm friend in

Bacchus as he had shared some of his bread with him. The horses had rested and grazed and so the foursome set off again without ceremony and without looking back. As the riders crested the low hill a lookout sounded the alarm and after a short wait Beadmund strode out to meet them his faithful hound at his side. Two armed men were dismissed when the group was recognised.

"Welcome. Your visit is timely. Rest from your journey and we will meet over wine. I will tell you all then." Beadmund embraced his brother in law and smiled at the other two, "Well Cedric, you have found a worthy master. Borvo will not be too demanding. You have done well. Aedylpryd begged me to free your woman and so Gwynne is also free. She will work for me until you return then you may set up together. She will not suffer from waiting." As they entered the safety of the courtyard Beadmund turned to Seofon, "Will you entertain us this night? We are sorely in need of distraction. You have heard of our troubles?" Seofon nodded, "You shall hear a story to set smiles on you all." The grooms rushed to see to the horses and each was shown where he would sleep that night.

Half an hour later Borvo sought out Sunny who was even then resting and feeling so tired being nearly three months into her time. "Little brother, how you've grown." She teased him as always but her face was sallow and lacking in light. "Sunny, how are you? Do you need my help? I've brought my scrip full of herbs and ointments that may give you relief." He knelt down and hugged her and the reunion was a happy one. "I will take what you give me for you have my undying trust. Have you heard of Godric? Can you help him? Beadmund is distraught as are the whole company. He is a much loved little one." "I will go and find him but you must rest and be easy. You have another life to care for and he will need all your strength. Beadmund is a large man and you may have big babies. I will give your woman the leaves for a tea. You will drink it and sleep. When you wake you will be stronger and more hopeful."

The serving woman went with him to prepare the leaves for her mistress. After that Borvo went in search of the young boy, who was eating his supper with his grandmother looking on to make sure he was well fed. He looked up at the stranger and retreated behind the safe skirts of his kinswoman. Borvo greeted the older woman with courtesy and then turned his attention to the young injured boy, "Well met young fellow. I am Sunny's brother come to talk with you and hold your hand for a while. May I sit with you while you eat?" As he spoke he sat down next to him and chatted about the journey from the king's spring palace. He told him of the damage done by the storm, of the sheep in the fields, of the bright red rays of the setting sun and how he must journey far to find some adventure. Quickly the youngster finished his meal and looked with interest at this man who told him tales. Borvo could see that one eye was dim. "Would you like to walk with me tomorrow? We can take your Gramma too and look out over the fresh hills to where Sunny grew up." Godric looked at his Grandmother who nodded her assent; the boy smiled and agreed that would be a good plan for the morrow.

That evening was pleasant if not lively. Seofon told a story of mythical sea creatures that played upon sailors who were too stupid to avoid their traps of seaweed and rocks. One or two minstrels joined him and the story took on a lyrical and soporific beauty. Seofon's voice was low and enticing. Most of those in Beadmund's hall slept better that night than they had since Godric's accident. On the following morning Borvo was up early to see in the dawn and after breaking bread with Sunny he took off with Godric and Rimilda to sit in the hills and try to mend the young boy's hurts. They found a place to sit where the sun had warmed the grass. Borvo encouraged the boy to lie down and look up at the sky. He prayed to Borvo his river god, he prayed to the Holy Spirit to give him the power of healing for this young blighted life. As he held the boy's head in his hands there was a rushing wind in the still of the calm morning, his hands became as though on fire and the boy closed his eyes and took on the look of sleep. He lay very still and Rimilda began to fear for him but Borvo quietened her with a look and carried on with his task. After nearly an hour the boy stirred and Borvo left him to come round while he walked some distance away. He looked back at the anxious woman as she fussed over the boy. As he watched the boy sat up and looked around him. He reached out for his Gramma and then hugged her. He stood up and ran over to Borvo and hugged him too. "My eye, it is clear. The wind has healed me." Borvo laughed and swung him round. "Be happy young man, your god has blessed you." His stammer had gone and his wits would never be quite as sharp as before but he would live a good life. Borvo had done what he could and now he must continue his journey. This had been a good deliverance and he would be sad to say goodbye to Sunny but she was in good hands and Beadmund would care for her and their children. Borvo must go on.

Elvina stood by the brook and thought of her children. Ayken was somewhere being feasted in the halls beyond the great river of death, while Borvo was off on his adventures with trusty companions and Sunny was bringing life into the world with her doting husband. Elvina had buried Esmund as he wished and as she had promised him. It had been a week now and still she could not get on with living. Hild and the children brought her food every day and stayed with her until she made it clear that she needed to be alone. Everyone was kind but she felt as though she had done her life's work and was needed no more. Her grandchildren were however a joy and so she turned her face towards the village to play out the rest of her life as best she may.

Epilogue

Ten years passed. Borvo had been to the place where the druids had met their gruesome end. He, Seofon and Cedric had finally crossed the straits with the fisherfolk of the northern hills almost a year after setting out from Beadmund's hall. Bacchus they had buried in the mountains after he lost the battle for life by fighting with a hungry wolf. He had saved their food and their lives. They honoured him, buried him and then walked on.

After living among the people of the island for another year where Borvo healed many, Seofon decided that the time had come to move on alone and so he left the island and made his way east to the seat of the Mercians where the king of the West Saxons daughter had married into their royal family. He needed to renew his store of stories and gather more information about the state of the kingdoms. It was after all his meat and bread and he had neglected his trade for too long. Cedric was released from his servitude to Borvo. He too went with Seofon as far as the northern mountains and then left him to strike south to where he had left his loving Gwynne. He hoped she had waited for him as they had a child together and expected to marry on gaining both their freedom and their small parcel of land that had been promised. He travelled hopefully and with a fresh store of songs in his heart for the land of the Celts was full of song and strange dialect that spoke to him of an ancient people.

Borvo stayed for another year and then decided to go by boat to the southern tip of his southern lands. He felt sure of a welcome when he landed back in his own country. So it was that ten years after they set out from the spring palace they found themselves once more in the land of the West Saxons. His journey had not been smooth down the rough channel between the land of song and the land of St Patrick. The boat had blown off course and taken him to the green isle and his adventures continued for many years. He healed as he went, he learnt of different ways and his tolerance, never really in doubt, increased. He spoke with any and all who would pass the time with him. Some were Christian, many others were not. He discoursed and argued his way across that wet and green island until he found himself once more in a boat heading for his homeland.

Borvo's hair had grown and was plaited once more. He sported a beard and wore ordinary clothes. His monk's habit had been left behind on the island of the druids, albeit with some reluctance as it had been a cover for many a night and had helped them in more than one risky situation in the wild lands of the Celts.

So it was that the man who walked over the old drovers' way, over Hambledon Hill towards Shaftesbury, was grown broad in the shoulder and long in his stride. His tanned face of thirty summers wore lines that told of experiences that were dangerous and had needed all his cunning from which to extricate himself and his sometime companions. He had been lucky in his choice of Seofon and Cedric, one had all the knowledge of travel and foreign ways, the other many practical skills and an instinct for survival.

He stood in the late autumn chill one evening as the light was fading and looked at the distant hilltop. He could see the massive walls of the newly finished abbey. He could smell the tanneries on the air where the tanners plied their skill at the bottom of the hill below the abbey. He heard the distant voices as they called to one another as the work of the day was called to order ready for the next and the next in harmony with their surroundings. Father to son, mother to daughter, it was the way of his lands and many others that the generations passed on their skills and protected their own in a huge effort to survive the daily grind. Into each life they may hope to survive each winter and create some magic with their scant leisure time. They carved, spun, wove and sewed such things of beauty that to them were priceless, as these were their heritage.

Although weary, hungry and rather damp he decided that his legs were too tired to continue his journey, the final lap would be completed in the morning. His weaker leg had improved mightily since he had walked hundreds of miles in his quest but even so it failed him that evening and he lay down and slept until dawn in the roots of a mighty elm that stood on the horizon like a beacon. As he closed his eyes he thought of his precious princess and wondered if she would remember his promise to return.

The next morning he walked past the washer folk in the lee of the abbey walls as they started their day by the river. He walked up Gold Hill to the abbey and waited for his knock to be answered. A fresh faced novice pulled the small wooden shutter back to reveal the visitor. "I come to speak with your abbess, sister." The young nun asked if he was expected at which he smiled and said a simple, "Yes. I am expected these ten years." He gave his name and she went away to ask for his admittance. After a few minutes the bolt was drawn back and he was ushered in to wait in an ante room while the mother superior finished her morning devotions.

The meeting was tender and reverential, he bowed low over her ring of authority and she smiled and bestowed on him a blessing of welcome. "Welcome back dear brother. You have altered somewhat since our last meeting. It becomes you well." "Your situation suits you too my lady. You have come home too I suspect. It is what you always sought. Does it bring you the pleasure of the spirit that you hoped?" He looked on her shining face and answered his own question, "I see that it does." "And you brother, have you found your spiritual home too?" "Mother Abbess, my lady, my princess, I have. It was with me all the time." He tapped his heart and his head at the same time, "In here, in here." He paused, "A good spirit is a good spirit. Naming it will not better it, it will remain always as it was."

In his head he heard a song:

The Fourth Song Of Borvo

Borvo Borvo hear my song
This is now where you belong
Stay awhile and help to mend
All the folk around your friend
She is duty bound by far
So can't see another's star
Take the time to help her see
You are how you're meant to be

The End

DNI Bradbury © 2011